Little
Red Rooster

Little
Red Rooster

GREG MATTHEWS

NAL BOOKS

NAL PENGUIN INC.

NEW YORK AND SCARBOROUGH, ONTARIO

PUBLISHER'S NOTE

This book is a work of fiction. Names, characters, places, and incidents either are the product of the author's imagination or are used fictitiously, and any resemblance to actual persons, living or dead, events, or locales is entirely coincidental.

Copyright © 1987 by Greg Matthews

All rights reserved. For information address NAL Penguin Inc.

Published simultaneously in Canada by The New American Library of Canada Limited

 NAL BOOKS TRADEMARK REG. U.S. PAT. OFF. AND FOREIGN COUNTRIES
REGISTERED TRADEMARK—MARCA REGISTRADA
HECHO EN HARRISONBURG, VA., U.S.A.

SIGNET, SIGNET CLASSIC, MENTOR, ONYX, PLUME, MERIDIAN
and NAL BOOKS are published *in the United States* by NAL Penguin Inc.,
1633 Broadway, New York, New York 10019,
in Canada by The New American Library of Canada Limited,
81 Mack Avenue, Scarborough, Ontario M1L 1M8

Library of Congress Cataloging-in-Publication Data

Matthews, Greg.
    Little red rooster

    I. Title
PR9619.3.M317L5   1987   823   86-28559
ISBN 0-453-00536-5

Designed by Leonard Telesca

First Printing, April, 1987

1 2 3 4 5 6 7 8 9

**a hat trick
for Jane**

Little
Red Rooster

1

There's this theory I've got about Neil Armstrong. What it is, I think he went and blew his lines when they got to the moon and he went down the ladder and spoke his piece before that final step down onto moondust. What he said was, "One small step for Man, one giant leap for Mankind." Right? I've seen it and heard it a million times on TV documentaries and stuff, so I've got it by heart. Everybody has. "One small step for Man, one giant leap for Mankind." Okay, but the thing is, there's no difference between Man with a capital *M* and Mankind. They both mean the same thing—all of us. What he was supposed to say, I bet, was, "One small step for *a* man . . ." Small-*m* man with an *a* in front of it—a man—namely himself. One small step for a man—Neil Armstrong—representing, or symbolizing or whatever, a giant leap, technologically speaking, for Mankind.

See what I mean? Only he blew it, what with being nervous about being the first guy to set foot on the moon and all, and got it wrong. He went and left the *a* out from in front of *man*, which made it Man with a capital *M*. So what he said was nonsense. The lines were supposed to take Neil's small step and contrast it with a couple hundred years of Science and Knowledge and Effort and all. And it would've been a pretty neat thing to say before putting the first footprint on the moon—poetic, even—but Neil went and blew it and left out that teeny little *a* from in front of *man*, and the whole thing went to shit. I mean *millions* of people must've heard him say the lines live on TV. He couldn't do a retake or anything. Once it was out, there wasn't a thing he could do except go ahead and step down off the ladder. Maybe he was saying to himself, "Shit, I fucked up," or maybe he was so excited about being the first man on the moon he didn't even *know* he'd blown his lines.

The point is, no one, I mean *no one*, has ever had the nerve to come right out and admit that Armstrong's lines were fucked, the very first words spoken *ever*, just a few feet above all that virgin moondust, a Big Deal of the first magnitude if ever there was one, strictly a *once-only* in history, and what happens? He blows it. I bet a few guys at NASA cringed when they heard him say it, especially the guys that wrote it. I kind of doubt that Neil wrote it himself, the occasion being such a huge fucking deal, et cetera. I bet they had a whole team of scriptwriters or whatever working weeks, maybe even months in advance of blast-off, figuring out a few appropriate words for the first man on the moon to say when he got there. And then Neil gets nervous and loses an *a* halfway down the ladder. No one's ever pointed this out till now is my whole point. I guess it's too embarrassing or something. One small step for a man, one giant leap for Mankind, that's what he should've said, definitely.

A couple of times I told people about this. The dumb ones, the ones that don't understand basic grammar or what words mean or anything, they say I'm wrong; I have to be wrong because nothing that important would've been screwed up that way, and anyway, how could *I* be the only one in the whole world to see that a mistake was made, like who the fuck am *I* to say if the lines were blown or not? That's what the dumb ones say, and the smart ones—that is, the *less dumb* ones, because I don't know too many people you could call smart, if you want the truth—they say, "So what?" They just don't appreciate the irony or anything. Here's the biggest event in history and the poor lonely guy up front of it all goes and fucks up his big history-making lines. It's more than ironic—it's sad, even. It makes me want to pat Neil on the back and tell him, "What the hey, the important thing is you got there and back and made history. What's a little screwed-up line when you compare it to that?" I'm not trying to put shit on Neil Arm-

strong, not a bit, I just want someone to *acknowledge* and *admit*
I'm right about it, just to set the record straight and not keep it
swept under the carpet like it's been for almost sixteen years
now. I don't want my picture on the cover of *Time*—BURRIS
WEEMS, MAN OF THE YEAR, POINTS OUT MASSIVE HISTORICAL
ERROR—nothing like that. I just want one intelligent person, or
maybe a bunch of people, to tell me, "Yes, you're *right*, by
God! Why didn't we see it before? Oh, how stupid of us all."
Words to that effect.

I told Charlene—she's this girl I know who's the same age as
me—and she hadn't even *heard* of Neil Armstrong! How's that
for dumb? So after I explained the whole thing she got mad at
me—who do I think I *am*, criticizing someone who's been to the
moon, et cetera, and she wouldn't even listen when I said I
wasn't criticizing him, just pointing out a very human error, for
Chrissakes; but she wouldn't buy it, said I was acting like a
smartass—no, acting like a smartass *as usual*, that's what she
said, meaning I'm always criticizing things. So I said, "I admit
I'm a little pedantic sometimes—" and she cuts me off and
says, "You're a little smartass." A few days later in front of her
dopey friends she calls me "a pedantic." See? Dumbness again.
Charlene is so dumb she thinks Moby Dick is a venereal disease. By the way, that's a joke I made up myself. If you already
heard it, that's because I made it up two years ago now and it's
traveled a long way to get to you. There's another joke I made
up myself a long while ago, when I was around eleven, and it's
this: What did Joan of Arc say to her judges when they asked
about the voices in her head? She said, "I refuse to answer that
question on the grounds that it might tend to incinerate me."
Nobody got it until I explained it. No one expects an eleven-
year-old to be that smart. Today I don't think it's such a terrific
joke, but for eleven it's not bad, I think.

The thing that makes the moon landing important to me,
apart from my being pedantic, is the incredible fact that I was
born the very *second* old Neil set foot on the moon. It's true! My
mom told me plenty of times how they had a TV right there in
the room, not a delivery room in a hospital, a room at the
Starlite Motel over on the edge of town, her and my dad, and

they're watching the lunar approach like everyone else on the planet when *bam!* she starts breaking her waters or whatever and feels me coming down, and my dad says they have to get her to the hospital, the car's right outside, but she says no, it's too *late*, I'm coming down *right now*, and he runs out to phone for an ambulance. There was a phone right by the bedside, but he forgot about it and ran to the manager's office and left my mom there on the bed with her knees up and the lunar module coming down between them and her grunting and groaning, and down the ladder comes Neil and blows his lines and *splat!* there I am on the sheets all slimy and new and there's a man on the moon and a new baby right here on Earth. How fucking symbolic can you get! I asked her once if she noticed at the time how Neil got his lines wrong, and she told me no, but she watched the whole thing right there on the coin-in-the-slot TV in Room 107 of the Starlite Motel, which has only got ten rooms anyhow—the first one's 101, see. I guess it makes the manager feel like he's in charge of a big place to slide a key across the counter and say, "One-oh-four" or "One-oh-six," instead of just plain old "Five" or "Nine."

The rest of the story's kind of anticlimactic, just an ambulance to the hospital and my dad wringing his hands and my mom telling him to shape up and stuff. Then he got drafted and went over to Vietnam and got killed, which she never forgave him for, not the getting killed part so much as letting the government draft him in the first place. She said they should've gone up to Canada, but he didn't want to leave town, which was his hometown with his parents living in it, and so they stayed and he got drafted and inducted and killed. It took about ten months. I don't know what he looked like. She never kept any pictures, what with being so disgusted with him for letting himself stay around and be drafted that way, and his parents both died in an auto smash when I was around three years old, and none of their stuff ever found its way to our house, so no photographs or anything. My mom isn't from around here originally. If our house hadn't been all paid for I bet we never would've stayed here at all, just would've left town and started again someplace else. She could've *sold* the house, though, and used the money to start up again in another town. That's an important point to consider. I've got this psychological theory that she feels guilty about being disgusted with him for letting himself get drafted. Staying here in Buford, which is a place she doesn't even *like* very much, is a way of punishing herself for not being too impressed by poor old dead Dad. Mind you, it's just a theory. I'm not a psychological expert or anything.

I forgot to say the reason they were in Room 107 of the Starlite Motel when Neil set foot on the moon was because the house was being fumigated for bugs and they had to stay out of it for forty-eight hours. They could've gone to my grandparents' place but my mom didn't want to, her not getting along too well with them, but making it less of an insult to them by letting Loretta—that's my big sister—stay with them while her and Dad went to the motel for forty-eight hours, even if she's big as a barn and getting ready to give birth to yours truly.

So by the time I got to be old enough to be aware of the fact that there's this place called *the world* and I'm *in it*, which happened when I was around five, there's just me and my mom, who I won't call that anymore seeing as she likes to be called Peggy, which is very appropriate because she reminds me of a cartoon dog in that old Disney movie *Lady and the Tramp*, the dog that has hair falling over one eye all the time and the voice was done by Peggy Lee. That's just what Peggy looks like, with a lot of whitish blond hair that's always falling in her face and sticking out everyplace else, but her voice is nothing like Peggy Lee's, which is kind of deep and slow and sexy; not like my mom's, which is high and snappy a lot of the time, especially if she's mad about something. So it's just her and me and my big sister Loretta, who's six years older than me with dark hair like mine, both from our dad, and who she looks like is Shirley MacLaine in *The Apartment*, with short hair and eyes that crinkle up like a Chinaman's when she smiles, which she does a lot on account of having a terrific sense of humor. She's a cabdriver. Everyone in Buford knows her. Myself, I look like Frederic Forrest in his first movie, *When the Legends Die*, which is on the late show pretty often. He's an Indian in it that gets to be a rodeo rider. I don't look as old as

him, naturally, but when I'm around twenty like Frederic
Forrest in that movie I'll look even more like him than I do
now. In case you haven't seen *When the Legends Die*, he isn't
what you'd call handsome or anything, but he looks friendly,
like someone you could go over and talk to and he wouldn't tell
you to fuck off. Also, I'm kind of on the short side, five foot three
and already I've quit growing, which isn't fair in my opinion.

We're the only Weemses in Buford, on the second-to-last
page of the phone book. There used to be my dad's folks, but
they were in that auto wreck, so their name probably got taken
out of the next edition of the phone book, which just leaves us
three, under just the one name—Weems Peggy 1404 Westwood
Dr 843 5104. Westwood Drive runs north and south, and there
aren't any woods in half a mile. I think when they name streets
they pull names out of a hat any-old-how, never mind if it's
appropriate or not. Town planners probably don't have a lot of
creativity; they just pull a bunch of typical names like Meadow-
view Road and Valleybrook Drive and Eaglewood Avenue and
Springdale Heights out of a hat and pin them on the map
any-old-how. Peggy's got creativity. She does those pictures on
black velvet you see getting sold outside the downtown mall, all
stacked against each other so they face outward, and the artist
herself under a beach umbrella with a little folding card table to
put the cash box on. The pictures she does are generally
stampeding stallions or lions and tigers, and Elvis and Jesus and
Kenny Rogers. Kenny's face is fatter than Jesus', and his hair
and beard are shorter, and Jesus doesn't have a mike in his
hand. She sells more Jesuses than Kennys, but more tigers than
Jesus. Elvis is a steady seller too. My own preference, if I *had* to
pick something I like, would I guess be the stallions, which are
always silvery to get a good contrast with the velvet. But when
you look at Peggy's stuff next to a book from the library with
guys like Rembrandt in it you can't help but see a big difference. There's nothing out of proportion or the wrong color or
anything, but it isn't the same thing at all, I have to admit. She
does too. "It's a living," is how she puts it, or "Keeping the wolf
from the door," which is not the most original phrase in the
world, but then her pictures aren't, either.

So Peggy does velvet paintings and sells maybe five or six a week for fifteen bucks each with a frame included, which she gets *real* cheap from Mack's Frame Shop because Mack likes her. Loretta pulls in more than that as a cabbie. She's the only lady cabbie in town, in the whole county, maybe in Indiana for all I know. Peggy one time phoned up *People* magazine and told them they ought to interview Loretta for an article, but they weren't interested, said being a lady cabbie wasn't unusual enough to be worth writing about. Peggy didn't buy *People* for a whole month after that, she was so pissed at them. I really don't think she minds about Loretta earning more money than her, even though Loretta's only twenty-one. You should see them together, they're like sisters. I mean, they don't *look* like sisters with Peggy so scraggly and Loretta like Shirley MacLaine in *The Apartment*, but they *sound* like sisters. If you close your eyes and just listen, it's like spying through a keyhole or cutting in on a crossed line. They talk about some really embarrassing stuff sometimes, even if I'm right there in the room with them, sitting at the table right under their noses. It doesn't stop them—no way, Rene. I say "no way, Rene," not "Jose"—*every*body says "no way, Jose." I could just about be a gynecologist from what I've heard them talk about between themselves, their insides and genitals and thrush, et cetera. I could write some pretty horny books, too, the way they talk about sex and men and everything. They both sit around and drink coffee by the bucket and discuss all kinds of stuff while Loretta does Peggy's hair or something, and I just put my nose in a book and pretend to read, but really I'm listening to every word. They know I am, too, but that doesn't make them quit.

"Seeing anyone new?" asks Peggy.

"Only Pete."

"I thought you said he was a lousy lay."

"He's improving. His wife never used to let him do anything oral."

"And you're educating him."

"Wouldn't you?"

They both thought that was pretty funny. You'd think Pete was some guy that runs around with his tongue hanging out and slobbering over everything, but really he's kind of ordinary with two little kids that his wife left him with. Loretta has this theory that his wife would've stayed around if only she'd learned to relax and let him lick her genitals. It's supposed to be very relaxing for a woman to have that stuff done to her.

Both of them smoke like a house on fire when they get together. They really stink the place out sometimes. Peggy smokes those bargain-brand cigarettes you get at the supermarket, the ones with no name that come in bright yellow packets, $5.95 per carton. Jesus, do they stink! I all the time have to empty ashtrays around the place because she and Loretta never do. I don't think they've got any sense of smell or they couldn't stand it, all those ashtrays piled up with squashed butts and filling the entire place with stink. I empty out the ashtrays and then wash them with dishwashing liquid and a plastic scrub brush. It isn't enough to just empty them, you have to scrub them to get rid of the rotten filthy smell of butts. And they go and fill them right up again. It's incredible. Loretta even blows smoke down into Peggy's hair while she tizzes it around and stuff. I always keep the door to my room shut so the smoke doesn't drift in there and stink the place up, but it gets in anyway. My clothes smell of cigarettes even when I'm outside the house. I could be way over the other side of town and I'd still smell like 1404 Westwood Drive. It's in my shirt and my pants and my hair, too, when it's long enough to bring a hank around to my nose and sniff it. I keep telling Peggy and Loretta they'll die if they don't quit, but they keep right on puffing. I bet if I stopped emptying the ashtrays they'd just drop their ash and stuff all over the floor. Neither of them is house-proud or anything. If the carpet gets vacuumed, guess who does it? And I'm expected to take out the garbage as well, which I don't ever forget to do or it'd *really* stink the place out.

Don't get me wrong, I like them, but let's face it, they're kind of slobby. You know the old comedy reruns on TV where the mother's always yelling at the kid to go clean up his room and pack his junk in the closet? Well, at my place it's the other way around. They've both got clothes and laundry and makeup and shit everywhere, spilling out of their dressers and ward-robes, all across the beds and the floor too. It's a real mess, believe me. The other day Peggy says to me, "Did you take the garbage out?" and I say, "No, I hid it where you'll never find it—in your room." It was the wrong thing to say. She can't stand it when I say something that's not only true, it's witty as well. "Little smartass," she says, just like Charlene that time, and I say, "It's true, I'm little and I've got an ass—everyone has—and I'm definitely smart. Thank you for the compliment, Madam." I call her Madam if we're having a fight. Sometimes, when I'm funning around with Loretta, I call her Miss. Miss and Madam and Smartass, that's us. And while we're on the subject of stink and mess, guess why we can't have a cat or dog? Because Peggy says they drop their hair and fleas every-where. Me, if I was a dog, I wouldn't want to live there with all that cigarette smoke. Or a cat. And a canary'd just keel right over and drop off his perch if we had one, just like those canaries they used to have down in the coal mines to warn the miners when the air got bad.

Loretta doesn't know what our dad looked like, either. She was too young when he went away and got killed. The reason I know for sure Peggy never forgave him for getting drafted is because when they finished the war memorial in Washington, that place with the black granite walls chiseled all over with dead names, she wasn't even interested in looking at it on the news, never mind we all go there and look for her *own hus-band's* name. I would've liked to see it myself. I've never been out of Buford except for a school trip to the state forest about seventy miles away. I read somewhere that the average Ameri-can family moves house every five years. Not us. We've got roots here, it seems like, and it's not even a wonderful place or anything, Buford, and our house is just a little old place with a teeny front porch, just a square wooden box. It looks like the kind of house little kids draw with crayons. There's a couple of trees out back in the yard that are older than the house, probably. The house I'm not crazy about, but the trees I like. I don't know what kind they are, but they give a lot of shade in the summer when you need it most. We don't have air-conditioning, not at the Weems's residence. When I was a kid I climbed in those trees pretty often, so I'm sentimentally attached to them. But the house is too small and ordinary to get attached to. It's just a place to live. It's hard to imagine living somewhere else, though.

I flunked all my classes, every one. Before school finished for the summer vacation they told me I'd have to repeat the whole semester. They hadn't had anyone flunk the way I flunked since 1967. The principal told me that. He said if I was embarrassed about being the only one in the whole school that has to repeat the semester, it served me right. He really laid it on thick. I don't care. I didn't *apply* myself and so I flunked. I knew what I was doing all the while I was doing it. I was riding for a fall and it really didn't matter, not one bit. My theory is, if you're intelligent you don't need school; you just need to be taught how to read and write and then you can go to the public library and find out everything you want to know about anything at all. You walk in, you pull out a book and read it, and then you know all about whatever the book was about. It's much faster and easier and more fun than sitting in class listening to boring stuff you don't even care about. They think if you don't get good grades, you're dumb. I'm the living proof that it ain't so, Cosmo. I know all kinds of stuff, none of which I learned in school. I got a real thrill out of letting the teachers and vocational guidance counselors and all think I'm stupid. They were real sympathetic about how dumb they thought I was, except for Mr. Kinney, who teaches Social Science. He told me to quit acting like I'm mentally retarded or something and start using the brains he knows I'm hiding. I acted like I didn't know what he was talking about. Then he wanted to know if I had problems at home, so I told him the toilet seat keeps coming off because the screws at the back are rusted. He told me to get out. I didn't fool him for a minute, but at least he doesn't like me and won't bother snooping into my life, trying to straighten things out. Nothing needs to get straightened out. They think their way is the only way, and anyone who doesn't get good grades is going to wind up a wino bum on skid row. What they don't know is, Burris Weems is *different*.

It's true, I really am different, and there are reasons for it. A smart person is someone who can sit down and think about things and figure out how come things are the way they are, or why someone is the way he is. You've got to understand stuff like that or you aren't smart, Bart. You've got to put all the pieces together, all the little bits and pieces from the past and fit them together so they're all arranged in a line, which is called *cause and effect*. This is very important, understanding this part. A lot of people can't figure out *why* they are *who* they are, and it's because they haven't been able to figure out the cause-and-effect thing that made them that way. They're all confused about not knowing, and it's a shame, because all you need is a clear eye and the mystery is solved. Even a halfway smart person can do it if he wants. In my case, figuring it all out was the proverbial piece of cake, Jake, partly because I'm smart and partly because there's nothing really complex about the stuff that made me different from the rest.

What it was, when I was ten I got a bike, a red one, very speedy with yellow tires, and I went pedaling like crazy around town, really enjoying it even if my legs got awful sore from pedaling. Then I got in an accident. It was my own fault, I admit it. What I did wrong was, I turned left without looking behind me first or making a hand signal or anything, just turned left and started across the road and *bam!* this car that was coming along behind me ran straight into me and I flew off the bike and landed maybe thirty feet down the road. It didn't even hurt at the time. I was just surprised, didn't know what happened. Then I saw the car up on the curb with a big dent in the hood, and over on the other side of the road is my bike with the front wheel all mangled and bent way out of shape. Then I looked at myself, and my leg's twisted right under me, my left leg. I can't feel it at all, and a leg that's twisted under you like that should be excruciating, so it just had to be broken. I even said it out loud, real surprised that it happened to me: "I've got a broken leg." Then people came out of houses, and the driver got out of the car, and everyone headed straight for where I'm lying in the middle of the road, and someone was saying an ambulance was on the way and that made it official.

I'll make this short. I got taken to hospital and X-rayed. A compound fracture of the left femur is what I had. My leg got put in a metal brace and a weight was tied on the end that went up and over a pulley on the bed frame. I asked the nurse what it was for, and she said to keep the two broken ends of bone from lying alongside each other and knitting that way. The weight and pulley is called traction, and I stayed that way for two weeks, then got my leg covered in plaster from hip to ankle and had to lie on a metal frame for a couple of months, but at least they let me go home for that part. I got made a big fuss over by Peggy and Loretta, which was a very big novelty even then. There were two drawbacks—one, I had to lie on my back *all* the time; and two, I had to crap in a bedpan, which is harder than you might think when you're stretched out horizontal, and very embarrassing when the poop has to be carried away by someone, even if they're family.

Then the plaster got cut off with these big bolt-cutter things, and my leg was just as thin as a fucking broomstick from not having moved all that time, and covered in dead skin, big brown patches of it that peeled off like autumn leaves. God, it was ugly-looking. Then comes the bad news—what they said about traction, it didn't work. The two broken ends had laid alongside each other just exactly the way they weren't supposed to and gone ahead and knitted that way, so when the doctor measured my legs it turns out the left one is a whole fucking two inches shorter than the right. They should've X-rayed me again before they put the plaster on, to make sure the weight and pulley had done the trick, but they didn't do it, I don't know why, maybe too long a line at the X-ray room, or somebody *assumed* it had been done already when they started putting the plaster on. Someone somewhere fucked up, and I've got one leg two inches shorter than the other. If I had've been X-rayed a second time, they would've seen it hadn't worked and they would've rebroken the bone and set it *right* this time. But now it's too late. The doc measured my legs twice to make sure.

"Will it catch up?" asks stupid me.

"It may," says the doc. "Your bones are still growing, so there's a chance."

Some chance. It didn't happen. The leg stayed two inches short, and here's where the trouble starts. I had to have this *heel* put on my left shoe, this fucking enormous hunk of leather three times as thick as the right heel. It's to make up for the missing two inches. Without it I'd walk with a limp, a kind of roll, "like a drunken sailor," Peggy said, trying to make a big joke out of it, but it wasn't funny, not to me. Frankly, I bawled my eyes out about it and said I wasn't going to wear such a stinking horrible ugly thing *ever!* But when you're ten years old you don't get things your way. Peggy even went and hid all my other shoes, all the sneakers and stuff I usually wore, and left just this fucking *boot*, so I had to wear it. And I had to learn to walk all over again, too, with the left leg being so withered away. For a while there I was on crutches, dragging this skinny leg around with this ugly fucking thing on the end of it, and gradually the leg filled out a little with muscle again. But it didn't get any longer.

There's nothing in the world that's worse than being stared at. If you're different, physically different, you get stared at morning, noon, and night. Okay, that's an exaggeration—who's going to stare at you at night? But all the rest of the time while you're out there in the public eye you get stared at all right. Jesus, some people are really rude. You'd think I was carrying around a big turd on my foot or something. I couldn't walk too fast at first, either. The worst thing was when I'm crossing the street with a green light, dragfooting along, going fast as I can but not fast enough, because *every time* I'm halfway across the street the goddamn light changes and I'm still dragfooting along and the drivers are honking like crazy at me for blocking the way, like I'm doing it *deliberately* to make them mad. And then there was school, dragfooting along the corridors and having everyone look at my fucking leg . . . Jesus!

It took about a year for me to walk at a normal speed again, and the left leg never did catch up with the right, so even though I didn't hold up the traffic anymore I still had this wonderful conversation piece clumping along with me wherever I went. I was ashamed to have one leg shorter than the other, that's what it was, pure shame that I wasn't like everyone else, with two legs the same as each other to walk around on. It was a real shitty time in my life, just the shittiest. Every night when I took off the built-up shoe and the normal one I stood there as straight as I could, hoping both soles would feel the same as each other on the floor, but the left one never did. It didn't even *touch* the fucking floor, just kind of swung back and forth two inches above it. Then I'd kind of tilt my body over so the left foot was on the floor alongside the right. Now my legs looked pretty near normal, even if my knees didn't match up too well, but my body was all bent over to the left. I looked like an idiot.

I was going to make this short. I want to get over this part quick as I can, so here goes. For three years I wore the special shoe, then I had enough of it. I threw it away down by the river where nobody would ever find it. I threw the other one away, too, left and right, sent them way back into the brush down there. I would've thrown the bastards into the water, but I was worried they might float. Then I went home with just my socks, and coming down the street I guess I *did* look like a sailor in a storm. Peggy came near to killing me, said I'd twist my spine out of shape and walk funny and have terrible backaches and all the other stuff the doctor told her the built-up shoe would stop me from getting. But I didn't care. At least with a limp you can pretend you're a wounded soldier or something, and that's exactly what I did, acted inside my head like I'm shot in the leg and limping for cover before the sniper gets me through the head this time.

Everywhere I went, I imagined stuff like that. It was the only way. After about six months the limp wasn't so bad, not so noticeable, but only because my spine got a permanent sideways curve to compensate for the short leg, which nowadays gives me this pain in the right hip. You'd think it'd be the left hip but it isn't, and I'll probably have it the rest of my life.

And another thing that happened was, the muscles on the right side of my back got strong, and the muscles on the left side of my back wasted away to nothing, I don't exactly know why, but it's connected with the crooked spine, definitely. If I stand in front of the bathroom mirror naked and lift my arms out of the way and turn a little bit sideways, first one way, then the other, I can see how there's a straight line sloping from my shoulder blade to my hip on the right side, but on the left side my body goes in like a girl's, like there's a whole section of flesh and muscle that's missing halfway down. If I started wearing the special heel again I guess my spine would straighten out and the muscles on the left side would build up again, but I'm not gonna do it. I took off that thing and threw it away three years ago now, and I'll never put it back on again. Never. I don't care how much my hip hurts me.

Anyway, that's how come I'm different. All that staring, all those hooting horns, all that standing in front of the mirror made me different. Now, the thing about being different is, you *think* different and *feel* different, so when you see everyone in school studying hard for their grades and fretting about straight *A*'s and all, you think to yourself—What's that got to do with me? Hey, I'm *different.* Why the fuck should I study to be a doctor or lawyer or computer programmer or whatever? I've got a leg that's two inches shorter than the other. I'm a gimp, and gimps don't do that stuff. That's how I figured it, and that's how I feel right now, like a gimp. You just need to watch me walk down the street and right away you know I'm a gimp. I carry one shoulder higher than the other and swing the short leg just a little bit. A gimp. It's too late now to start thinking I can fit in, way too late for *application* to my *studies* for Chrissakes. I don't know if I'll repeat the semester or not. Maybe I'll quit school. I don't know how old you have to be before you can quit school in this state. I don't *want* to know right now. I can leave the decision till September. There's the whole summer ahead of me yet.

Peggy was kind of pissed about me flunking, not that she ever gave a fuck about going to PTA meetings or anything. She's never been pushy about school, never asked if I shouldn't be doing homework instead of watching TV. But she was pissed at me for flunking, so maybe deep down she wants me to be a Big Success like all the other moms want their darling boys to be. It doesn't seem like Peggy, but you never know. I knew for sure she was pissed when she told me I had to get myself a summer job. She's never done that before. She says I can spend some time working for a living like herself and Loretta. I don't want to. Summertime is when I like to laze around and read books and generally kind of do nothing. I *like* doing nothing. But she means it, I can tell.

I've been looking for work but not looking too hard, I admit. What I did this afternoon, after I went for an interview that went out the window when I told the guy I didn't really want the job, I went to Radio Shack and stole this little tape recorder that fits into my pocket just right, and from now on, every couple of days I'll talk into it like I'm talking now, make a secret diary on tape and kind of keep track of things that happen. Now it's late. My room's hot and the windows are open, and there's about a million crickets out in the yard sawing away and making a racket you can probably hear behind my voice. I can't think of anything more to say right now.

Ten-four.

2

Still no luck jobwise. Memorial High closed down for the summer, so every kid in town is looking for a summer job. I've been in every supermarket and plenty other places, too, warehouses and light manufacturing, all those places. No luck, yuk, yuk! I'm really crying into my beer about it. Peggy says it's my clothes. See, I wear these army-surplus combat pants with the leaf-pattern camouflage all over them. You see them everywhere nowadays, but it was me who started it all way back before baggy military pants got to be fashionable. What I wanted was some pants that'd kind of hide my leg so it wouldn't be so noticeable, being shorter and a little punier than the other one, so tight jeans were out. I was the only one in school to wear camouflage baggies back then, and now those same idiots that said I looked weird are jumping over each other to get hold of a pair. Only they don't wear them to job interviews like me, which is probably why they get the jobs and I don't. What a fucking tragedy. Also, I bet they smile a lot and act real *enthusiastic* and call the guy that interviews them sir, practically sit with their paws up and beg for the privilege of sacking up customers' groceries at the checkout and replacing canned goods on the shelves and walking around with a dinky little price-label gun on their hip like a little kid playing cowboy. They get these Joe College haircuts and put on a shirt and tie and shine their shoes till they look like they stepped out of a time machine from 1953 or something. And it works. They get the jobs. No way am I getting into that suckhole, smiling, yessir-I-want-to-be-a-credit-to-the-store-and-my-parents-are-counting-on-me-sir-can-I-please-have-the-job-sir bullshit. I had a big fight with Peggy about it. She said she'd buy me some decent clothes if it meant getting me a job, but I said no. We had a big yelling match that would've ended up in a fistfight if Loretta hadn't stepped in and taken my side.

"You've never encouraged him to *be* anything," she says, and Peggy hits the roof.

"What was I supposed to be encouraging him to be! He doesn't have any *aptitude* for anything! Look at the way he wanders around town for hours, doing what? Doing nothing! He probably hasn't even been *going* to any interviews, just wanders around in a *daze*."

"I *do* go to the interviews. I just don't get the jobs!"

"Of *course* you don't! *Look* at you!"

"I'm not wearing any goddamn suit!"

"How about a normal pair of pants, then? Even jeans would be better than those stupid *soldier* pants."

This is psychologically revealing, I think. It means I remind her of the old man getting his head blown off or whatever in 'Nam. I don't mean to remind her deliberately, but I'm not changing my pants for some lousy job just because she's all screwed up about having a dead soldier for a husband that she didn't even respect because he let himself get drafted.

"Since you're dressed for the occasion why don't you join the *army!*" she says, practically screaming now. "Why don't you learn how to kill women and children and destroy their homes!"

She'd gone crazy. What could I say? Her face went all dark and her mouth got all twisted. Loretta went over and tried to calm her down, and Peggy ended up calling me a little shit and then crying, with Loretta holding her and trying to get her smoothed over. Then, just when things have quieted down some and I think I've won, for the time being anyway, Loretta turns to me and says, "It wouldn't hurt you to spruce yourself up a bit, Burris."

Spruce myself up a bit? It sounds like something out of a movie, some spit-and-polish officer telling a shit-covered private to "Spruce yourself up a bit!" And I thought Loretta was on my side! Naturally I walked out. I can't stand unreasonable behavior. You'd think the world was going to end just because I haven't got a fucking job, for God's sake!

The big fight happened after supper, so it was getting close to dusk when I left the house. What I needed to do was go for a long walk and forget it. So that's what I set out to do, only I couldn't stop thinking about jobs and stuff. What I'd like to be, for a while anyhow, is a cabbie like Loretta, but I can't be because I won't be sixteen till July 20 so I haven't got a license yet. I like driving. I taught myself. Peggy's got this beat-up old Impala, a real rustbucket with a Mondale-Ferraro sticker on the rear bumper, not that Peggy even bothered to vote or anything, it's just that she can't stand old Uncle Ron. She says he's a moron. She was incredibly pissed when he got back in for a second term. And Geraldine's making Pepsi commercials now. Don't tell me politics isn't all bullshit. Anyway, the Impala. One day I just took the keys, got in the car and drove around town awhile. It's got automatic gears, so what's to learn? You just steer on the right side of the road and don't hit anything is all. I've taken it out a few times since then and Peggy doesn't seem to mind, but she says if I get caught, she'll let the police charge me with auto theft, which is an empty threat if ever I heard one. Peggy's great like that, but about this job business she's getting to be a real pain in the ass.

So I'm walking along, still jumpy from the big fight, watching the sun go down, which is a nice time of day because it makes everything look like it's dusted with powdered brass or something. It's true what Peggy says: I really do like wandering around town, even at night, maybe even more so at night. See, my hip keeps me awake a lot, especially in summer, I don't know why. It's cold weather that's supposed to bring out the worst in joints and stuff, you know, some old farmer rubbing his arthritis and predicting rain, but with me it's the exact opposite, so even though I like summer in lots of ways, it's a fact that I sleep better and get less pain in winter. Which means in summer I sometimes get up practically in the middle of the night and go for a walk to forget about my hip throbbing away, not real painful, but *there*.

I headed down Westwood to Wilkerson, then left along Trail Ridge, which goes kind of up and over, then down to the freight yard. It's pretty crummy around here. All the fancy homes are in Harland Heights, way over on the other side of town. But I like walking along here anyway. The sun's gone now, but it's pretty early still, maybe nine o'clock. I don't have a wristwatch. You can see light from TVs flickering across ceilings where the curtains haven't been drawn, kept open for the breeze, not that there *is* any breeze. It's around eighty still, not too hot for a stroll. I'd stroll anyway, even if it was a hundred. There's no one else around, just me on the street, walking on the road because the sidewalks around here are all cracked and tilted and the streetlights are only at crossroads, so you can't see what's under your feet most of the time. You could break a leg on these sidewalks at night, so that's why I walk in the road. You can hear the TV voices, all hollow-sounding, drifting from windows and open front doors. Most people around here don't have air-conditioning same as us, but now and then there's a house that does, only it's not the steady hum you get from an expensive unit, more like the clattering sound you get when the wind blows through venetian blinds that need adjusting. I don't know how people can sleep with a racket like that outside their window. I'd prefer to stay hot.

And while I'm walking, it comes to me that the reason I like doing this, the explanation for it is, no one can see me. That's what it is. No one's watching me walk, and the fact is, when I'm alone at night I really let the short leg swing plenty and kind of lurch along like a regular gimpy bastard, all because I know there's nobody around to stare. And I'm happy. It sounds dopey, I know, pathetic even, but just about the best times in my life are when I'm walking down some road in the middle of the night with the moon over my shoulder and the next street-light glimmering way, way off and a moon shadow stretching out in front of me, with the houses along the road getting darker as all the TVs are turned off and everybody goes to bed and there's just me left, gimping along, listening to moths kill themselves on the blue bug light somebody left working on his front porch—*snap! zap!*—and every now and then a cat crossing the road without a sound, stopping to look at me for just a second, then *zip!* he's gone into the shadow of somebody's yard, and sometimes a dog'll hear me even though I'm wearing sneakers, and he'll start woofing like crazy and keep it up till I'm way down the block and he figures I'm not going to break into his goddamn master's house after all. I really *like* it then, Jesus I do.

Sometimes I pretend there's been a plague and everybody's been wiped out except me. I'm the last man on Earth, and in my pocket there's a little golden ball, and inside the ball there's about ten million teeny tiny weeny little pinhead things that are the souls of everyone that died, every little microscopic thing a human being; and what I have to do, I have to get this ball to a secret scientific research lab way up in the north in a hidden valley, and I have to put the ball in a giant machine and pull a switch and every single one of these itsy bitsy pinheads will turn into a person, not all at once or they'd squash the shit out of each other, but like one per minute for years and years until they're all humans again. The plague's long gone by then, see, so they won't catch it again or anything, and they all go back to their different countries and everything starts up again the way it was before, but I don't stick around to get thanked for saving the world, nothing so cornball. I just kind of slide out the door after the first few people start getting created, and when the world's full of people again I don't tell anyone they owe it all to me, nothing so egotistical, I just keep the knowledge to myself and go about my business, knowing it was *me* that did it. Even when people say, "I wonder how we all got to be born again? Who put the golden ball in the machine?" I don't say anything, just shake my head along with the rest and say, "I'd like to know that myself, I really would, but I guess we'll never find out."

That's what I think about when I'm roaming around the town at night like this, and another thing I think: I make believe the road's the only solid thing in the universe. Everything on either side of it is false, a dark mirage or something, and if I step over the curb onto the grass and sidewalk the mirage'll disappear and I'll be standing on thin air because the road is laid along the top of this incredible wall like the Great Wall of China, and the sides of the wall go down and down forever, so as soon as I realize the big mistake I made stepping off the road, I start to fall, down and down, with the wall zapping by on one side of me, and on the other side there's just nothing, nothing at all except darkness like outer space without any stars, and I don't know what's at the bottom because it'll take *forever* to reach it.

So I stay on the road, and when I get to a crossroad where there's a light hanging over the very center on wires from the telephone poles at the corners, I stop and stare at it hanging there with this silvery blue light coming out of it like a star, and moths and bugs flitting around it like little planets. The sun is a star. Plenty of people don't know that. This guy at school, Robert Lapato, he said the *Earth* was a star, the stupid fuckhead. I told him all the stars in the sky are like our sun, and all on fire, which is why we can see them, but this stupid *fuckhead* says *planets* are stars. What a *moron!* He says if I know so fucking much, how come I flunked science two semesters in a row? End of argument. I wouldn't even bother *trying* to explain to a dork like Robert Lapato.

After I've looked at the light hanging over the crossroad, I walk on. I'm almost to the end of Trail Ridge now, and there's spaces between the houses, vacant lots with junk and weeds. The houses get kind of old and shitty around here where the road starts sloping down toward the freight yard. I followed it down past the last house and walked along the chain-link fence that's supposed to keep railroad property off-limits, only it doesn't, because I found a hole in it about a hundred yards along where one stretch of wire ends and another begins, and the part where they're spliced together wasn't done too well, so there's this triangular hole you can pull apart and step right on through, which I did. There's always two or three freights made up and standing on the tracks, waiting to get hauled out sometime tomorrow, and what I like to do is walk along them and read the names off the boxcar sides, like I'm a hobo making up my mind which direction I'm going to head off in come daybreak. There's supposed to be a night watchman patrolling hereabouts—there's a sign that says so—but I've never seen him. I don't make any noise, though, just in case. I like the smell here, a machinery kind of smell, iron and steel and rust, and oil and grease and diesel that's soaked into the ties and ground. I like the way those extra-long boxcars look so fucking *heavy* sitting there on the tracks, like it'd take a loco the size of an ocean liner to get them moving. If I'm lucky I get to the yards when a night freight comes cannonballing through with its horns blatting, a real arrogant, sneering sound. You can feel the engines and wheels right through the soles of your feet and up into your belly, with the loco like a one-eyed monster tearing along maybe sixty miles an hour, really hammering your eardrums, and all the freight cars coming along behind, clickety-clacking over the points so fast and loud you think they're going to jump the tracks. But they never do, and the caboose flies past with the brakeman maybe looking out the little window that pokes out from the side so's he can see along the train, or maybe he's making himself a cup of coffee on the stove in there and having a ham sandwich, or jerking off, what the hell do I know? Then there's just the red light getting smaller and smaller, then it's gone.

I walked across the tracks to the other side of the yard and climbed up on a stack of wooden pallets that's been there for years, up on top and over the fence. It's an easy jump down to the ground. I'm sweating plenty now, mainly under my left arm. I mean, both armpits sweat the same, but on account of my hip tilting over to the left, it means the top part of me, my shoulders, they tilt to the right to compensate for the bend in my spine, which means my right arm kind of hangs away from my ribs, and the left arm lies smack alongside them, so the right armpit has a kind of space for the breeze to blow through and cool the sweat; there's never any on my shirt there, but the left armpit gets good and soaked.

Okay, now I go across a wide stretch of asphalt where trucks park through the day but it's empty now, and then I'm at the Interstate that cuts around the edge of town. For about seven miles it's called the Buford Thruway, but really it's the Interstate. There's a fair amount of traffic still, big tractor-trailer rigs mostly, and it's too risky to race across, so what I did, I went along to the footbridge that crosses over a couple hundred yards down, and when I got halfway across, I stopped to watch the rigs go howling along underneath me with their tires whining and their smokestacks coughing out dirty clouds you can actually see swirling around in the weird light that comes down from these incredibly tall poles that go straight up—I don't know how high—then kind of curve out over the highway and end with a long hooded rod of this weird purplish light. You can smell the diesel exhaust, too, even more than you can see it. I went on across and down the steps on the far side. There's gas stations all along the highway here—Chevron, Gulf, Amoco, Exxon, Texaco, Shell, Fina, Phillips 66, you name it, and in between there's places to eat—McDonald's, Hardee's, Chicken Shack, Wendy's, Pizza Hut, Kentucky Fried, Domino's, Dunkin' Donuts, Taco Bell, Burger King, and all, and in between *them* you get the motels—the big ones like Motor Inn, Red Carpet, Ramada, Best Western, et cetera, and the not so big—the All Nite, the Friendly Inn, Harry's Highway Haven, which when I was a little kid I thought was Harry's Highway *Heaven*, a place where you went if you got killed on the road, and plenty more—Lay-Z-Days with Pool! Phone! Cable! Restaurant! the Mercury, the Traveller's, the Passin' Thru, the Conway, and way down at the end of the line, way out on the edge of the dark—the Starlite. I always end up there. That's where my nightly constitutional ends. That's where I stop and turn around and head for home again.

The Starlite looks like all the rest of the cheapo motels, built out of cinder blocks just one story high with a big old neon sign out front that's always got a piece of it flickering on and off when it ought to be steady. The words STARLITE MOTEL are in this real bright poison green, and over the top there's this big pink, I mean really bright candy-pink neon star with five points. Tonight it's the left arm that's blinking. Last week it was the right leg, if you see what I mean. The star isn't supposed to go on and off or anything, it's the letters that do that—STARLITE MOTEL blank STARLITE MOTEL blank. You can see it from way off.

What I do is, I go around the back to Room 107, which is second from the end, then I generally go in a wide arc around the office so the night man in there doesn't see me prowling around and call the cops or something, and cut through a gas station to get back on the highway. But I always stop for just a minute outside 107. That's where I was born, right in there. Tonight there's someone hiring it out. It's pretty near always occupied when I come by. There's a Corvette parked outside, and that made me think that whoever's in there is screwing some girl. If it had've been a boring old four-door Chevy or something, I'd figure whoever's inside is just sacked out after a hard day's driving, but a Corvette doesn't make you think that way, not the way it looks, like a shark on wheels. I'll be honest. I was jealous. I got hot under the collar just standing there because I didn't have a Corvette or a girl or fifteen bucks or whatever for Room 107. I really got mad about it there for a minute, which was very dumb of me, then I went away. One day I'll hire Room 107 for myself, just for a night, just because it's where I was born. Just *because*.

I didn't go home the same way. I backtracked along the highway past all the fast-food joints and gas stations and motels, a solid mile and a half of them, and went across another footbridge down that way that lets me go under the railroad tracks where they go across a big concrete-and-steel bridge. It's a longer way home, but I don't have to jump any chain-link fences, and anyway, I wanted time to think. What I thought about was Room 107 and what was happening inside it. Maybe nothing was happening inside it except some guy brushing his teeth, but that's not what I felt. I *knew* some really disgusting stuff was happening in there, and it didn't include me. I hated them, whoever they were, I really did.

See, I've only ever done it one time, and that one time was no big deal, about twenty seconds of deal, in fact. I knew it wasn't supposed to happen that quick even if I'd never done it before. It's supposed to go on for minutes and minutes, sometimes *hours*, and the girl is supposed to be groaning and biting your shoulder and clawing the skin off your back and stuff. It wasn't like that. *Nothing* like it. The girl was the same Charlene who didn't know who Neil Armstrong was. I mean, I didn't even *like* her, never mind *love* her or anything. Okay, I'll be honest. Love was the last thing on my mind. I just wanted to get laid so I could relax and figure I'm a man at last, not some wimpy little virgin. But what I meant was, I didn't even *go* for her—sexually speaking, that is. I mean, she isn't good-looking and she doesn't have a terrific body or anything, none of which would've mattered if I thought she was an okay person, but she wasn't even *that*. Charlene, let's face it, is a complete moron, not just dumb but *nasty* dumb when she wants to be. But she's got this rep for *doing* it, and on this particular night she made it pretty clear she was prepared to do it with *me*, so I wasn't going to say I had to go do my homework or something. I mean, normally she probably wouldn't have wanted to do it with me, but she was kind of drunk. To be honest, I think that's why she put out for me, no other reason. Maybe she felt sorry for me or some fucking thing. Anyway, even if I didn't really want to, her not being the girl of my dreams who takes first bite of my cherry, I had to go through with it. You *do not* turn down a fuck, especially if it's the first one you've been offered, not unless you want to start building a reputation as a faggot— excuse me—a person of alternate sexual persuasion. I *had* to do it. Isn't that just the feeblest thing, to fuck someone because you feel *obligated? Try* to fuck someone, I should say, because what I did doesn't even qualify as a fuck. It was an *attempt*. Your Honor, I plead guilty to attempted intercourse. To tell the truth I'm not even sure it was properly *in* or anything, everything was so goddamn mushy down there, and Charlene had a fair amount of wiping to do afterward. Jesus, was she sore at me.

"Is that *it?*" she says. We're in the backseat of her brother's Pontiac that's parked outside this party that was going on. It's a Saturday night a whole year ago now. *A whole year.* "Is that *it?*" she says. You know how you read in a book about someone's lip curling with scorn? Well, that's what she did with hers, curled it with plenty of scorn. Then she says, "God, you're pathetic."

What could I say? She's right. Stupid me, I tried to save

face. "Maybe if we waited a little while . . ." But she wasn't having any of that, no sir.

"For what?" she wants to know. Very encouraging. So I took the resolute, upright, manly approach.

"Awww, come on, Charlene . . ." Burris Weems a crawler? *Never.*

"Oh, fuck off," she says.

There's nothing worse than having a girl tell you to fuck off. There's no way you can continue a conversation after that. She was already wriggling back into her panties anyway. I felt very depressed and panicky watching her pull her jeans on, depressed about how my dick let me down and panicky about how she'd probably blab to her friends how useless I am, and depressed again about how *that* would affect my chances with other girls, the old grapevine you know, and here's a weird thing—behind all of that stuff I felt sorry for Charlene, I really did; sorry, I guess, because she might suspect that I hadn't felt any actual *desire* or anything, which would be a big insult to her femininity and stuff. What I did, I turned my depression around in about thirty seconds from *me* to *her*. Is that crazy or what? I shouldn't have wasted my time, though, because after she's got herself all zippered up she opens the door and gets out, then leans back inside the car and says, "You're an asshole. Everybody says so." Then she slams the door.

I didn't go back to the party. I didn't have the nerve. I could imagine Charlene telling everyone what happened, making a big joke out of it, and would you believe it, the very second I finished picturing it in my head, there's this big burst of laughter from the house. It came out through the open windows and straight into my head like a spear or something. I *actually thought* they were laughing at *me.* I don't think it now, but I did then, and I got out of that Pontiac like it was on fire and walked away without looking back to see if there was a bunch of people hanging out the windows to watch the *asshole* slinking away with his tail between his legs. I can kind of laugh about it now, a year later, but it must've made me feel pretty bad deep down because from that night right up till now I haven't put any kind of moves on anyone, haven't had the guts to try again with some other girl. God, I'm pathetic, just like she said.

And here's another weird thing. For that whole year, what I thought about, apart from going over and over what happened in the Pontiac, was these two dogs that live down Westwood Drive a little way. The first dog is called Mukluk, a Siberian husky, you know the kind with the black-and-white face and blue eyes, a real *handsome*-looking dog, and what he's also got, Mukluk, he's got *dignity*, which you don't expect a dog to have, but he's got plenty of it all right. He never gets excited and jumps around or does goofy stuff like you expect a dog to do, nothing like that. He's just the coolest pooch on the block. But this *other* mutt, God, what a fucking *idiot!* He's called Buster, and he's I don't know what, some kind of mongrel, and he's the cowardliest, most sniveling ass-licker of a dog I ever saw, a real belly-crawler that grovels when you just *look* at him, and rolls onto his back all submissive if you take a step toward him. He doesn't walk, he *cringes* along, always looking over his shoulder like he's expecting a boot to come out of the sky and kick him in the balls. Know what I saw him do one time? I saw him kind of squat on the grass and rub his nuts on the ground until he came, and then guess what he did—he ate it. He ate his own come off the grass! I mean, I think I'd be less disgusted if he'd squeezed a loaf and eaten *that*.

Anyway, the point is, I kept thinking to myself that Mukluk was how I *wanted* to be, and Buster was how I *was*. I couldn't shake it. I was Buster. That's how I saw myself. It's true, and it means I've got a very serious problem with my self-image. I guess it's understandable if you're a five-foot-three virgin with a short leg, but it can't be *healthy* to see yourself in the same light as a dog that humps the ground and licks up its own joy juice, it *can't*. What I've got to do, I've got to start thinking I'm Mukluk. Maybe if I think it hard enough it'll rub off on me and I'll really *be* like Mukluk. It's not so weird when you think about it. I mean, for practically a whole year now I've thought of myself as being no better than Buster, a kindred spirit even, for God's sake! That has to stop. It's got to stop right *now!* Definitely.

Talking all this shit out is a good thing. I used to think all that stuff about lying on a psychiatrist's couch and spouting your problems was all bull, but since I got this recorder I can appreciate what a little out-loud talking can do, I really can. I only stole it for something to *do*, the way everyone does, but it's turning out to be something special. Anyway, I've talked plenty for tonight. I guess I'll look for another fucking job tomorrow. *Yeccccchh!*

Over and out.

3

Just did a couple minutes of play-back, the bit about sex. I'm a little bit shocked at how honest I'm being about everything. Talking to a little electronic box kind of liberates something inside you. It does *me*, anyway, and I'm going to keep it up, keep on being honest, I mean. What's the point otherwise? I mean, if you're talking to another *person* you change things around, just little things, to make yourself look better. Every time you talk to people, I don't care who *you* are or who *they* are, every time you talk to someone it's a *public relations exercise*. But talking to yourself is different. You don't have to try and impress anyone.

Anyway, I ended up by saying I'd go look for more jobs. Well, I did for another couple of days. . . . Honesty, honesty, *honesty*. I *pretended* to look for jobs. What I really did, I spent a lot of time in the library. I read a very interesting book about monsters that are maybe still alive today, Bigfoot and the Abominable Snowman and the Loch Ness monster, stuff like that, and I looked through a big book of pictures by some famous photographer. There weren't any in color, but some of them were pretty good anyway, especially this one of a statue, just the face. It's this little kid with fat cheeks and a dopey little smile, only his face is all pitted with age, the stone he's carved from is, and he's got those blind eyes all statues have, and also he's got vines growing all over his face. It makes him look dead and evil at the same time, even if he's just a fat-faced little kid. It's called *Head of a Cherub, Villa Garzoni, Collodi*. It's spooky.

That was Thursday. On Friday I read this terrific book by this English writer John Wyndham called *The Chrysalids*. It's set in the future after an atomic war that was so long ago, everybody's kind of forgotten the details of it. There's no machines or anything, just the Bible, and anyone that's different from what they call "the norm" is killed, because the Bible says we're made in God's image and we're supposed to have ten fingers, ten toes, one head, all the regular parts, and the hero's this kid who's got this girlfriend who lives way out in the woods with *six* toes on each foot. He doesn't care if she's got twelve toes, only it's got to be kept a secret from everyone else. But the girl gets found out, and her and her family have to head for the Fringes, which is this desert place miles away where nobody in their right mind would go. Then later the hero finds out *he's* different, too, only no one can see it because how he's different is he can *communicate telepathically* with a few other people, and they're all scared shitless they'll get found out, which they *do*, of course, and they all have to hotfoot it to the Fringes, only they're chased by all the normal people and only get saved at the last minute because this little girl that's with them can communicate telepathically *halfway around the world*, and this flying saucer comes to rescue them from a very advanced place where *everyone* communicates telepathically, so the hero and his friends can go home with the people in the flying saucer and not feel like freaks or be scared anymore. It's just about the best book I ever read. I'm definitely going to read it again someday, which is something I don't usually do with most books. If I was in that place where everyone has to be normal, I would've been okay, because you have to be *born* peculiar to be judged unfit and put to death, like there's this cat they talk about that's got no tail, but it's okay because it had it cut off, but if it had've been *born* with no tail they would've drowned it. My short leg is accidental, not a birth defect or anything, so I would've been okay.

Friday night I borrowed a few bucks off Peggy in return for promising to give her a hand Saturday with her pictures, and I went down to the Junction. That's this place down on LaVista and Marion, which is why it's called the Junction, and a lot of

guys hang out there that aren't old enough to go to a bar, so
what they do is they go to the Junction instead and smoke a
little dope and maybe do pills if there's any around. I don't do
that stuff myself except for once in a while to prove I'm not a
Prince. What I did at school was, I divided everybody up into
categories. Princes are the ones that never do anything wrong
and get good grades and are jocks on the team and their parents
are real proud of them and they get extra-big pictures in the
yearbook and their names mentioned about fifty times because
they're so fucking wonderful. Princesses are the same thing,
only girls. A Prince and Princess practically always get to be
Prom King and Queen every year. Princes look like they're in a
razor commercial and Princesses look like they piss Pepsi and
shit Oreo cookies. Then there's the Plodders, who work real
hard but aren't glamorous or anything. I had this friend, Ray
Siegler, who was a Plodder, a real nice guy and interesting to
talk to, especially about stuff like Atlantis, but his family
moved out of state two years ago. Then there's the Paupers,
from families with not too much cash. There's lots of black kids
in this category. Me too—I'm a Pauper.

Anyway, a bunch of the Paupers generally hang out at the
Junction, so that's where I went. There's a jukebox and a Coke
machine and some pool tables and a cigarette machine and no
paint on the walls since around World War II. You should
smell the toilets, they'd make a cockroach barf. So in I went,
not feeling too confident or anything because I've only been
here a few times before and there's no particular bunch of guys
I know real well or anything. I mean, I don't *belong* here like
the rest of them. There's this book we had in English class by
S. E. Hinton which we had to read and which we're supposed
to *identify* with or something, and it's all about juvenile delin-
quents, real dopey bastards with leather jackets and all that
old corn, a real boring book but a lot of the Paupers loved it, I
bet, because they act just like the dopey bastards in the book,
like they've done *every*thing and get laid every night of the week
by these girls that do real disgusting things with them and beg
for more. These guys are kind of a subspecies of Pauper that I
call Posers. What they do is, they act tough, and how they do it

is they look down their nose at you and are always glancing around while they talk like they're expecting the cops to come busting in with pump-action shotguns to arrest them for being so fucking *dangerous to the community* or something. It's all an act, it really is, and I can see right through it, same as I can see through just about anything that's phony. These Posers really get into the role, playing pool with cigarettes hanging out of their mouths, which is just terrible for aiming the cue when there's all that smoke in your eyes, but it looks *real tough*.

So I got a Coke and pretended to watch a game while I see who's around that I know from school. I bet there's a few other guys here that flunked pretty bad, too, only in their case it's because they're genuinely dumb or their father beats them up and their mother's a dipsomaniac or some sociological reason. I guarantee I'm the only smart guy that flunked. It's hard to see who's around, there's so much smoke in the air, and the only bright lights are way down close to the pool tables. Then I see this guy Tony Hunsinger that got to be real famous last year when he was expelled for calling Mr. Seddon the math teacher a cunt and then not apologizing for it. He looks about twenty, but really he's only seventeen. He could go in a bar and they wouldn't ask for his ID or anything. He's talking to this other guy so I hung around waiting for them to finish, and when the other guy turned his head to see what everyone around the nearest pool table was oohing and aahing about, which must've been a spectacular shot or something, I saw a chance and stepped right up.

"Hi, Tony!"

He looked down at me like I'm a turd on the sidewalk that's stood up on its pointy end and *talked*.

"What the fuck you want, Weems?"

He remembers my name! It's pathetic how grateful I am.

"Nothin', Tony, nothin'. Just passing the time."

"Well, pass it somewhere else."

"Just wondered if you had any grass . . ."

He does a little pushing sometimes. The other guy turned around then to see who Tony's talking to, and *he* looks at me like I'm a turd that *tap*-dances. "Who's this?" he says, acting real bored.

"Some asshole," says Tony.

"Beat it, asshole."

"Just wondered if there's any grass around . . ."

"There will be tomorrow," the guy says, and he winks at Tony.

"Yeah?" I say, and my voice is all squeaky, the way it goes when I'm nervous. Sometimes I sound like Betty Boop.

"Yeah. My old man's gonna mow the fuckin' lawn."

They both yuk-yukked like it's the funniest thing anyone said *ever*, and stupid me, I laughed, too, which was a big mistake because when I'm nervous, I've also got this laugh that in the funny papers would sound like this—Tee hee hee—which only female characters like Minnie fucking Mouse get to do. It made Hunsinger and the other prick laugh even more, and what do I do? I make things worse. This is what I say—"No, I mean *real* grass. . . ."

Jesus. I really said that. How stupid can you get. *Real* grass. It really broke them up, those *morons*.

"Anyone ever tell you you're a creep?" says Tony's pal. He's a real dorky-looking bastard now I come to think of it, a real conehead. I bet he can't even *read* the funny papers.

"Not lately," I say. Very witty. Very *cutting*.

"Well, I'm tellin' you for free," he says. It's obvious he thinks I'm too pathetic to even make fun of anymore. The situation called for a fast exit, but you can't turn around and walk off just because you've made an asshole of yourself. You have to try and get some of your pride back, really you do.

"Okay," I said. "Fine. Well, don't read too much S. E. Hinton, you'll strain your eyes."

Quick about-face, march to the door, but before I take two steps, the other guy grabs me. "What?" he says, and pulls me around to face him again. "What?" He actually wanted me to *explain*.

"Forget it," says Tony.

I was getting scared, frankly. I can't stand the thought of

someone hitting me. It's just about the worst thing you can
think of, getting *hit* by someone.

"What the fuck didja say, creepo?"

"Leave him alone," says Tony. "He's a gimp."

Jesus, that hurt. That really hurt. Gimp, he calls me. You'd
think I had one leg and a crutch and a tin cup or something.
Gimp. I can't think of a single thing to say. I want both of
them, but especially Hunsinger, to be squashed by a dump truck,
one of those big fuckers with the twelve-foot tires and about
fifty tons of rock in the tipper. I want their kneecaps shot off
with a Magnum .357, and then I want them left to die of
gangrene in the desert, but I'll leave food and water so they
don't die too quickly. The conehead's looking down at my legs
to see what's so gimpy about me, but he can't see anything in
particular that's crippled-looking or anything. I practically felt
like bawling. It was so *uncalled*-for!

"Don't *call* me that. . . ."

What a fucking hero! I actually managed to *say* something.
But it must've come out soft and squeaky because the other guy
leaned closer and said, "What?" He's still looking at my legs,
looking for gimpiness. Then Tony gave me a shove.

"Fuck off, Weems."

Then he turned his pal away and they both had their backs
to me. I stood there like an idiot, wishing them both staked out
naked on anthills while I pour sugar and honey all over them,
especially their dicks, which are probably bigger than mine and
get plenty of use inside those slutty Pauper girls that are always
hanging around shitty bastards like Tony Hunsinger.

I had to get out. I got out. I went to the 9.30 show at the
Hillcrest, a real fuckhead movie about teenagers. The plot you
wouldn't believe unless you've got a cabbage for a brain. It's
about this college that's going bankrupt. They only have boys
there, it's this big tradition going back to the Pilgrim Fathers
practically, and what they have to do to get their enrollment up
is let girls in. The principal doesn't want to because he's an old
fart that never had his dick sucked or anything and hates
women, but the board outvotes him and girls start arriving by
the busload in about ninety seconds, and every single one of

them has got this perfect complexion and around three yards of hair, blond mostly, and big tits and short shorts. They shot this piece of garbage in summer so the girls can wear these short shorts and tank tops so you can see how sexy they are. I mean, it's really *obvious*. Naturally all the guys at this college go batshit when they see them and get all horny and everything, and the big problem in their lives is the girls' dorm is in one building and the guys' dorm is in another one, so they can't prong them or anything because there's a curfew and even a *dog* patrol to stop these horny freshmen getting from one side of campus to the other. Then this guy who up till then was just a standard-issue nerd says he's got this ultrasonic whistle that brings dogs running, and they use this fucking whistle to keep the dogs occupied while the guys race across to the girls' dorm. According to this movie everybody in the whole place just wants to get fucked, like it's all they ever talk about, and after the dogs are gotten out of the way everybody *gets* fucked, no problem, with this big orgy happening. Then the principal wakes up and smells a rat and goes to investigate and practically has a heart attack when he finds out, but even though he's at death's door he's got to stop the orgy, so he sets off the fire alarm and two seconds later there's tits and asses flying everywhere with everyone scrambling to get the hell out. That's only the beginning, the first forty minutes. It gets too stupid after that to even talk about, but there's plenty more T and A, and even the principal gets laid in the end by about a dozen girls and winds up dressed like an ancient Roman in this fucking sheet and says it's just fine with him if everyone fucks their brains out. What a piece of *crap!* But when it ended everyone came out all laughing and smiling and saying what a terrific movie it was. I swear, sometimes I think I'm the only smart person in town.

I started walking home. Every few minutes a bunch of cars'd go past me with plenty of screaming going on inside and about a million decibels of music coming out the windows, all of them heading for a party someplace where they'll scream a whole lot more and get drunk and feel each other up and smash their cars on the way home around dawn. Fuck that for a caper. Who needs it. I got about a mile along Timberland when this car comes along and pulls up just behind me and honks. Cops! is what I think, getting all scared, I don't know why, I never break any laws hardly. I even keep my gum wrappers in my pocket till I pass a trash can. But it isn't cops, it's Loretta in her cab, so I got in and we drove off. The meter isn't going, naturally, seeing as I'm her brother. She's not supposed to do stuff like that, but she does it anyway.

"New in town?" she asks, like she always does when she gives me a free ride.

"Yes, ma'am," I said. It's this game we play.

"Looking for a good time?" she says next.

"Oh, absolutely. The gooder the better."

"Us cabbies know where the good times are, Bub." She calls me Bub.

"Please take me to where the good times are, cabbie."

"It'll cost you plenty."

"I don't care. I've got to have a good time or bust."

"Health insurance all paid up?"

"Just last week. I'm covered for everything."

"Including diseases they haven't put names to yet?"

"Weeeell . . ." I do this doubtful part real convincingly.

"You like seafood?" she says.

"Splendid!" I say. It's one of my favorite words, *splendid*, but I don't ever use it except when I'm with Loretta. I say it like Basil Rathbone in the late show— "Oh, splendid!"

"That's good," she says, "because you'll be eating crabs this place you're going." She's got this pretty disgusting sense of humor, Loretta, but it's funny-disgusting, not dirty-disgusting.

"Maybe I've changed my mind."

"Chickening out, Bub?"

"Weeeell . . ."

"I know this other place."

"Okay, let's go there."

Where the other place is, is 1404 Westwood Drive, naturally. We pull up outside and I look at the house and start massaging my forehead, like I'm real puzzled and trying to figure something out.

"But . . . but I have the strangest *feel*ing . . . It's as though I've been here before . . ." I'm still doing Basil Rathbone. "These peculiar sensations . . . they're overpowering . . . yes, yes! I *have* been here before!"

"Take it easy, Bub."

"I tell you I *have* been here! In the living room there's a sofa . . . and a TV!"

"By golly, you're right. There *is!*"

"And . . . and . . . in the crapper there's a *roll of toilet paper* and . . . and . . . a Renuzit *fart-killer!*"

"Yes! This is just incredibly amazing!"

"And *people* live here . . . a warmhearted family of four—no, *three*—decent, hardworking, God-fearing Americans all . . ."

"Sorry, Bub. That settles it. You've got the wrong place."

We quit then and laughed at each other. We do a pretty good job in the acting department, believe me.

"Uh-oh," says Loretta, and I looked where she's looking and saw this van parked a little way along the road. I know what's on the side—"Mack's Frame Shop. You WANT it framed, you GOT it framed." It used to be called Gandalf's, but Mack's accountant told him it wasn't the right image for a viable business. He said Gandalf's sounded like a vegetarian restaurant.

"I think Peggy's got the colored lights going," says Loretta. That's a line from a Brando movie. What it means is Peggy's fucking Mack in there. I like Mack, he's okay, even framed a picture of an eagle for me for nothing, but I don't want to go in there while him and Peggy are pounding away in the bedroom. Then Loretta's radio spits out a crackle and she's got to report where she is, and two seconds later she's on her way to a fare. She knew I didn't want to go inside.

"If I drop you off on Delancy will you be okay?"

"Sure. I'll go on home later. It's early yet."

"What we need is a bigger house."

"Yeah."

Loretta never brings her boyfriends to our place, not to fuck them, anyway. She'll maybe bring them around to show them off to Peggy and me, but she always goes to their place or a motel for sex with them. I think she thinks it's kind of crude for

Peggy to be fucking while I'm around. Sometimes I think that, too, then again, sometimes not. I can always see the other person's point of view. It's Peggy's house, after all. I don't pay rent or anything. And she's got a perfect right to fuck people if she wants. To be honest, I'm probably just jealous. Sometimes I *hate* anyone who's got someone to fuck, I really do. It's kind of disturbing how at school I'd feel good whenever news went around the grapevine about So-and-so breaking up with Such-and-such. That's a pretty fair indication of how fucked up I am about sex. It's all very negative and immature, but I can't help it. I just don't see why any sane female would want to fuck me, honest I don't. I'm being very candid here. *I* wouldn't fuck some gimpy girl. I wouldn't care if she was short like me, but I wouldn't fuck a gimp, no sir. It's really sick for me to think that way, but that's the way I think. I'd hate for anyone to hear this tape. I keep it pretty well hid in my room, though, and I'm talking softly into it so no one can hear and start asking why I'm talking to myself.

I could tell Loretta felt sorry for me, but there's nothing she could've done. She's on the night shift till 4 A.M. She reached in her pocket and pulled out five bucks and gave it to me. "Take in the midnight show at the Hillcrest," she says.

"I just came from there, and it's already started, anyway."

"Well, keep the cash. Sooner or later you'll need it."

"Thanks."

A few minutes later I'm on my own again. What do I do? I head for home all over again. Maybe Mack'll be gone by the time I get there. Walk, walk, walk. My hip is killing me. I want to take a shower too. I really stink. I generally take a lot of showers in summer. When I was a little kid, Peggy used to call me Hygiene Boy, like Astro Boy or Superboy. Hygiene Boy. What a goofy name. I was a goofy kid. I still am. I'm a goofy, gimpy *kid*. Jesus, I really feel like killing myself sometimes. I hate it when I get this way. *Forget it*. I'm walking home for the second time tonight and I'm thinking about that eagle picture Mack framed for me. What made me cut it out of a magazine is, when I was a kid I used to imagine I was an eagle flying way, way up in the air, only I'm walking down the street, see, and this eagle that I am is flying through a world of gigantic things, everyday things like trees and houses, only they're a hundred times bigger than usual, so although it looks like my eye is about five feet from the ground, really I'm about two miles high, looking around at this colossally huge enormous world made for giants, an eagle the size of a pinhead floating high, high above that sidewalk way down there, a massive sidewalk like an airfield made for planes so *huge* they'd never leave the ground, and those trees so tall their top branches must be dying in the stratosphere, and those *houses* . . . A skyscraper on the same scale would've touched the moon! It made walking down the street interesting. I still do it sometimes. But not at night. It's better in daylight.

Then this smell of fresh-baked bread came to me on the breeze. Where it was coming from was the Holsum Bread Co. on Whitney, and I got this brilliant idea to go get a loaf *directly* from the oven. I was pretty hungry by then. There's nothing in the world better than the smell of fresh-baked bread, and the taste of it comes in a close second. I know the way around to the back of the bakery because Loretta used to go with this guy Steve that works there, and a couple times I went with her when she picked him up in the cab. I think she took me along those times just to let him know *he* doesn't automatically come first the way most guys expect things to be. I didn't go out on dates with them, nothing like that, but I figure she was letting him know she isn't the type that brushes family under the rug just because she's met some guy. He was okay about it, though, even gave me some of those cream horns. It's called the Holsum Bread Co. but they make other stuff, too, pastry and stuff. But they broke up anyway, Steve and Loretta. She never did tell me why. That was around eight months ago. He seemed like a nice enough guy to me. Loretta's had four different guys that I know of. I could be jealous of her if I let myself.

So I went around the back to the delivery bay where there's this big door they keep open a little bit in summer to let the heat out. It gets really hot in there with the ovens and all. I went in, and first off no one noticed me, then this guy comes over and asks what I want, and I told him I'm looking for

Steve. He turns around and hollers, "Steve!" and there's Steve way down the other end of the room, which is a big room with tables to slap the dough around on, and here he comes with his arms all white and this crazy white cap on his head and a long apron. "Hi, guy," he says. He always said that when Loretta brought me around those few times.

"Hi, Steve."

"Looking for a summer job?"

Well, I wasn't, not really, but it's not a bad idea.

"Yeah."

"We got anything?" he asks the first guy, who's still hanging around, the nosy type, I bet.

"Nothin'," says the guy, then he says, "Keep an eye on seven," which must mean oven number seven, then he goes off and starts doing baker stuff, so maybe he's not so nosy.

"Sorry, Burris. We're pretty much full-handed right now."

"That's okay. Did you just bake some bread? It smells great."

"I sure did. You want a loaf to take home?"

"Yeah, please."

"Come on down here."

We went over to the cooling racks where there's all these long, square tins full of bread set out to cool off.

"Just out of the oven," says Steve.

You could practically eat the smell, it's so wonderful.

"Better wait a minute," he says. "They're still hot."

"Okay."

"How's Loretta, still cabbying?"

"On duty right this minute."

"How's she doing?"

"Pretty good, I guess."

"She seeing anyone these days?"

"I dunno. Yeah, I think so. Some guy."

"Well, tell her I said hi."

"Okay."

There's nothing more to say for a little while, just a few seconds, but they were awful long. Then he says, "Let's turn this sucker over."

He's got these mittens on strings around his neck like little kids have in winter so they won't lose them, and he pulls out a tray and turns it upside down over a table. It's a double-loaf tray with two loaves in it end to end, and when they fall out they're joined together till he pulls them apart. When he did that the smell just about laid me out.

"You just want a half?" he says.

"Yeah."

They call a double loaf *one* loaf and one loaf a *half*, don't ask me why.

"How much is it?" I ask him.

"Seeing as you're a buddy, fifty cents."

"Deal," I said, and pulled out a buck. "Got change?"

"Not on me. How about making life simple and taking the whole thing."

"Okay."

He put both halves in a paper bag for me.

"Well, thanks a lot."

"Take care now," he says.

"I will."

"And say hi to Loretta for me."

"I'll do it."

It's kind of embarrassing, I don't exactly know why. Maybe I shouldn't have gone in there now that Steve isn't with Loretta anymore, but I really wanted that bread. I had to keep passing the bag from one hand to the other, it's so hot.

"So long." It's all I can think to say.

"Let it cool. You eat it while it's doughy, you'll get indigestion."

"Okay, thanks."

Out I went. Fuck indigestion. I pulled out a hunk of hot bread and crammed it in my face. Deeeelicious! I'm munching away and walking down the delivery ramp when this kid comes up to me. It's hard to see his face because he's got this baseball cap on and the light over the delivery van parking lot is behind him. Then he speaks and it's a girl, a real skinny girl.

"Is that where you go to get the bread?" she asks, and she's pointing behind me at the door I just now came out of.

"Yeah."

I've got a wad of bread big as a fist in my mouth.

"Can you just walk in and they'll sell it to you?"

She must've smelled it on the breeze, same as me.

"Sure."

"How much?"

"You mean, how much bread or how much dough? I mean, do you mean how much actual bread will they sell you or how much does it cost?"

I felt real stupid, real *pedantic*.

"How much does it cost?" she says.

"I dunno. I know a guy in there so I got mine cheap."

"If you went in with me, would he sell it to me cheap too?"

"I dunno. Maybe."

I don't know if she's got a nerve asking me for a favor like that or not. Anyway, I don't want to go back in there, not after Steve asking about Loretta that way and giving me a special price on the bread.

"Did you just want one loaf?" I ask.

"I guess so."

"Here," I said, and pulled the loaf I'm eating out of the bag and gave her the other one plus the bag to keep it in. It wouldn't have been polite to give her just a naked loaf.

"But you got this for yourself," she says.

"No, I only wanted one, but I had to take two because he couldn't make change. I don't need two loaves."

"You sure? I don't want to take your bread."

She's got this drawly accent like she's from Texas or someplace, but it doesn't sound dumb or country hick or anything. I still can't see her face.

"I couldn't eat two."

I pushed the bag at her again. I just wanted her to take it so I could get going. I felt like an idiot standing there with a loaf in my hand that's got a big chunk torn out of it, like I'm a kid that's been caught with his hand in the cookie jar.

"Well, thank you," she says, and takes it at last.

"Don't mention it."

I can be very polite when I want to be. What I want her to do in return for my being so polite and generous is to turn around and go away so I can do the same.

"Is it good bread?" she wants to know.

"Yeah, the best."

"It sure smells good."

I'm starting to think maybe she *is* dumb after all. How long can you stand around discussing bread?

"Well, thanks again," she says, and then she's walking away. She's even littler than I am, which I couldn't tell before because I was still a little way up the delivery ramp while we talked, but now I'm at the bottom and watching her walk away and she's got to be five foot or even less. There's short hair sticking out from behind her ears, and she's got this peculiar kind of *loping* walk that makes her head bob up and down. Definitely funny-looking.

I started walking again and got home limping pretty bad. I practically walked my hip to death tonight. I didn't have any bread left. I ate half on the way, then got sick of it, all that flabby dough, and the crust wasn't anywhere near as thick as I like, so I threw the rest away. Mack's van was still parked outside. I went in the back door and the fluorescent clock in the kitchen says 2:11. No wonder my body's killing me. Then the kitchen light goes on and Mack's standing there with no clothes on.

"Hi, Burris," he says, and goes over to the refrigerator.

"Hi."

He doesn't care if he's nude or anything. He's tall and skinny and he's got all this hair and beard that makes him look like Moses or someone, all dark and curly like his pubic hair, which is pretty long, too, with this big zoob hanging out of it. He hauls open the refrigerator door and stands there looking inside, just stands there and looks and looks, like there's a TV in there or something. Sometimes I think Mack's totally spaced-out, but his business does okay, so maybe he's just not a big talker.

"Feels good," he says.

"Huh?"

"Cold."

He means the cold air spilling out onto his shins and feet.

"Yeah, I bet."

"Got any chicken?"

"I dunno. I haven't looked lately."

"Cold ham'd do."

"Well, maybe there's some there, I dunno. I'm going to bed."

"Okay."

I left him with his hairy head blocking half the light from inside the refrigerator and went to my room, which is the back room, right next to Peggy's studio. I couldn't go to sleep straight off, so I've added to the tape. Side one's just about finished. I'll turn it over for the next entry. Jesus, I'm tired.

Signing off.

4

Saturday I had to help Peggy like I promised. We stacked about thirty pictures in the Impala's backseat and trunk and headed for the mall. Mack was already gone when I woke up. Peggy didn't say anything about him. Loretta didn't come home after she finished her shift, so she must've stayed at Pete's. I think she must like the guy, because it's got to be a problem staying around at his place with the two little kids his wife left him with running around underfoot. Or maybe she *likes* kids, I don't know. I forgot to say Pete's a lineman with the telephone company.

The mall is the biggest shopping center in town, bigger than K-mart or Wal Mart or Shop City. You can get everything from a napkin ring to a catamaran at the mall. Where Peggy sets up her stuff is over in a corner of the parking lot where just about everyone who parks his car has to pass by on his way to the main mall entrance. There's a strip of ground there where you can hire a few yards from the mall committee and sell stuff. It's mostly handmade sandals and belts and perfumed candles and all that junk. I wouldn't buy any of it. Some do, though. I mean, about fifty thousand people must walk by on a typical Saturday, and maybe a few hundred'll stop and actually look at the stuff, and maybe fifty'll buy something, a belt or candle or one of Peggy's pictures, whatever. If the stuff belonged to me, if it was something I'd *made*, I'd get pissed off with the way most people just walk straight past like they do. But seeing as the goods aren't mine, and seeing as I think they're pretty much junk, anyway, all I feel when I stand there waiting for a customer is *embarrassed*, because I don't want all these dorks to think *I* painted these tigers and mountain scenes and Jesus Christs.

Frankly, I think it's kind of cynical of Peggy to do pictures of Jesus. She isn't a Christian or anything. She thinks Christians are idiots. "How can one man take the sins of the world on his shoulders?" she says. "It's ridiculous. It's wish-fulfillment." She's probably right, but to go ahead and do pictures of him is pretty cynical and two-faced, I'd say. She watches the religious channels sometimes just to prove to herself it's all dumb, and I bet even Jesus would say it's dumb if he saw some of those shows with those dickhead preachers with their phony purr-raise the Lor-rud voices. They're pretty funny, even if they don't mean to be. My favorite is this woman that's got hair looks like it's a wig made from horsehair and crop-sprayed with about ten gallons of Superglue. She's got a voice like a crosscut saw being twanged. Peggy's favorites are that chubby couple that praise the Lord in this set that's supposed to look like someone's living room, with chintzy curtains on the fake windows and a chintzy sofa and chairs and a chintzy carpet and fucking little *dolls* sitting on the bureau. Mr. Chubby's got a big smile and styled hair that's never out of place, and Mrs. Chubby's got eyelashes like tarantulas. Peggy calls them Bim Bim and Boom Boom. They just love the Lord, those two, and they practically burst into tears whenever Bim Bim reads a few lines from the Good Book or Boom Boom gets up off the chintzy sofa and sings a song. Plenty laffs there, believe me.

"Get that look off your face," says Peggy when we got the table and umbrella and pictures all set up and ready.

"What look?"

"That *pained* look. Try smiling. Oh, God, is that supposed to be a smile? You look like someone who's just peed himself."

"I didn't get enough sleep."

"Neither did I, and *I* don't look like that."

"Same amount of sleep, different reason," I said, and for a moment there I thought she was going to crack me one across the face.

"You said you'd help me today, Burris."

"Well, I *am*."

"No you're not. Can't you put a pleasant expression on your face?"

"No."

"Thank you very much. Next time you sit down at the table, ask yourself where the food's coming from."

"Your veteran's widow's check."

"*And* the paintings."

"Right."

"So you can just help me sell a few. You don't have to enjoy doing it, just *look* as though you are."

"Okay, *okay*."

Bad day ahead, I could tell. She's got this bitchy look in her eye. About eleven o'clock the parking lot really started to fill up. Eleven till three is the mall's rush hour on a Saturday. I don't know why Peggy needs me there. If someone wants a picture, they pick it up and pay their $15 and walk away. It doesn't get wrapped up in paper or anything. She sold a wild stallion and an Elvis in the first half hour, no sweat. All I'm doing is taking up shade under the umbrella.

"You don't need me here," I said.

She gave me a real dirty look.

"You just can't stick at *any*thing, can you?"

"Guess not."

"Are you going to be like this the rest of your life?"

"No, I'm gonna write away for nine ninety-five's worth of Tenacity."

Her lips went all hard and straight, the way they do when she's really pissed. "Go away from me, Burris," she says, very cold.

So I did. I went inside the mall where it's cool. There's about fifty different stores in there, on two levels. I got myself a corn dog and strolled around. If I'm in the right mood I can enjoy crowds. I read the faces moving by me. I've got this talent, this *faculty* for reading faces. That girl over there is frantic because she thinks she won't be able to find exactly the right kind of shoes she wants for the big party coming up. She's real unhappy about it. Unbelievable. Her friend with her hopes she *doesn't* find them, because her friend hates her deep down for being better-looking and better-dressed and making her look frumpy by comparison. That guy over there with his wife in the fancy furniture store is looking confident because he knows he can afford to buy anything they've got in stock. What he doesn't know is, his wife isn't impressed by his wallet; in fact she's not impressed by *any*thing he's got and deep down wishes she had've married that other guy that asked her and like a fool she turned him down. She wants to spend hubby's cash because she's miserable and angry and bored, real *bored*. There's a big hole inside her, and she keeps trying to plug it with dollars. Have I got news for you, lady—it's bottomless. She's looking around for the most expensive thing. Yep, there it is, the grandfather clock, a genuine colonial imitation, a bargain at a mere $1,295. Why not buy two and put one in the garage to keep the BMW company!

Those young guys going into the sports store want some of those cutoff T-shirts that show your belly. Summer's here and it's gal-impressing time, gang. Let's get out there and *flex* those pecs, *clench* those glutes and *bunch* those lats. Their conversation'd make Fred Flintstone look smart but boy! can they parade their bods. Fill that gap, fellers, strut yer stuff. Ten, fifteen years from now you'll be behind your old man's desk running the family business—matching bathroom fittings—a very risky trade because the basins are the same shape and color as the toilets and someone who's just a little bit stupid might take a crap where he's supposed to wash his hands afterward, and you'll be getting fatter and balder and remembering those wonderful days before you went away to fucking college to learn how to become a citizen and the old man bought you that going-away present, remember? Was it a Camaro or a Trans Am? Who cares! It's a great life if you don't ask questions! Bounce that basketball! Get them grades! Yaaaaaayy, *team!* Rah! Rah! Rah! Repeat after me—I yearn to learn to earn more coin to burn. . . . The girl looking for the shoes'll find the guy looking for the cutoff T-shirt and they'll fall in love over a Thick-Shake, and after he's graduated, they'll do their best to increase the population of the ever-growing nation and in time their kids'll agonize over shoes and grades, and when they're old enough the old man'll buy them a car to drive off to college in, only because he's made such a success of the business he'll buy them *Porsches*, because this is what America's *all about*, guy!

I'm outside the Organ Center. With a name like that you'd expect to see bits and pieces of human beings in the window, Frank N. Stein, prop. There's a sign out front so no one can miss it—DEMONSTRATION TODAY AT 12 NOON. Oh, boy! I'm just in time for the *demonstration!* All the organs have been pushed back to the walls and there's camp chairs set up for the audience. Everybody there is *at least* fifty. The star of the show is a fat lady in this long black evening gown with spangles. She must've looked pretty strange coming across the parking lot like that. Maybe she changed in the back room. You can tell she thinks she looks pretty damn good, smiling and nodding at the whole room like she's the queen of England or something, then she figures these good people must be just *dying* to hear her tickle the old ivories, so down she sits. She gets most of her ass on the stool and starts playing churchy music. It's kind of familiar, but I just can't Name That Tune. I started watching the audience. Most of them I can't see because they've got their backs to me, but some of the ones at the back have got profiles. There's this one old lady, I mean *real* old, all dressed up for her big treat of the week, which is shopping at the mall, and she's got *tears* rolling down her face she thinks the music is so beautiful. She wants this tune at her funeral service, which isn't far away now because her guts are all eaten out with cancer and she knows it, even if the prick of a doctor told her it was something else, something an old biddy like her could *handle*. She knows her son and daughter-in-law are just waiting for her to die even though they keep telling her she's got *years* left. Everything is a lie. The only clean thing left is the funeral, and she wants this drony-phony music to get sent off by because it reminds her of how things were when she was a little girl before the sky got filled with planes. Don't ask me how I know this stuff, I just *know*. I've got this third eye in my forehead and it sees Truth, and now it looks to me like the Organ Center *is* a church, and they're all sitting there waiting for a corpse in a coffin. Now the *organs* look like coffins, all squared-off, polished wood with candlesticks on top. The whole crowd is *surrounded* by coffins. The coffins are moving closer all the time, inch by inch, but no one notices, they're all hypnotized by the music, and Fats at the keyboard keeps right on playing, with this big *exalted* smile on her face. Look out, lady! The coffins are coming! And I'm going. From farther down the mall I could hear her cranking up with her next number, "The Battle Hymn of the Republic." Go get 'em, Fats!

I started to sweat, like someone tipped a cup of water down my back. Am I sick? Into Orange Julius for a quick juice to cool off. The air-conditioning puts little tears of ice on my brow. The place is just full of kids my own age, but I'm old, old, *old!* I'm a gimpy old man that's seen it all. The girls behind the counter couldn't find Greenland on a map if you told them it's in the northern hemisphere. They've got $30 permanents. Isn't there a girl left in this town that lets her fucking hair just *grow?* Back in the booths there's plenty of giggling and talking. The girls back there are all color-coordinated in their dinky little blouses and short shorts from Merry Go Round and their pink sneakers and little white socks with a pom-pom at the back like a rabbit's tail. They're just as cutesy-wutesy as you can get, with Shine Free makeup and tennis-star sun visors that years ago only came in green and got worn by the late show's fat city editor behind a desk full of phones with a cigar stub in his mouth shouting down the line, "Get me that story *fast* or you're fired!" but now visors have been *rediscovered* and come in all the colors of the rainbow. It takes ten minutes to put one on so the headband doesn't crush the permanent, but it's worth the effort because they know they look so fucking *cute*, and their tight little cunts get all gooey over MTV heavy-metal monsters from another planet, but they wouldn't actually *date* anyone that looked like that, no sir, it's strictly boy-next-door for these gals. High-school jock is as high as they aspire in the *real* world, and when they find one, they'll put out, but only if they *really* like him a lot and putting out'll turn what *he* feels into true *lerv*, baby. They're like sisters, all of them exactly the same, jabbering and interrupting each other and squealing non-stop like a flock of colored geese, and the topic of *interest*, the one and only topic under discussion today and every day is guys, guys, guys, but not guys like me, not geeks in any shape or form, thank you very much, only guys with Clearasil skin and Aquafresh smiles, hair by Snip'n'Style, body by Health'n'Fitness, mind by Home'n'Family, wardrobe by Adidas, wheels courtesy of the old man, but it's *got to be a two-door*, because four-door means over twenty-five, means *babies*, and that's a long ways over the horizon yet, so let's have fun! fun! fun! while we're young! young! young!

They've noticed me staring at them. Now they're whispering and looking at me. One little bitch poked her tongue out. Fuck this for a caper. I couldn't even finish my juice, just up and left, back out into the river of shoppers, down past the Music Store—25% OFF ALL TAPES—the Donut Shoppe—EVEN OUR HOLES ARE D'LICIOUS!—the Fashion House—BARGAINS! BARGAINS! BARGAINS!—Camper's Supplies—YOU TOO CAN OWN A CANOE!—the Cut'n'Blow Job . . . Blow *Dry*—TODAY'S SPECIAL, CUT'N'PERM $12.95!—the Supa-Value Drugstore—SUPA SAVINGS ON SUPA SATURDAY!—the Portrait Studio—WEDDINGS! BIRTHDAYS! ANNIVERSARIES!—Sears—THERE'S MORE FOR YOUR LIFE AT SEARS!—the Home Appliances Store—COME ON IN, WE'RE FRIENDLY—the Treasure Chest—SEE THE MISS TEEN USA JEWELRY COLLECTION—the Cookie Jar, the Crock of Shit, the County Morgue, the Last Exit . . . I don't feel good. I'm sweating like a pig. I gotta get *outa* here!

In the parking lot it's pushing toward ninety, but there's a lot of sky overhead crisscrossed with jet trails and only cars around me, rows and rows of them, sneering and grinning with their grilles, turning their taillights and bumpers to me.

I caught the bus across town to the pool. I didn't have a swimsuit with me. I don't own one. In a swimsuit you can see how different my legs are. I'm whiter than white from the neck down. I just wanted to hear water splashing. Just *hearing* it can make you feel cooler. I didn't waste a buck fifty getting in, just stood outside the wire fence and watched. It's really packed in there, with all the splashing my ears can catch. Around the pool, all along the grass border there's these tilted plastic sun lounges, every one of them occupied, even the spaces in between, just crammed with meat, brown and pink, all held together while it cooks by little bitty pieces of colored string and cloth, legs and arms and backs and bellies and tits and asses all in tumbled rows like seals on a beach. There's a Labrador in there going crazy, chasing around and around the pool, just loving all the splish-splashing and getting chased by the lifeguard seeing as pets aren't allowed. The lifeguard's around seventeen and really pissed at the dog because she doesn't want to be scrambling around on the concrete trying to catch some stupid mutt, she wants to be up on her perch under the umbrella where she can show off her terrific legs and check out all the guys that come in for a dip. She's got on a little shorty dress with no sleeves like the mad scientist's daughter in *Forbidden Planet*. Hearing the water made me cool for a little while, but standing there in the sun just made me hot again.

No joy for Burris at the pool, so I went to the library and got another book by John Wyndham that wrote *The Chrysalids* and took it home this time. This one's called *The Midwich Cuckoos*, and I read it on the back porch in the hammock there. It's shady and I can concentrate. The story's about this little village in England that gets cut off from the rest of the world for twenty-four hours by this invisible wall, and when the wall disappears, I mean when it goes away—an *invisible* wall can't disappear—when it isn't *there* anymore, no one in the village can remember what happened during those twenty-four hours. It's like they were asleep or something and have got amnesia. It's a big mystery, but things get even more mysterious a couple months later when all the village women find out they're pregnant, whether they're married or not. It's a pretty old book and stuff like that was a big deal back then. Anyway, they give birth to these kids with blond hair and funny-looking eyes, and these kids are *telepathic*—telepathy again, like in the other book— and they make people do what they want even if they're still only little. In fact, they're not like human beings at all, with no emotions or anything, and they're super-intelligent and everyone's scared shitless of them.

Then Peggy came home in a bad mood, even if she sold five pictures. What she's pissed about is me. She won't talk to me. That's okay. I stayed out of her way and went back to reading. I could expect to feed myself. When she's pissed at me she only makes food for herself. Okay again. There's stuff in the freezer I can whip up in a jiffy later on when I feel like it. Back to the book, and things are getting bad in the village, which I forgot to say is called Midwich. The kids are the cuckoos, see. The creepy little fuckers are killing people who get in their way, not murdering them outright but using their *will* to make whoever pissed them off go and commit suicide. That's the kind of talent I wish I had sometimes. The kids don't live with separate families anymore because they've quit pretending they belong to anyone the way an ordinary kid belongs, and they've all moved into this big old house together and got the guy who's telling the story to educate them, give them real advanced stuff way beyond their years. And what he does, this guy, he decides to blow them up because he knows in a few years these little kids'll be powerful enough to rule the world. So he rigs up a time bomb in his briefcase and turns up at the kids' place same as usual to give them a lesson in nuclear physics or whatever, and he knows they can read his mind so the *last* thing he can let himself think about is the bomb in the briefcase right there on the desk in front of him, but the kids pick up his intentions with their minds and gang up on him to make him spill what's in the back of his thoughts, and he does something very clever to hide the bomb's existence from them—he thinks of a brick wall. A brick wall, a brick wall, a brick wall . . . and all the time the little bastards are probing his mind, the bomb is ticking away right under their noses. He's only got to hold out a half minute more, but the wall's beginning to crumble, crumble away, and behind it is the briefcase and in it is the bomb, and the very second the kids realize how he tricked them, it explodes and wipes them all out, kids, teacher, house, everything, and Earth is saved. Wow! This Wyndham guy has got to be about the best writer that ever lived. How come they didn't give us *him* in school instead of S. E. Hinton?

"I'm going out tonight."

Peggy's standing in the back porch doorway. It's getting dark now, and I had to turn on the outside light for the last few chapters. There's moths and other bugs flitting around and she swatted at them to keep them off her face.

"Where to?"

"A party at Mack's. You're invited."

"Nah, I think I'll stay home."

"Suit yourself."

You can tell she's relieved. She wants to get away from the house, and I remind her of it. It's understandable. And I really don't want to go. I've been to Mack's parties before and they're always the same—about fifty loaves of hot *garlic* bread—*yeeecchh!*—and this cheap wine and skull-bust tequila and dope by the handful, and Mack always, *always* puts on this boring music from when he was young—Iron Butterfly, Vanilla Fudge, Buffalo Springfield, all that crapola, and everyone ends up completely zonked out. No thanks. I like having the house to myself about as much as Peggy likes to get out of it, so we're both happy with the situation.

Loretta came home then, and she and I made something to eat, which was frozen pizza with extra cheese—we both go crazy for it—then she's off to the movies with Pete. Peggy gave her a lift to Pete's place seeing as Loretta hasn't got the cab tonight. And then I'm all alone. On goes the TV. First comes the eight o'clock movie, Elvis in *Wild in the Country*. Elvis is this "rebellious youth who becomes involved with three women." That's what the *TV Guide* says, and it ain't lyin'. If this is rebellion, I want *in. Three* women! Totally unbelievable. But the title song isn't bad, even if it's kind of corny. Sat at home on a Saturday night. Is this any way for a red-blooded boy to behave? No sir, but I don't care. The rest of the world can party all it wants, I'm doing just fine. Then it's ten-thirty, time for another movie. Oh no! The umpteenth rerun of *Von Ryan's Express*. Shit! I practically know the lines backward, so what I do instead is flip back and forth between the rock video programs. There's always three or four on a Saturday night. Also I got very drunk on Peggy's stash of Budweiser. I have this problem with beer. It goes right through me in around two minutes, so every second or third video I'm up on my way to the john again. My bladder must be around the size of a thimble. I'm *really drunk!* Some of this tape's gonna sound ker-ayzee. I've been in front of the tube for seven hours. There's a late, late movie on, some dumb Western. I turned the sound way down. Madam and Miss haven't come home. I can hear the crickets zinging away outside. They'll keep it up till daybreak. I'm recording this on the sofa, stretched out with my feet up.

Th-tha-tha— Th-th-tha— Th-th-that's all, folks!

5

Sunday. A day of rest. I decided I'd go see Goliath crush a few cars over at the Mazda dealership. In case you don't know what Goliath is, it's a four-wheel-drive pickup, only it's got this special chassis with huge wheels and tires, tractor tires, so the cabin sits about ten feet off the ground. I mean, those tires are *enormous*. It looks pretty silly, like something you'd climb inside to ride around on the moon, but it's a big draw, Goliath, and the forecourt is jam-packed with people waiting for it to do its thing, which is to get put in low gear, rev a lot, and then climb up on the backs of these old junked-out cars that aren't worth anything and squash the fuckers flat. It looks like some weird kind of machine-mating ritual, like mechanical turtles making out. It's entertainment with a capital *E*, very uplifting, a challenge to the mind. It really makes you *think* when you see something like that. It took about thirty seconds in all. There were guys there who'd been waiting *all morning*. For *this?* You betcha. I bet they would've *really* enjoyed it if there'd been *people* inside the squashed cars. I don't know why I think that, I just do. My third eye tells me so.

That's all I did Sunday.

Monday I got a job.

I said a *job*.

I went to the Servex Box & Carton Co. They had an ad in the paper. Loretta took me in the cab, so I had no excuse for not getting there early. And I *got the job*. Jesus, I couldn't believe it.

It's only a shit job for lousy pay, but even so, did they really *have* to go and hire me? I didn't dress up or *any*thing. I didn't even make any effort at the interview. But they went and gave me the job anyway, the bastards. Basically, what I do is I stack cartons, big flattened-out cardboard cartons about six feet by ten, stack them up twenty high on this special table on wheels, then push it across to a banding machine—that's a machine with a kind of giant hoop with a gizmo inside it that whizzes around and wraps plastic banding tape completely around the stacked cartons. I have to put two bands around each stack. These big cartons are for putting refrigerators in. They've got the manufacturer's name and a picture of a refrigerator already printed on them. When they've been banded they get stacked up five high on pallets, and a forklift takes them away to the loading bay. Whither they goest from there I know not, nor do I give a fuck. This place makes all kinds of cartons, from little milk and orange juice cartons right up to the big boys that get put around refrigerators, but I'm strictly a refrigerator carton man—me and my partner, that is.

His name's Lee Trimble and he's from New Mexico. First off, when they put me with him and he got told to show me the job, I didn't like him for a few minutes there, I don't know why, just the look of him or something. He's peculiar-looking, Lee. He's around five ten but straight up and down like a telegraph pole, so he looks taller than he is. He's got no shoulders at all, I mean absolutely none. His arms are just joined to the sides of his chest where his neck ends. It's very strange, but he's not deformed or anything, just kind of out of proportion. He's got an average kind of face, nothing handsome about it and nothing ugly, just real average, and he's got this long lock of hair falls down one side of his forehead like Leo Gorcey in those old Dead End Kid movies, flopping right across the real old-fashioned glasses he wears with thick black frames, Buddy Holly glasses.

"Hey, how ya doin'!" he says.

"Okay!"

We had to shout because it's pretty noisy inside the Servex Box & Carton Co. He showed me what to do in around ninety seconds, it's such a simple-pimple job. He must've been doing it on his own till then. The cartons aren't heavy or anything, even when they're banded together, but being so big, they're kind of awkward to move from the table on wheels to the pallets, so I guess he was glad to have someone help him. He's got this big grin, very friendly. He looks about nineteen, I'd say, but it's hard to tell. He hadn't shaved for a few days, and whiskers make you look older. They don't make *me* look older because I haven't been shaving long enough, but Lee had a real raspy-looking growth sprouting out of his face all right.

"This a vacation job?" he hollers.

"Yeah! Just for the summer!"

"You get your finals?"

"Nah! Flunked!"

"Too bad!" he yells, and from then till lunch break we didn't talk, just did the work. They've got a cafeteria out at Servex that isn't too bad, and we went in there to eat. We got food from the self-service line and found a table, and that's where I found out his name's Lee Trimble and he's from New Mexico. I gave him my name too.

"Burris," he says. "What kinda name's that?"

"I dunno. I think my old man's old man was called Burris. It's in the family or something. Do you live around here?"

Sometimes I ask the dumbest questions. Of *course* he lives around here. He doesn't commute from New Mexico, idiot.

"Just temporary," he says. "My wife's kind of looking after her dad. I mean, she's looking after her *mother*. She's sick, so we came on up here to look after her awhile."

"How long have you been married?"

"Oh, a couple years now. You married?"

"Do I look it?"

I was kind of flattered he thinks I look old enough to be married, even if at the same time I know he's not serious. You just have to look at me to see there's no way I could be married.

"I guess not," he says. "You look like too much of a swinger to be all settled down."

Both of us laughed, and I think that's when I really started to like him. He's got this laugh that's even goofier than mine, a real hoot. Everyone turned around to look at us, and that made us laugh even more, you know how it is when it's a funny us-and-them type situation.

"Boy, this burger tastes like it was carved off something squashed by the side of the road."

"Yeah."

It tasted okay to me, but you don't disagree when someone says something like that, trying to be funny.

"What kind of job did you have in New Mexico?"

"Construction work mostly, some of it in Tucumcari, that's my hometown, and some of it other places. There's plenty of work down there. It's a go-ahead state. I would've stayed there, but Diane, that's my wife, she didn't want to come up here on her own. It's just temporary, though, so I don't mind doing a little crap work for a while."

He asked a few questions about me, who I live with and stuff, then he says, "How'd you hurt your leg?"

It's strange, but I didn't resent him asking, the way I would've with someone else. "Fell off the high wire," I said.

"The what?"

"High wire. We used to be a circus family before my dad died. He fell off the high wire, too, doing a triple back flip with no net. That was his specialty, working with no net."

"Jesus. That how you got hurt?"

"Well, I wasn't good enough to work without the net, but I got my leg busted anyway. I hit the net so hard I bounced right out again onto the ground. I was pretty lucky."

"Awwww, shit. I believe you made the whole thing up, you liar, you."

"Almost had you convinced, though."

He wasn't sore or anything; he had this big grin on his face.

"Was it the truth about your mother painting pictures and your sister being a cabbie?"

"Gospel. Loretta's the only woman cabbie in Buford, and you can see my mom's stuff outside the mall every Saturday."

"That big place with the fancy bricks and glass roof?"

"Right outside the main entrance."

"I went in there once, but it was a Sunday."

We talked about other stuff, like how dry the summers are in New Mexico, not all humid like here, ordinary stuff like that, then it was time to go back to work. We banded and stacked and banded and stacked, and the foreman came by and watched us awhile, then walked away without saying anything, so we must've been doing it okay. Then it's quitting time and we washed up along with everyone else. We were kind of ignored because what we do isn't really connected with anyone else, except maybe the forklift driver. The cartons come to our corner of the floor on a conveyer belt and go away on the forklift, so there's not much contact except with each other. But that suited me fine. I'd rather work with one person I know I like than a whole bunch of mixed personalities, some of whom might be a pain in the ass.

So after we're all washed up we clocked off and went outside. "You got a car, Burris?" he wants to know.

"No, but the crosstown bus comes out this far."

"No need for it. I've got wheels."

We went over to the parking lot. It was full of slamming doors and guys shouting to each other as the day shift left and the night shift came on duty. Lee went over to this decrepit old Dodge pickup with a paint job like a pinto horse, just patches everywhere, brown on dirty white, and fenders so dented and dinged they're like the surface of the moon. Then I looked in the rear window, and what I saw made me realize Lee isn't just the good ol' country boy I originally had him figured for, because what I saw was a rifle rack like you'd expect to see in any pickup, generally with a Winchester and maybe a big hunting rifle with a 12X scope or a shotgun, stuff like that, but what Lee's got resting on *his* rifle rack is a walking cane and a rolled-up umbrella! That just isn't country-boy style. There's parts of the country I bet they'd lynch him for poking fun at rifle racks like that.

He saw me looking and said, "Think you need that gimp stick, Burris?"

I didn't get offended. I even laughed! Anything that comes out through that big grin just can't be offensive, somehow.

"Nah, I'll hobble along without it."

We got in and Lee picked up this hat off the seat, a big cowboy hat, black, with a dent along the crown like you'd make with the edge of your hand. It didn't have turned-up sides or one of those faggoty feather hatbands like country-and-western singers wear, was just a helluva hat. He put it on and it looked kind of peculiar sitting on top of those Buddy Holly glasses and that complete lack of shoulders. I forgot to say he doesn't wear cowboy boots or anything, just lace-up Kodiaks, which must make his ankles hot in this weather. He's the unlikeliest-looking cowboy you ever saw, and he knows it.

"Burris," he says, "I tried to get a white hat, honest I tried, but the state authorities wouldn't let me have one, said I'm too much of a mean dude and bad guy, so I'm stuck with this one."

He jammed the key in the ignition and the engine turned over like a dying elephant. "Come on, baby, come *on!*" he yells at the dash. "A half tank of super ethyl if you'll just fire up before dark."

Finally it started up after plenty of backfiring and we drove off with this big cloud of oily smoke left behind us. I told him where I live and showed him how to get there, because he hasn't been in town long and doesn't know all the streets. We pulled up outside 1404 and he says, "How do you figure on getting to work?"

"The bus, I guess."

"Forget it. You're on the way from my place to the plant. I'll pick you up around eight-thirty, okay?"

"Thanks a lot, Lee." I got out. "See you tomorrow," I said. I was actually sorry that was the last I'd see of him till the next day. I really *liked* the guy. And he didn't have to offer to drive me. That was plain generous. He drove off with that crazy walking cane and umbrella bouncing in the rifle rack.

Inside, Peggy said, "How'd you make out?" She didn't know I'd gotten the job, probably figured I'd been wandering around town all day. I gave her the facts. Normally I would've hated the way she was all pleased about me finding a job, but I didn't mind so much under the circumstances, because I didn't resent the job the way I expected I would. That's on account of Lee.

The first week at Servex went by on wings. We didn't do

any other work except banding and stacking those refrigerator cartons. If we had've been regular workers that intended staying there for years, they would've taught us other stuff, but seeing as we're only summer help they left us alone and couldn't care less if we got sick and tired of doing the same thing all day. We got to be so good at the job we were like a team, working together, moving back and forth, back and forth, between the bander and the pallets. We horsed around plenty, too, just to make it less of a chore. On the way back, empty-handed from the pallets, we'd kind of leap around and spin and jump like a couple of mad bastards. Lee had this trick where he'd join hands above his head and pirouette like Baryshnikov or somebody. He looked really dumb and clumsy doing it, but that was the whole point. He knew it broke me up, and he did it a dozen times a day. One time he even tried to do this scissor thing they do in ballet, jumping up and kicking the legs, kind of fluttering them real fast before coming down again, only Lee couldn't do it properly, natch, and kicked shit out of his ankles while he's up in the air. It really had me cackling, the way he came down like a stork with a hernia. He didn't do that trick again, but he kept up with the pirouetting. Some of the other guys saw him and whistled and asked him for a date, stuff like that, but he didn't care. He'd kind of drop his wrist at them and say, "You're not my type, big boy," something like that, really killing me with this faggoty voice he put on, and whoever asked him for a date or whatever would say, "I guess little guys are more your type," meaning me. They weren't serious, but they couldn't treat the whole thing like a joke, just clowning around, the way Lee and I did. Frankly, I think it's because they're totally lacking in smarts. They're nine-to-five factory bozos with baseball caps and those dorky little lunch pails, always talking about the big fucking game on TV last night, so it doesn't matter what they think.

When we quit work Friday evening, he says to me, "How about a beer?"

"They won't let me in a bar."

"We don't need a bar. I've got a refrigerator full of brew back at my place."

"Well, okay."

So we went to his place, which is the Green Acres Trailer Park. There's acres there, all right, but it's mostly asphalt and gravel. There must be around forty trailers parked there, some still with wheels but plenty without, just sitting on jacks and piles of brick or cinder blocks. Some were so permanent they had flower beds around them, but they all looked pretty much the same, long and square with little windows backed by venetian blinds and a TV aerial on top. There's also a section for overnighters, mainly out-of-staters on vacation, passing through Buford on their way to someplace interesting with their campers and Winnebagos with a motorbike stashed on the back bumper, or even a little car being hauled along behind for local touring along the way.

Lee steered us over to this very typical trailer, one with no wheels, and we got out. I was kind of nervous about meeting his wife, but she wasn't there when we went inside. "Over at her mother's," said Lee, and got us a couple cold Buschs. "Your very good health, sir," he says, and I came right back with "The regiment and the queen." We drank that first one down fast. It was so cold, I could feel it trickling down through my chest. A cold beer on a hot day is just the greatest.

"I'll go get her after a little bit," he says, meaning his wife.

"Does her mother live here too?"

"Yeah, she does."

"How sick is she, if it's not a personal question?"

"Not as sick as she makes out," he said, and chugged his beer empty.

It sounded kind of heartless, but then I figured he's come all the way from New Mexico so his wife can be with her mother, which must be pretty inconvenient. Or maybe it's just the traditional bad feeling that's supposed to come between a guy and his mother-in-law, the thing all those jokes you hear are about. We had a second beer and I looked around the place. It's narrow and cramped like you'd expect a trailer to be, and kind of untidy, with clothes lying around and dishes in the sink— not as bad as my place, though. Lee talked awhile about how it is to live in a trailer, which isn't so bad according to him, but I could tell he's distracted by his wife not being there. Finally he said, "Back in a minute," and left.

I got up for a quick nose around while he's gone, the way you do in someone else's place, but there wasn't much to see. It was like the inside of a thousand trailers, I bet, with not much to show what kind of people lived there except the magazines, *Cosmopolitan* and *Rolling Stone* mainly, and someone's halfway through *Dune Messiah*. I sat back down in case he came back sooner than I expected. I'd hate to get caught snooping. There's a clock on the wall, one of those with all the sun rays coming out of it, and Lee was gone thirteen minutes. It seemed like something bad must be happening, some kind of argument about his wife not being there when he got home. I don't think Lee's the kind of macho idiot who wants his wife in the kitchen slaving over his supper—it's just that he brought a guest home and it's only right to have her meet me. Maybe it's not her he's sore at, it's her mother for keeping her over at the other trailer.

Then he came back. He was mad all right. "That stupid fucker," he says, and pulled more beers out. He slammed them down on the table and twisted the top off his like he was wringing a chicken's neck.

"Trouble?" I asked, very diplomatic.

"Nothing new. She'll be along in the wink of an eye."

So I don't know if the "stupid fucker" is his wife or her mother. I preferred to think it wasn't his wife. It'd be awful for a guy to call his wife that.

"So what are your plans?" asks Lee.

"For tonight?"

"For the rest of your life."

He sounded very pissed off, very aggressive, almost like it's *me* he's mad at.

"I haven't got it all worked out yet."

"Well, take your time. My old man *told* me I was going into construction, same as him, when I was fifteen. I never questioned it."

"Don't you like construction?"

I could see him way up on some girder about thirty stories

high, with a hard hat and utility belt, or riding a cement hopper up to the fiftieth floor.

"It's okay. It's a living, but you build one house pretty much the same as another."

So he doesn't build skyscrapers. Maybe they don't have them in New Mexico.

"Is there something else you'd rather do?"

"You bet. Chopper pilot, but it costs thousands of bucks to learn unless you join Uncle Sam's fighting forces. I can't see myself doing that. I can't stand for someone to tell me what to do. Discipline isn't what I'm good at."

Then someone opened the screen door and came in, and if I hadn't been expecting a girl I would've thought Lee had a kid brother he forgot to tell me about, because this girl has got very short hair, about half as much as me, kind of mousy-brown-colored, and no tits at all. Lee's got no shoulders and his wife's got no tits, absolutely none. What also made her look like a boy is these khaki overalls and sneakers she had on, like she's just been checking out the carburetor on an army tank or something. They really are a weird-looking couple, believe me. And the funny thing is, as soon as she came in the door, I thought I recognized her.

"Hi," she said.

"Hello."

"Diane, Burris, Burris, Diane," says Lee. He still sounded pissed.

"I think we've met," she says.

"I was just thinking that too."

"It was you gave me that loaf of bread, wasn't it?"

"Yeah. You had on a baseball cap."

"Well, that's charming," she says, looking at the bottles on the table. "Where's mine?" She was just kidding around, you could tell.

"Keeping cool," says Lee.

She went and got one and sat down. She's got a little nubbin nose and those little teeth that are rounded off at the bottoms, not square like most people's. Her hands were small, too, but she twisted off that Busch cap in around half a second. It takes me twice as long because I don't like the way the serrated edge cuts into your flesh. So call me a wimp, I don't care.

"How do you like your job, Burris?" she asks.

"It's okay. It's just for the summer."

"Lee just needs it for the summer too."

"Lee *better* just need it for the summer," says Lee, and she gave him a look that says to can it. She looked around seventeen or eighteen—it's hard to say for sure with a face that unusual. Her eyes are a bit slanty too. I don't mean she looks Chinese or anything, but it's one more thing that makes her different. She chugged the beer down pretty fast, straight from the bottle like us guys, but it didn't look unladylike, the way you'd expect, just natural. It saves washing up glasses, too, which their sink had plenty of already.

"I've been over with my mother. She had an operation a little while back. She hasn't recovered properly yet."

"That's too bad. I hope she gets better."

"I'll drink to that," says Lee. It was pretty rude of him, but Diane just ignored what he said, kept looking at me, not him. "It's a crazy kind of coincidence, you giving me that bread and now working alongside Lee."

"Yeah."

"It's not that big a town," says Lee.

If I hadn't been a little drunk by then I would've felt uncomfortable about the atmosphere in there. But Lee got mellowed out after another beer and pretty soon they were both telling me stuff about Tucumcari, and how they both knew each other in school and dated for years before they got married, real cornball Pat Boone stuff, but it didn't seem corny because they're both so weird, definitely not a Prince and Princess. I mean, you could tell just by looking at them and listening to them they'd never in a million years wind up in a house with one of those adjoining garages that's supposed to *blend* with the house so the garage windows have shutters and white lace *curtains*, even, a house with concrete pineapples standing both sides of the front door, and they'd *never* buy a new car and park it out front with the specification sheet still stuck inside the window—you know the sheet with the sale price and all the extras listed and the *grand total* down at the bottom, parked out front so the fucking neighbors can *see how much they paid for it.* No sir, not these two.

Diane told me how her and her girlfriend flunked science and they decided to get their revenge by blowing up the science lab, so they snuck in there one night—the alarm system was shit, everybody knew it—and they turned on all the gas taps you plug Bunsen burners into and then left a lit candle burning away down the other end of the corridor leading to the lab. The plan was that the lab would fill up with gas, and eventually it'd spill out the door and start coming along the corridor, and when it finally reached the candle—*kaboom!* No more lab. But it didn't work because the candle burned out before enough gas built up to drift along the corridor and reach it, and the janitor smelled all the gas first thing next morning and called the fire department, and they had to send guys in with gas masks to turn off the gas mains and open the windows. But the thing that really gave Diane and her girlfriend a kick was the way every guy in school was given the old third degree about it, but not one girl got questioned, because no one ever would've figured girls are capable of doing stuff like that. You could tell she was proud of it, and Lee was proud of her, too—in fact it was him that made her tell the story, so he's definitely not the macho type who wants women to keep their mouths shut, which was a big relief. I mean, I didn't want to be *disappointed* in him.

"Hey," he says to me, "you better tell your mother where you are."

"She won't be worried. Peggy doesn't expect me home most nights of the week."

It's a big lie, and they both saw through it, which was embarrassing.

"Show Burris where the phone is," says Diane.

"This way, pal."

He took me across to the manager's office where there's this pay phone on the outside wall under a little porch. You could hear traffic howling along the Interstate, maybe half a mile away.

"Got a dime?" he says.

"I think so . . ."

I didn't have one but Lee did, and he wandered off a little way because he knew I didn't want him listening to me while I talk to my mom. It was very considerate of him. Peggy was in a good mood about something, probably amazed that I'm still working after an entire week, and she didn't squawk too much about the way I missed supper without telling her in advance, which usually gets her very pissed at me. It's around eight o'clock by now. Time passes fast when you're drinking beer with your buddies.

"Do you want me to come pick you up later on?" says Peggy.

"No! Lee'll drive me."

Jesus, can you believe it? What a cringe-making situation. So long, guys, my mom's outside waiting to drive me safely home. Sometimes she's so *dumb* it's incredible.

"Well, you tell him to drive carefully. I can tell you're drunk, so he must be too."

"Okay, and I'll also tell him to shake the pee pee off the end of my dick for me."

Oh, shit. Did *I* say *that* to my *mom?* I'm definitely drunk. But it's okay! She's laughing! She must be drunk herself, or Mack's over there giving her a pronging. Nah, too early.

"All right," she says, still laughing. " 'Bye."

Click. I went over to where Lee's watching the moon come up. There's still light in the sky, but you can see the moon, too. I like that time of the evening. Lee was walking in circles and humming to himself, an old Smokey Robinson tune, I forget which one.

"Everything okay?"

"Sure."

We started back, going along between the rows of trailers. You could hear radios and TVs blasting away inside them, and somewhere someone was shouting at someone else about something, a domestic argument.

"Which one's Diane's mother's?" I asked.

He pulled up short and grabbed my arm, not tight or anything, just enough to stop me. "Listen, Burris, her mother's not her mother."

"Huh?"

"Awww, forget it. Let's get drunk."

I thought about what he said on the way back. I figured it meant Diane was adopted. Her mother's not her mother. Okay, big deal. I did what he said—I forgot it.

Diane had made culinary arrangements during our absence. No, I'm kidding. She put a bowl of tortilla chips on the table, that's all. "Noses down, gang," she says. More beers, more stories, more laffs. I really *like* these guys. They're my friends. It's like we've known each other *forever*. They don't talk down to me and they *listen* when I talk. I really appreciate that. Guess what I did. I told them about Neil Armstrong's big screw-up on the moon. Diane made me go through it again, slowly, then she says, "God, he's right! It should've been *a* man!" And Lee agreed. "Not only good-looking," he says, "the little fucker's *smart* too!" That's *me* they're talking about. They weren't pretending to understand, either. I could tell they really had digested the point of my argument. They *knew* I was right, and they *acknowledged* it. I'm telling you, I was in heaven. More beer, more tortilla chips. Diane made us all toasted cheese sandwiches, even if it's still around eighty degrees. Then Lee made us some more. You get really hungry when you're drunk.

The only problem was my bladder. All that beer had to come out sometime. I must've gone in their teeny tiny toilet about ten times, and even when the door's closed you can hear everything right through it. You'd have to be married or real good friends with someone to put up with being able to hear them crap and fart all the time in a trailer like this. But I only went in there to piss, which I did sitting down so I wouldn't make a lot of splashing, which could've been embarrassing. Diane's littler than me, but she only went in twice. You could hear her both times seeing as girls piss straight down. There's definitely something wrong with my bladder. Lee went in just *once* and it sounded like Niagara Falls. He didn't care. In the end I didn't care either. We were all three of us very relaxed together. It was like those beer commercials where all the guys in checkered shirts and jeans and hard hats and cowboy hats slap each other on the shoulder and shake hands and stuff. I forgot to say Lee kept his black hat on all the time. I didn't think it looked dopey on him—in fact it suited him in a crazy kind of way.

Then there's a tapping at the door, not the regular door that's hitched back to let the breeze through, just a tiny little tapping on the screen door. I don't know how long it was going on before any of us heard it. Lee got up and went to the door. He stepped on my foot on the way. God, he's drunk. Me too, I didn't feel a thing. I could hear a voice outside, a real soft, worried-sounding voice, then Lee says real sharp, "Diane. For you."

She was already on her way to the door. She went out and her voice and the other one drifted a little way off. Lee looked good and mad. "It's her fuckin' *mother* again," he said. "Jesus, she can't be by herself for five fuckin' *minutes* without Diane has to go hold her hand."

"Well, if she's recovering from an operation, I guess—"

"Operation *bullshit*. She had it over a year and a half back. I talked with the goddamn surgeon myself. He said it went off *perfectly*. She's just totally *fucked up*. Diane *indulges* her. She shouldn't *do* that."

What could I say? Nothing that would've helped. I couldn't think straight by then, anyway.

"Listen, Burris, things are gonna get flaky around here pretty soon. I think I better drive you home."

"Uh . . . okay."

I didn't want to go, but when the host offers, you can't say no. We went outside. I couldn't hear Diane or her mother, so I guess they must've gone to the other trailer. The Dodge started up without any trouble, the way crummy engines often do at night, I don't know why, and pretty soon we were heading along the Interstate. Lee wasn't in a talking mood. We went past the Starlite Motel on our way to my end of town and I said, "That's where I was born."

"Say what?"

"The Starlite Motel. We've passed it now. I was born in there in Room 107 the very second Neil Armstrong set foot on the moon."

"You're kidding."

"Nope. Gospel truth."

"Do you know his inside leg measurement?"

"Huh?"

"Neil Armstrong's inside leg measurement, do you know what it is?"

"How would I know a thing like that?"

"I thought you were some kind of Neil Armstrong expert, checking out what he said wrong on the moon, getting born right when he said it. You sure you haven't got some of his old socks or a toothbrush or something?"

"No."

I must've sounded teed off, because he laughed. "Don't get sore at me. Just a little harmless fun is all. Hey, gimme a smile."

I cranked one out and he laughed some more.

"That's the sorriest-looking smile I ever saw. Isn't Neil Armstrong the one that advertizes photocopiers?"

"That's Gordon Cooper, and Wally Schirra advertizes Actifed."

"It's kind of sad, you know, those old astronauts doing stuff like that after they're not heroes anymore."

"Yeah."

"Listen, about tonight. You probably think I'm an asshole, right?"

"No."

"We've got a family problem. It makes me mean-tempered sometimes."

"I know what family problems are like."

"Right. Okay, 'nuff said."

Westwood Drive. He pulled up by the curb and I got out.

"See you Monday, Burris."

"Yeah. Thanks for the beer."

He drove off. I went inside. Peggy's not there, most likely over at Mack's. I'm just in time for the regular *Twilight Zone* rerun. Tonight it's the one about the convict who has to serve a life sentence alone on an asteroid. He's given a female robot to keep him company, and when he gets a surprise pardon from Earth he has to leave the robot, which he's fallen in love with, behind on the asteroid, because there isn't enough room for her in the rocket. I'd seen it before. I've seen them all before. Then it's the Late Movie, Robert Taylor in *Bataan*. It's full of guys with names like Jake and Bill and Barney, all gung-ho guys that volunteer to stay behind the rest of the army and keep the Japs from crossing this very important bridge. They all get killed, one by one. In the end there's Japs everywhere, and whenever they come charging through the jungle the film is speeded up, which makes them look like jerky puppets or something, and when they get blasted by Jake and Bill and Barney's machine guns they flop over real fast, like their strings were snipped. It was pretty corny. They made it during the war. I bet everyone loved it then. I wonder what the big problem with Diane's mother is? Lee isn't the kind to get worked up over nothing.

This has been another late-night monologue with your host, Burris Weems, a Burris Weems Production, written and directed by Burris Weems, starring Burris Weems, who is solely responsible for its content. Burris Weems wishes at this time to deny allegations of egocentricity. Burris Weems is not that kind of guy.

This is Burris Weems wishing you good night, faithful listeners.

6 I've started going around there on
a regular basis, Green Acres that is. We've had a heat wave
these last few days. It's been too hot to even talk into my
recorder. I'm making up for lost time now, though. It's so hot,
guess what happened. A bird died in the sky and landed right
at my feet. I don't know what kind it was, just a brownish bird,
but it didn't look old or anything. I think it had a heart attack
or something in the heat, which was 109 degrees at 4:30 this
afternoon, and it conked out on the wing and dropped right at
my feet. If I had've been walking a little faster it would've
dived headfirst into the top of my skull. Imagine a beak going
into your brain like a nail! It was a lucky escape. I left the bird
where it was. I bet some cat took it home.

It isn't fair to drink their beer all the time, so when Lee stops
at the supermarket after work and gets beer and potato chips
and dip, et cetera, I pay half. Next stop is one of the burger
joints for quarter pounders and fries for three, then it's on to
the trailer park for TV and booze till around one A.M. They
never go bowling or to the movies or to a bar. They're saving
their cash for when they go back to New Mexico. Diane told
me she'd prefer to work through the day rather than hang
around looking after her mother, but that's not possible right
now. For the first couple of times I think Lee must've told
her—the mother-in-law, that is—to keep away from his trailer
and not come interrupting like that first time, because I didn't
see or hear her, but then I got to meet her at last. Jesus . . . I

better tell the whole story the way it happened tonight, which is Friday.

How it started, we were watching this horror movie, all about these indestructible Nazi zombie storm troopers left over from a World War II experiment, really hilarious it's so bad, when there's a knock at the screen door, only before Lee or Diane can get up and answer it, the door opens and in comes this guy wearing a dress. That's what I thought—a guy in a dress, about forty or fifty years old. He's really tall and thin, and he's got deep lines in his face and a real pathetic wig that's got this curled up bit around the bottom, the style they liked around 1963, and the dress didn't look right, either, not with those long skinny shanks coming out from underneath. And the makeup job was just awful. It wouldn't have fooled anyone for more than two seconds.

"Something wrong, Gene?" says Diane.

"My set's broken," says the guy, and he sounds really sad about it, like he's going to cry.

"Come and sit with us," says Diane, and I saw her shoot a look at Lee that says he better not make a fuss or there'll be a big fight, and it was that look that made me realize who this guy is, namely Diane's mother that Lee doesn't get along with. But she's a *guy!*

"I was watching *Benson*," he says, "and the set just went blank. It went *fzzzzt* and the picture went dark."

"I'll take a look at it," says Lee, and stood up. "You make yourself comfortable here, Gene." He sounded okay, not pissed at the interruption or anything, more like he's resigned to the situation. Or maybe he's leaving because he can't stand to be near this creepy guy, and taking a look at the busted TV is a good excuse to leave. Anyway, he left, and the guy sits down on the pull-down sofa Diane and I are on. He sat between us where Lee was until a few seconds ago. It made me feel very weird to be sitting next to a guy that looks like a sailor who got drunk on shore leave and had his duds stolen and had to dress up like a woman to get back to his ship. In a movie it would've been funny, but not in real life. He smelled very sweaty, too.

"Gene, this is Burris. He works with Lee out at the plant."

"How do you do," says the guy, and put out his hand. I shook it. It was a big hard hand but the grip was weak, which didn't suit it at all, like the guy's *acting* physically wimpy to go with the role he's playing. I wanted to let go of that hand fast but out of politeness kept hold of it till Gene dropped mine.

"You're becoming quite a friend, I hear," he says.

His voice wasn't faggy or lispy or anything, not even high like you'd expect from someone trying to pass himself off as a woman. It wasn't all that deep, either, just an average kind of voice, but like I said, sounding kind of sad and afraid.

"Yeah."

"Lee and Diane need the company. They do. They don't know hardly anyone in town, being new arrivals. I don't know anyone here myself, so we appreciate finding new friends."

"Yeah, I know what you mean."

I'm thinking, wow! this Gene's a freak all right, with the soft handshake and drag routine. Then I saw he's not wearing a wig at all, it's his real hair, only it's way too thin, and that's what makes it look like a cheap wig. So if he's grown his actual hair and had it permed and all, it means he isn't a transvestite that dresses up like a woman every now and then, he's an actual full-time dragster. I felt kind of sorry for him because it didn't work, all his efforts to make himself look feminine with lipstick and eyeliner and everything. He must be Diane's *father*, and because he's a gender-bender, Lee and Diane have to make out to other people like he's Diane's mother. Also, I got the impression he's not quite right in the head. Maybe the operation was a *brain* operation! If it happened a year and a half ago he's had plenty of time to grow his hair back after having it shaved off for the tic-tac-toe pattern they draw on your scalp with ink, and the knife and electric saw. That must be it, a *brain* operation. Maybe he thinks he's a woman because the operation went wrong and they hacked out the wrong piece of brain. But Lee said he spoke to the surgeon and everything went perfectly. I'm very confused. The guy's only been in the trailer about ninety seconds.

"What are you watching?" he asks Diane.

"*Death's Head Zombies.*"

"Could we see the end of *Benson*? It was only on for five minutes when the set stopped working."

"Sure," says Diane, and changes the channel.

I thought Gene had a nerve asking that. I didn't want to watch fucking *Benson*. That show gives me a pain. It gives new meaning to the word *garbage*, but what could I do? Nothing. So we watched this totally stupid show. Gene's taste in TV is pretty much equal to his taste in women's clothing. The dress is hopeless, one of those neck-to-knee numbers with a print on it, leaves or something, very corny-looking, like a dress Audrey Hepburn might've worn around twenty years ago. And the shoes! He's got these size-twelve feet, the poor bastard, and they just don't make women's shoes for feet that big, so he's wearing those Japanese sandals with the straw sole and fat thong that goes between your toes, very comfortable I'm sure, only they let the world know he's got bunions the size of hens' eggs sticking out of both feet. It was real ugly, believe me. I couldn't help but feel sorry for him with those feet in front of me. He had one leg crossed over the other, see, and kept bobbing the raised foot up and down, up and down—nerves, I guess. He liked the show, though. Every dopey line got him laughing this sad little spooky laugh. He thought the house-keeper, the Kraut or Swede or whatever the fuck she is, was just the funniest thing ever. She just had to open up with that phony "Vot iss diss?" accent and he's practically off the sofa and rolling on the floor. It's hard to describe how it all felt. I mean, I'm sitting there four-fourths drunk watching *Benson* with a girl that looks like a grease monkey and a guy that looks like Gary Cooper in drag. It definitely was not a normal situation.

Then Lee came back in, and weird as Lee is, he looked like Mr. Straight by comparison. "It's shot, all right," he says, mean-ing the TV in Gene's trailer. "You're gonna have to get a new one."

"Mmmmmm," says Gene, still watching *Benson*, not really paying attention to what Lee's saying, which was pretty rude of him, seeing as Lee went to all the trouble of checking it out.

"What happened to the Nazis?" Lee wants to know.

"We switched over to this," says Diane.

"Shit."

Lee went into the bedroom and pulled the concertina partition closed. He was pissed for sure, and I don't blame him. Why any human being would actually *choose* to watch *Benson* is a big mystery. You'd have to have the intelligence of a sandworm or something.

The episode finished after what seemed like about four hours, and Diane switched back to the zombies, which were surrounding this girl who already had half her clothes torn off in a previous encounter with these guys and hadn't learned a thing from the experience, namely they die if you rip their goggles off. It wasn't explained *why* they die if you rip their goggles off, but they did, and the girl already tore off one pair accidentally and saw the zombie fall down dead at her feet, but she's so fucking moronic, she can't connect the two things—removal of goggles and zombie death—so now they're coming for her again and all she can do is scream her lungs out, the stupid bitch. Wait! Here comes the hero swinging an iron bar! He doesn't know about the goggles either. If his girlfriend wasn't mentally retarded they could finish off this whole Nazi platoon in around three minutes, those zombies move so slow and all, just rip those goggles off and watch the fuckers die. They don't give a shit about iron bars because they're indestructible, but he batters a way through them to the girl and then starts battering his way out again. The girl didn't even try to make things easier for him by meeting him halfway. This is a really dumb movie. Even being drunk doesn't help much.

"I don't like these horror movies," says Gene, shaking his head, and it's like Clint Eastwood saying he's scared of snails or something—the words are just totally out of place coming from a face like that. "I think they give children nightmares and affect their mental development."

I didn't say anything, and Diane didn't either. What can you say when someone says something like that? And who's Gene to talk about mental development? He's a fucking *Benson* fan.

Diane called out, "Lee, we're watching the movie again!"

"So what!" he called back, and stayed in the bedroom.

We kept watching it, even Gene, and the guy and girl

eventually get away after all the zombies fall into a big hole in this cave where they all started out from, frozen in there ever since the war, and our hero and heroine hold each other and say, "We're saved!" and stuff, and they go off to get her a brain transplant, which she needs very urgently.

"I'm glad we didn't see it all," Gene says, sounding very worried about the influence all those Nazi zombies might have had on him. Then things got awkward. It was only the movie that was holding things together in there, bad as it was, and now that it's over no one knew what to do next. Lee stayed in the bedroom.

"Lee, honey, come on out here!" Diane called, but he didn't answer, so she tried again. "Don't be a party pooper, Lee!"

She really wanted him out there, but he wouldn't budge, sulking in the bedroom. I could understand why he didn't like being around Gene, but shutting himself away like that didn't help things any.

"I can't afford a new set," says Gene.

"We'll get you a secondhand one."

"But not black and white. Black and white doesn't do a thing for me."

"We'll find something."

"She can have ours if it'll get her out of here!"

That was from the bedroom. Time for me to go, I think. There's a large portion of family discord on the way. I stood up.

"Nice to meet you, Gene."

I shook hands again, just to be polite.

"Nice to meet you, Burris. Lee and Diane need friends. Everybody needs friends."

"Yeah, you're right."

"Honey, Burris is going now!"

"So long, Burris!"

I looked at Diane. She looked at me.

"Aren't you going to drive him home?"

"I'm all drove out!"

Uh-oh. Major embarrassment looming on the horizon. Lee's

being a turd, and *I* didn't do anything wrong. He must really hate Gene to be acting this way.

Diane gave this disgusted little snort, then says, "I'll drive you."

"There's no need. I can walk home easy. . . ."

"No. Just because *someone* is behaving like a child doesn't mean we let a guest walk home."

"Is Lee upset about something?" asks Gene.

That pancake makeup must be hiding skin thicker than a rhino's, or else Gene is a little simple-minded. I followed Diane out to the Dodge and we got in. Then she realizes she hasn't got the keys, so she went back inside. She was in there a few minutes and then Lee came out. He got in and we got rolling.

"Sorry, Burris. I turned into an asshole again."

"You really don't like Gene, do you?"

"Nope."

"Is it because he's . . . uh . . . gay?"

"He isn't gay. You won't believe this. Gene's a woman."

"He dresses up like one . . ."

"He's legally a woman. He's Diane's father. *Used* to be. Her mother divorced him two years back. She found out he used to wear her clothes when she wasn't looking. He was a transvestite, you know, not really *gay* or anything. I mean, so far as anyone knows, he didn't fuck guys, nothing like that, just the dressing up. But he wanted to *be* a woman, wanted his cock and *balls* cut off, for Chrissakes. And it happened. They actually *did* it, chopped it all off and gave him a cunt. Excuse me, a vagina. They can do stuff like that. They even gave him silicone tits and ran electricity through his whiskers so he doesn't have to shave anymore. It cost nine thousand bucks. He had to go around as a woman, wearing dresses, the whole thing, for a whole year before they agreed to do the operation. They have to be sure a guy isn't gonna change his mind and want to get back into pants. They did it, and now guess what. He wants his dick back, says he made a big mistake and can they please give him his dick back, he doesn't want to be a woman, after all."

"Jesus. Can they do it?"

"No way. It's not reversible. He's broke, anyway, and he's so fucked up mentally he can't work, won't even *try* to find a job. He used to sell outboard motors. *She* used to sell them. I just can't get used to Gene as a woman. He calls himself Jean— J-e-a-n—nowadays, signs his name that way. *Her* name. I can't get used to it, Burris. I remember him as this loudmouthed guy that was always telling me to get Diane home by twelve, all that crap, just your regular guy. Nobody knew about the funny stuff till the divorce. Cathy, that's Diane's mother, she hasn't gotten over it yet. That woman's a mess because of what he did. And Diane's kind of screwed up about it too. She doesn't show it, but she is. I'll give her this, though, she's stuck by the son of a bitch. He came up here to get away from everyone that ever knew him back home, then he has a nervous breakdown and calls up Diane and begs her to come take care of him, and she did it. I wasn't gonna come along, then I did. Shit, why should she have to do it on her own? I was between jobs anyway. I figured she'd smooth him out in a week or two. We've been here seven weeks now. It's one big fucking mess."

"Yeah."

"You know what really gets me? The bastard won't admit I hate his guts, talks to me like I'm his favorite nephew or something. If I get nasty, he just turns all fretful and starts sighing and wringing his hands and asking what's the matter. It's *crazy*. He wants to be a man again, but he's acting more and more like some old spinster aunt."

The thing I was thinking while Lee was saying all this, the big thought in my mind was, he must really *like* me to be telling me this awful stuff. No one ever told me tragic stuff like this before, so it's a big step forward, a giant leap for Burris Weems. I felt real good about things being so bad for Lee and Diane, if you see what I mean. Gene's right about one thing— even if he *is* a fruitcake, they do need a friend. And I'm it. It was enough to give me the chokes, pretty near, two people older than me confiding this stuff because I'm their friend. Okay, it was only Lee doing the confiding, but I bet Diane wants to talk about it too. I'd say Lee's unhappiness on one side of the Dodge was just about balanced on the other side by my happiness. I didn't have a clue how they could solve their problem—in fact, it was the *problem*, in a screwball kind of way, that made them *need* me, so I guess deep down I was glad they *had* a problem. All of which sounds kind of perverted, I know. I'm being honest, that's all, trying to tell how I feel about everything. I don't think I'm a sick person or anything.

"I've been thinking, you know," he says quietly.

"About what?"

I expected him to say, "About what a good pal you are, Burris," but he says, "About taking off."

"Taking off?"

"Just leaving Gene to figure his own way out of this fucking mess. He got himself into it, he can damn well get himself out."

"What about Diane?"

"She's gonna have to make a choice."

"Won't that be kind of hard? I mean, he's her father and all. *She's* her father."

"No one ever said decisions were supposed to be easy."

"I don't know, Lee, I just don't think you should leave her here with him . . . her. It'll just make things twice as tough for her—Diane, I mean."

"Maybe so."

He sounded doubtful, but I couldn't tell if it's doubt about leaving or doubt about whether it'd make things tougher for his wife.

"I really don't think you should go. It's not the answer."

"Well, what *is?*"

"I dunno. You can't leave, though. It isn't right."

"You sound awful sure about that."

He sounded a little bit amused and a little bit pissed off at me.

"I *am* sure."

"You're no expert on problems, Burris."

I could've told him I've had problems for *years*, so I *am* an expert, but I was kind of teed off with him for saying that. It sounded like he thinks I'm just some little *kid*, after all. I resented that, I really did.

"Maybe I'll phone up Dr. Ruth," he says. He means the lady on TV.

"Dr. Ruth does sex problems."

"Right."

"Well, she's not gonna be able to help you with this. I mean, she does sex problems between couples, not this family problem stuff."

"You think this family problem stuff doesn't affect my sex life?"

"How do you mean?"

"Forget it. Gene comes knocking on the door all hours, right in the middle of things, you know. It's very fucking irritating."

But that's not what he meant, I can tell. Guys don't like to tell other guys they've got sex problems. There's probably two reasons why Lee told me all this before he took it all back again with that knocking-on-the-door bullshit, and the first reason is he's pretty drunk still, even if he didn't have another beer after he went over to check out Gene's TV, and the second reason he let the cat out of the bag is because he doesn't count me as a regular guy—I mean, someone who's had intercourse and lived with a woman, et cetera. I mean, he probably guessed I'm pretty much of a virgin still, so telling me he's got a sex problem doesn't really matter that much, kind of like telling the dog or something. At least he had the decency to deny it a half minute later. If he hadn't done that, it would've been proof he *really* doesn't count me as one of the guys. But it's pretty insulting anyway. I mean, he didn't start to confide in me because I'm his *friend* or anything, only let it slip out because he's a little drunk and feeling plenty mean about things and not keeping a lock on his lip the way he normally would've, and I came pretty near to being *disappointed* in him because of it.

We didn't say anything more after that. He dropped me off at my place and I went in and watched TV for a while. Peggy was home but already in bed. No van outside, so she's in there by herself. Loretta was out cabbying. There's a movie half over, *Mysterious Island*, the one with the giant crabs. It's not as good as the book. Then there's a commercial for Coke. This is the summer Coke changed their secret formula after about a hundred years, and there's been a whole lot of publicity about it. Bill Cosby holds up a can and says how wonderful the *new* taste of Coke is. The *new* taste of Coke is sweeter than the old taste of Coke because more and more people were ditching Coke and buying Pepsi, which is sweeter than Coke. *Was* sweeter. If you can't beat 'em, *join* 'em! Coke fight back by making Coke as sweet as Pepsi, and here's Bill Cosby pushing it like he's been pushing Coke since forever. But a year ago one of his commercials had him saying how Coke tastes better than Pepsi because Pepsi's too sweet. He preferred the taste of Coke, he said, because Coke isn't so sweet. He made a big point about that—he prefers Coke because it isn't all yukky sweet like Pepsi. And now that Coke have gone and changed their formula and made Coke as sweet as Pepsi, here's Bill holding up a can and telling us the *new* taste of Coke is just fine and dandy with him. Bill Cosby's a funny guy, also very intelligent, but how can he say he prefers the taste of Coke because it *isn't* sweet and then turn around and say he likes the *new* Coke that *is* sweet?

Stuff like that makes you think to yourself, "More lies. More bullshit." That's all it is. Practically everything is like that. What with Bill Cosby pushing Coke and Geraldine Ferraro pushing Pepsi, it's enough to drive a feller to Sprite.

Cheers!

7

For the last week things have been different somehow. Lee doesn't do any pirouetting at work, no clowning around at all, and if I speak to him, he just grunts. It's almost like he regrets opening up to me on the drive home last Friday and just wants to forget it ever happened, practically forget he even *knows* me. I can understand how he feels. I can put myself in his shoes. I can put myself in just about anyone's shoes. There's no need for him to give me the silent treatment, though. I haven't done anything to deserve it. Frankly, it hurts. It's no fun working with someone who ignores you all the time and just looks at you like you're an idiot if you do something to make him laugh.

"What's the matter?" Peggy asked me the other night.

"Nothing."

I couldn't tell her what's on my mind. It's not that she wouldn't understand or anything—Peggy's pretty smart—but I just didn't want her to know my business. Or Loretta. She and I kid around a lot, but we've never talked about serious stuff, I don't know why. It's like her and Peggy don't talk to me like they would to an ordinary kid because if they did they'd have to stop and say, "My God, there's a kid in the house. Are we conducting ourselves the way adults ought to conduct themselves around a kid?" Maybe they don't want to ask themselves that question, so they don't see me as a kid. Okay, I don't see myself as a kid, either, but you see what I mean. Or maybe you don't. Maybe you're thinking I'm just jealous of the way

Peggy and Loretta have got sex lives and I haven't. Maybe you think that deep down I want them to forget about Mack and Pete and stay home all the time and play Trivial Pursuit with me. Maybe you think there's Freudian stuff involved here. Well, there isn't. I just haven't gotten into the habit of talking to them and confiding in them, and it's too late to start now. It's *my* problem. Actually it's Lee's and Diane's problem, but because I like them so much, their problem's gone and rubbed off on me. But even they don't know it. Maybe to them I'm just some pesky kid demanding attention while *they're* trying to cope with some pretty heavy *adult* problems. I couldn't stand it if that's what they think. I couldn't stand it if Diane puts her hand to her head and thinks, "Oh, Christ, *Burris* is coming around again tonight. I wish Lee wouldn't encourage him the way he does. He's such a little jerk-off." It's *crazy* the way I torture myself thinking stuff like that, but the way Lee's been acting, I can't help it.

I knew things were breaking down fast when Lee was driving us away from the Servex plant this evening. It's Friday again and I thought it'd be the usual thing, but he drove right past the supermarket where we usually load up with beer. He says to me, "I'll take you straight home. Things aren't too good out my way. It's kind of ugly right now."

"What kind of ugly?"

"The kind you don't want to know about."

That's all he said. It was like a slap in the face. He might as well have said, "None of your fucking business."

When he drove away from my place, I didn't go in. I didn't want Peggy asking how come I'm home after work for once. So I started walking. I walked through town, crisscrossing back and forth from one street to another, up one and down the next. I went down streets I hadn't been down in years. Nothing had changed. I walked and walked. It'd been a hot day, and now it was a hot evening that looked like turning into a hot night. Everywhere I look there are people setting out to have fun as the sun goes down and the weekend starts. I've slipped back weeks in time, back to before I knew Lee and Diane. They've shut me out. I'm back on my own. I blame Gene. We were all getting along fine before Gene came inside Lee's trailer. Up till then everything was fine. Then Gene pokes his dumb-looking head with the pathetic hairdo and makeup into our lives, into *my* life with *them*, and fucks it all up, the bastard. What kind of moron pays nine thousand bucks to have his dick cut off and then changes his mind? If he'd been happy after they took it off I wouldn't hate him. I'd think he was a real ugly woman, but I wouldn't hate him. I don't give a shit what sex people want to be. But he changed his mind and wanted his dick back and couldn't *have* it back, so he had a nervous breakdown or whatever and is leaning all over Diane, which makes Lee mad—and I can see why. It's all Gene's fault, is my point. If he'd only accept that his dick is gone forever maybe he'd be okay. Someone should tell him, really they should, for his own benefit. Why not me? It wasn't such a dumb idea. I bet Lee told him plenty of times already, and Diane, too, but they're family, too close to the problem for Gene to take any notice, if you see what I mean. What he needed was an outsider who'd step in and give him the straight poop about how he's fucking everybody's life up. I know it sounds crazy—I mean, I've only met the guy once for an hour or so while we watched TV, so how come I think I'm qualified? I'll tell you—because I felt like it.

It was eight o'clock by then, and I was walking along the Interstate, heading for the trailer park without really being aware of it. It must've been my subconscious that directed me there or something, because I only just now decided I'd go see Gene. Or maybe what took me there was I wanted to see the old Starlite again, from close up, not driving past in Lee's pickup. But first I had to eat.

I went into Wendy's. The place was full. On Friday night everybody gets filled up with burgers and fries before they get filled up with booze. I could've gone to another joint, but they all would've been the same, so I stayed where I was and put up my tent of silence, which is this thing I do if I'm in a crowded place when I'm not in the mood for crowds. Did you ever see *Lawrence of Arabia*? What a great movie! Anyway, in the middle of the day when the sun's at its hottest, the Arabs get down off their camels and sit cross-legged on the sand and hold these sticks upright in front of them—the ones they whack their camels with—and throw part of their long robe over the top of the stick, which is just above the top of their head, and they sit there inside their own little pointy tent until the worst of the heat has passed. Well, that's what I do in a crowded place, only I don't use a stick and cloth, I do it all in my head, build this cone-shaped tent of silence around myself. When it's up and operating, it means no one'll bother me and I can concentrate on whatever it is I'm thinking about without really hearing all the racket around me. What I was thinking about was if it's the right thing to do, give Gene a lecture like I intend to. Well, I decided it was, so after I finished my burger, which had been a pretty good one, I folded up my tent of silence and left.

I headed along the Interstate again, figuring to head straight for Green Acres, but on my way past the Starlite I saw something *awful*. Right under the big pink-and-green neon sign there's another sign, just a flat billboard-type sign a couple yards long and it says: COMING SOON ON THIS SITE—JODY'S OLD-FASHIONED PANCAKE HOUSE. Awwww, *no* . . . they're gonna tear down the Starlite and put up another fucking food joint! It shook me, it really did. The place where I was *born* is coming *down*! I went straight in the office. I don't know what I expected, some big sleazy-looking slob with a cigarette hanging out of his face, all set to wink at the customer and remind him there's vibrating beds and adult video available, but who there is behind the desk is this old guy around seventy.

"Help you, sonny?" he says.

"When are they tearing it down?" I said, gone all squeaky I'm so upset.

"Next week they start."

"But *why?*"

"Earliest we could arrange it."

"No, why are they tearing the place down?"

"Too many motels. Can't earn enough bucks, not with the competition."

"You can't tear down the Starlite . . ."

"I'm not gonna try, sonny. Got a demolition team coming in. Thursday they start. You wanna room?"

"No."

"Well, you still got time, you change your mind. Thursday they start. You got a girlfriend?"

"No."

"Only seventeen-fifty a night. Bring your girlfriend while the old Starlite's still here."

Then this nice-looking lady, his daughter probably, came in from the back and asked if I want a room, like she expected the old man hadn't already asked me and was just jawing away, wasting time. There isn't any time to waste at the Starlite, not anymore. Jesus, I can't believe it, not the Starlite . . . not the place I was *born*.

"Excuse me."

"Huh?"

"Do you want a room?"

"No. No thank you. Is there really gonna be a . . . *pancake* parlor here?"

"In a couple of months there will be. We have the franchise. We wouldn't sell without them giving us that. There's always been a family business on this section. We won't be making the actual pancakes, just running things. They'll bring in someone else to make them."

She's looking at me like I'm an escaped lunatic or something. I can't say a thing. She's being very polite to me, very chatty. The old guy's looking out the window, not seeing either of us. They're gonna pull it *down*. . . .

"Do you like pancakes?" she asks. She's smiling at me, but it's one of those fake smiles, about as genuine as the "Have a nice day" you get from checkout girls at the supermarket. She thinks I'm weird, so she's smiling. It's supposed to disarm me or some dumb thing. She probably read it in a book: Reassure the lunatic by smiling broadly. Do not raise your voice. Speak in moderate tones. Engage him in topics of conversation he finds convivial until help arrives.

"Pancakes are shit."

That wiped the smile off her face.

"I don't think we need that kind of language," she says.

All of a sudden I felt weak, like my legs have turned to marshmallow. I wanted to sit down awhile but I couldn't, not here, not after I said *shit*, and also because it's the Starlite and the only way I want to spend some time here is in Room 107. . . . Then I had a brain wave. It came into my head like a howitzer shell, practically took the top of my skull off. I would've thought of it weeks ago, I bet, but I'm still not used to having wages in my pocket. I've got *money!* I can do what I always wanted and hire 107!

"Uh . . . ma'am? I *would* like a room after all. Please."

"All righty," she says. She wanted to be friends again.

"Uh . . . not for tonight. For the last night."

"Pardon me?"

"I want to have Room 107 for the last night the Starlite operates as a motel."

"The last night?"

"Yes, ma'am. I'm booking in advance. I've got the money right here. . . . You haven't hired it out already, have you?"

I got real anxious all of a sudden. Jesus, what if someone else had 107 on that last night . . . ?

"No," she says, thinking she was right all along and I *am* a lunatic. "No," she says again. "We generally only get prior bookings on a Friday or Saturday night. You'll be wanting 107 on Tuesday. That's our last day of business. Wednesday we'll be removing the furniture and fittings, and Thursday is when they begin demolition. Originally we were going to close down operations this Sunday, make the most of one last Saturday night—that's our best night for trade—and just close things down next day. But then we thought, why not keep the place open till the last minute, just for sentiment's sake."

"Get a few extra bucks that way," says the old guy.

"It's got to be 107," I said, hauling dollars out of my pants.

"I'll just make a note of it," she says, writing in the register. You'd think she would've asked me *why* it had to be 107, just out of curiosity or something, but she didn't. Maybe she thinks it's my lucky number. I handed over eighteen bucks. She gave me change, still smiling, but she doesn't fool me with her family business and sentiment's sake bullshit. She'd rent to Jack the Ripper while they're unloading the bulldozers.

"There we are," she says, showing me this gray tooth around the side of her mouth—a really rotten one, it looked like. "Room 107 is yours for the evening, next Tuesday."

"Thank you very much. I appreciate it. Thank you."

I practically backed away, bowing from the waist. They watched me go, the woman still smiling, the old guy kind of letting his eyes slide away from me, because once I'm more than five yards away from him I may as well be on Mars. My third eye tells me he's getting so decrepit that by the time he finishes his cornflakes in the morning, he can't remember if it was the first or second bowl he just ate. And her, she's really looking forward to when the pancake parlor opens, because she'll be able to boss the staff around. They'll be kids mostly, like in all the other food joints along the Interstate, and they won't give her any back talk, not like the maid they've got working at the Starlite. The old guy'll be happy having kids around the new place, too, high-school girls with dinky little caps and big smiles and smooth skin. He'll like that all right. It'll get so bad she'll have to ban him from the place to keep him from pinching their asses and stuff. Can't have old Pop getting in trouble with the law for molesting minors, no sir.

Then I'm outside again. I only went in a minute ago, and now the whole world is different. They're tearing the Starlite down, but at least I've got 107 all to myself on the *last night!* I felt like a little kid waiting for Christmas just around the corner, four days away. I felt sad and happy at the same time. Being in 107 on the last night would be *very symbolic.* I felt confident now. I'd go out to the trailer park and talk to Gene without Lee and Diane knowing and get him to see the error of his ways. It's a shame about him having no cock and balls anymore, because he's never going to make it as a woman—not with that face and being about six foot high, he's not. But he'd just have to make the best of the situation. He couldn't keep on fucking up Lee and Diane like he's been doing. They're my friends and I owe it to them to straighten Gene out, which is bound to be a tough job because any guy that pays nine grand to have his equipment lopped off has got to have more kinks than a sack of snakes.

When I got out to Green Acres I ducked along through the shadows so no one can see me. Sometimes I have this very overdeveloped sense of the dramatic, because the only ones I really can't let see me are Lee and Diane, and I wasn't anywhere near their trailer yet. I couldn't help it, though, being dramatic, and I sneaked along, going from one trailer to the next like Sylvester scooting from tree to tree while he sneaks closer and closer to Tweety-Pie. Then I had this thought I should've had before—I don't know which trailer is Gene's. How dumb can you get! I stood there like a moron behind someone's trailer—it might've been Gene's for all I knew—and wondered what to do. Now it didn't seem like such a good idea anymore, but I'd come all that way and my hip was killing me from all the walking I've done, so I wasn't going to just turn around and walk back home again. What I could've done is wait around till 11.30 when *Benson* comes on and go listening under all the open windows till I found someone stupid enough to be watching it, but that plan had two drawbacks—one, it's not even nine o'clock yet; and two, Gene's TV doesn't work. Maybe he got himself a new one in the past week, but I couldn't count on it. Shit!

When in doubt, do the obvious. I went to the manager's office and asked which trailer was Gene's. "Gene who?" says the guy behind the desk. Shit again! I don't know Diane's maiden name. What a complete fuck-up!

"Gene . . . uh . . . the guy that looks weird."

"The cupcake?"

"Yeah, I guess so. What's a cupcake?"

"He a friend of yours?"

"I'm a friend of the Trimbles."

"So?"

He was chewing a mouthful of food because I interrupted his supper when I came in. There's a TV going in the room back of the reception area.

"Well . . . he knows them."

"Does he?"

Uh-oh, am I giving away secrets? Doesn't the manager know they're related? He's looking me up and down, up and down, trying to make up his mind if I'm a cupcake too.

"So which trailer's his?" I said. I hate being stared at.

"If you know him, you'll know what trailer."

I couldn't be bothered explaining. It's none of this guy's business anyway. I just hope I haven't blown what Lee and Diane might've wanted kept secret, namely that Gene's her father. I wouldn't want people to know if he was *my* father.

"Look, would you mind telling me what I want to know, please."

"I've got a responsibility to my customers," he says. I think he meant tenants—*customers* sound wrong somehow. "I can't let strangers just roam around the place. This is private property, not City Park."

"I don't *want* to roam around. I want to go directly to Gene's trailer, so where is it, if you don't mind?"

This guy's an *asshole*, a real brown fundament.

"And there's morals too," he says, sucking his teeth where there's food stuck between them. "I'm responsible for the morality around here. How do I know what goes on when cupcakes get together? It's dirty stuff, makes diseases they don't have cures for, see, and seeing as I'm responsible for the health of the customers, I get to say what goes and what don't."

"So you're not gonna tell me."

"Not till you can explain yourself."

It was almost funny the way this complete idiot thought he was important enough to have *influence* over people. He probably sits in here all day doing nothing but jerk off, getting dumber and dumber by the hour because his brain doesn't get used, and then along comes me with a perfectly civil request for information and *bingo!* he steps out from behind his scabby-looking desk with this skintight colored suit on and holds up this gloved hand and says, "Hold it right there, buddy. No perverts allowed. Captain Kleen says cupcakes are a definite no-no in family-oriented Green Acres." What a fuckhead! The good thing about meeting retarded people like this guy is the way it reassures you that you're smart. In a way I'm grateful to him for being such an imbecile.

"Thanks a lot," I said.

"Don't mention it," he says, with this dumb little smile on his face. He really thinks he's *won*, the moron. It was really pathetic to see.

"You're a terrific guy," I said.

"Don't start any cupcake stuff with *me*," he says, going all tough and threatening. It was just so incredibly funny I even laughed. He didn't like the sound of it. Nobody ever has, it's so goofy.

"Go on, now," he says. "You've had your one and only warning, I'm warning you."

This guy's just hysterically funny. I can't believe he doesn't know what a complete cretin he is. If it was any funnier it'd be tragic, somehow. I went to the door.

"I'm going now," I said. I'm still smiling. I know he won't hurt me. He's only a little guy who doesn't like it if you look at the top of his head, which is going bald.

"I don't want to see you around here again. I know a couple guys on the force," he says.

"Do you? I like cops. I like the way their gun belts hang down low over the bulge in their pants."

"Get outa here, ya faggot creep!"

He really *said* that, I'm not making it up. "Get outa here, ya faggot creep!" Pretty incredible, huh? I walked away from the office feeling very, very good. My head was so filled with things whizzing around in there and colliding with each other, it was like being stoned, just everything happening at once and all of it interesting. I had to remind myself I'm on an errand of mercy here, making moves to give Lee and Diane a less compli- cated life so they'll invite me around on Friday nights the way they used to. It's an important job, and I haven't even started yet. And I still don't know which trailer is Gene's.

I saw this little girl jumping rope under one of the light poles and went over. "Excuse me," I said, and she quit right away. Kids love it when you talk to them politely, like they're grown-ups or something. "I'm looking for my uncle. He's a tall guy that wears a dress like a lady."

She knew who I'm talking about, all right. She points down the row of trailers that's nearest. "Not this one, not the next one, not the next one, *that* one."

"Thank you very much. How many times can you jump rope without stopping?"

She thinks awhile, then says, "A thousand!"

What a fucking little liar. "That's very good," I said. "The Olympic record is only one thousand twenty-eight, so you're almost the best in the world."

"I *know!*" she says. She's all defensive because she knows she told a whopping lie.

"Well, 'bye now," I said.

She ran away. She won't go directly home in case I call in there and tell her folks their daughter's a *liar*. I wonder if I was that weird when I was little? It's just awful the way you forget stuff. Not that one, not that one, not that one, *this* one. I knocked on the door. It was shut even though it's a sweltering night. It won't start cooling off till just before dawn. An experienced insomniac like me knows about that stuff. A psychologist would tell you that the closed door was very symbolic, or symptomatic, one or the other, of Gene's state of mental health. It means he's got a closed mind and won't admit he's fucking things up for everyone. Well, the mind-opener is here, Gene, so open up! Which he did at long last and stood there looking like Tony Perkins in *Psycho* after he's put the dress and wig on. And *stood* there and *stood* there . . .

"Hi, Gene."

"Who is it?" he says, very suspicious.

"Burris."

"Burris?"

"Yeah, Burris Weems."

"Who *are* you?"

"Last Friday. Lee and Diane's trailer. *Benson*, remember?"

"Oh, *Burris*. Yes, yes."

I waited for something more, but that was it.

"Uh . . . can I come in, please?"

"Did Lee send you over?"

"No, he doesn't even know I'm here. I came to see you."

"Came to see me?"

"Yeah. Can I come in?"

"Lee didn't send you?"

"For the record, no."

Sometimes if I'm talking to an idiot I can get sarcastic, I admit it.

"Would you like to come in?"

"Thanks, Gene. Now that I'm here I'll just come in for a minute. Great idea."

So I went in. The place stinks. It's like a bear's den in there. Does a bear shit in the woods? Nope, in Gene's trailer. Okay, I'm exaggerating, but it was powerful in there, believe me.

"Won't you sit down, Burris." He pointed at a chair with a plate of food or something on it. "Oh, excuse me," he says, and hurried the plate away down the other end to the kitchen, then comes back and jerks his hips down onto the sofa, trying to do it like a woman would, with his knees and ankles together. It didn't work. I just couldn't imagine a vagina under that fucking awful dress he's wearing. A vagina just doesn't suit him at all. Gene and a vagina go together like a camel and a tiara. But that's what the doctors gave him. And they said Frankenstein was crazy!

"Well," he says, kind of breathless. I think he tried to do it like Bette Davis would. He looks like Bette Davis's brother. "To what do I owe this pleasure?"

He's been diving into the cliché bin, Gene has. He probably thought it sounded pretty sophisticated. I wonder if he was as big a dork when he was a man as he is now, or if the operation affected him mentally. I know this sounds pretty patronizing, and maybe even sexist, but if you saw this guy you'd just be amazed that he convinced *doctors*— I mean, men of supposedly advanced intellect—*convinced* them that he's a suitable candidate for dick-docking. How did they fall for it? Couldn't they see he's a dork that doesn't even know which way is up, never mind whether he wants to be Arthur or Martha? Maybe they don't take intelligence into account when they decide who gets

chopped and who doesn't. They wouldn't want to be accused
of prejudice against idiots or anything, I guess. It's just very,
very sad to see him sit here in this smelly trailer, trying to act
like a woman when I know, because Lee told me, that he
regrets having had his bag burgled, wishes now he hadn't *done*
it and wants his dick back again, wants to be a man again. But
he's acting like a woman still. What he *was*—a man—and what
he *is*—a woman—and what he *originally* wanted to be—a woman
that's happy to stay a woman—and what he wants to be *now*—a
man again—must all be boomeranging around inside him, and
he's trying to put on a brave face and fit into the dress he's
obliged to wear. If he didn't have tits he could cut his hair and
get into pants and ditch his makeup kit and pass for a man
again, dickless or not. But the tits are there, even if the doctors
didn't give him nine thousand bucks' worth.

Just looking at him made me feel pretty damn sympathetic,
but it didn't help me open the conversation, because it just then
occurred to me that Gene doesn't know that I know he's had a
sex change and wishes he hadn't. So how do I approach him?
As a man? As a woman? Both, maybe?

"Did you get your TV fixed?"

"No. Lee wanted to take it away and dump it, but I said no,
maybe it can be fixed. But Lee won't take it to the repair shop.
He says *I* should. He knows my back is bad. I couldn't lift a
TV. It's not a portable, it's full-size."

This was a big revelation to me, seeing as the TV is about
two feet away, looking very big and useless with its screen all
blank.

"That's too bad. I guess you and Lee argue a lot."

"Well, I don't know if I'd say that. We have differences of
opinion. We're very different personalities, Lee and I."

"I think he wants to go back home," I said, and when I said
it a little door in my head popped open and a voice said: *Yes, he
wants to go home, and if you talk Gene into not being fucked up
anymore, it'll mean all three of them won't have any reason to stay
around here anymore and you'll be left the way you were before,
namely on your own.* Now, why didn't I think of that earlier? I'm
not stupid, so why didn't I think of it? I've got a choice

here—do I unfuck-up Gene and have the whole crew skedad-dle, or do I let things ride and let the situation keep Lee and Diane here, even though it looks like they might not invite me over to see them again? But maybe they will. Maybe Lee didn't invite me around tonight because he's feeling worse than usual about the way things are here. Maybe next week he'll be back to normal. Yeah. Which means I don't have to try and straighten Gene out. What a relief! I don't know how I would've gone about it, anyway.

"Go back home?" says Gene. "Well, of course he does. Everybody misses their home. It's only natural."

If I follow up that comment by asking how come if Lee wants to go home he doesn't up and do it, Gene'll have to admit it's because Diane's here, which'll lead to an admission that she's here because Gene's here, which is a point that might have serious repercussions, like I said.

"Yeah, I agree with that. I think you're right. I miss my home sometimes too."

"Don't you live at home, Burris? I thought you did."

"Yeah, well . . . I spend a lot of time away from it. I've got friends all over town I crash with, a night here, a night there, you know."

"Young people are very independent nowadays."

"Yeah, that's very true. I agree."

The little voice in my head is telling me I goofed coming around here. I should've stayed away to accomplish what I need to accomplish to keep Lee and Diane here, namely noth-ing. But here I am. And I bet Gene'll tell them I came around, and they'll think I'm some kind of sneaky bastard poking my nose in where it's not wanted, which'll get them pissed at me and Lee *won't* invite me around next week. I've gone and fucked myself up with a vengeance here. And I call myself *smart!*

"I've had an operation," says Gene out of the blue.

"Yeah, I know."

"I suppose they told you."

"Well, yeah."

"It was a terrible mistake, Burris."

"I know . . ."

"You *can't* know. Only someone who's lost what I've lost can know."

"Sure, I agree. I only meant I sympathize . . ."

"Please don't," he says, and turns his head away and looks at a calendar on the wall. It's a railroad calendar with a yellow Union Pacific locomotive on it. He looked like Bette Davis's brother again, showing me his profile like that. "I don't want sympathy," he says, which is just bullshit because he got Diane up here to hold his hand, and what's that if it isn't needing sympathy?

"I'm sorry. I didn't mean to sympathize . . ."

"You're a generous person, I can tell, but sympathy would only weaken me now."

I thought it was pretty funny the way he's still looking at the locomotive on the wall. It'd be a very dramatic pose if there was a big window there with a sunset or the ocean or something behind it, but there's just the wall and calendar. It was very pathetic and, like I say, kind of funny. Then I didn't think it was funny anymore, because he's gone and started crying. Really, he's crying. This guy with a vagina he doesn't want is looking at the wall and crying.

"A very cruel trick was played on me," he says, his voice gone all froggy. "I believed at an early age I was a girl put somehow inside the body of a boy. I thought I was being punished for something, I don't know what. I tried very hard *not* to feel what I felt. No one knew I felt that way. I didn't look like a girl, I looked like a boy—an ugly boy, even. I didn't tell a soul. They would've locked me away. I grew up and got married like a man is expected to do and had a daughter I thank God for. I'd be lost without Diane. She's been the only one to stand by me. For forty-one years I stayed inside that prison, then I found out I didn't have to be there. Don't ever underestimate the importance of television, Burris. I saw a documentary program on PBS about a certain operation that could change people in my situation into the people they *truly are* inside. It was a revelation, it really was. I saw that I wasn't alone and there was a way out. I sold my business to pay for the operation and told my wife what I wanted to do. She didn't understand. She *couldn't*. I don't blame her for divorcing me. At least Diane stood by me. Lee hasn't forgiven me for what I've done, I know. He's very bitter. I feel very sad about that, but I felt I had to do it."

"A man's gotta do what a man's gotta do," I said, and right away felt like a total jerk for saying something so dumb.

"The thing is, Burris, I *shouldn't* have done it. I *don't* feel at home in a woman's body. I was supposed to, but I don't. Everything was supposed to work out fine, but it *hasn't*. I made an awful mistake, and now they can't *give me back my penis!* Imagine that, Burris. Imagine having no penis after half a lifetime of *having* one. Imagine having breasts you *thought* you wanted, but when you've got them you *don't* want them, they're just something you have to *carry around* in front of you like one of those baby holders. I should've listened when everyone told me I was making a mistake. For a whole year before the operation I lived like a woman, wore dresses all the time, even sat down to pee. I truly believed it was what I wanted. I was *happy* then, just waiting for the day they'd let me go to hospital and become a woman. It never once occurred to me I might change my mind later on. It seemed so natural to perm my hair and wear heels and panty hose. I thought all along I was doing the right thing. But I *wasn't*. I was doing the *wrong* thing. Oh, I know most men who have the operation are better off for it. They truly *were* intended to be women, and the knife is a blessing to them. But not to me, Burris. I'm the exception to the rule. I convinced myself, I convinced the doctors . . . and I was wrong. I'm *not* supposed to be a woman. Do you know what I think, Burris? I think I was supposed to be a homosexual. That probably sounds shocking, I know, but I think, on mature reflection, that's what I was supposed to be. I shouldn't have gotten into the cross-dressing thing at all. That was my first mistake. I should've joined in the gay scene instead. I've never had sex with a man, I want you to know that. But maybe I should've. Maybe that would've let the female side of me find satisfaction without surgery." He said it again. "Satisfaction without surgery . . ."

It was just the saddest thing, listening to him. He's not such a moron, after all. I thought he was because he likes *Benson*, which was a pretty trivial reason for thinking he isn't bright. I mean, I don't think he's a genius or anything, but hearing him explain what happened to him like that made me see things from his side, and it's the sorriest story I ever heard. At the same time it's kind of pathetic too. They'd never make a Movie of the Week out of it, because everything in the story is wrong, most of all the fact that Gene turned out looking ugly and stupid. If he'd come out looking gorgeous they'd make a movie of it in about two minutes. But they won't, because everything went wrong. The wrong decisions gave the wrong operation to the wrong guy. No happy ending in sight, no book deal, no Movie of the Week. Nothin'.

"Maybe if you had your . . . uh . . . breasts removed. I mean, they're silicone, aren't they? They could just take the stuff out and they'd go flat again."

But he shook his head. "I have to take hormones, female hormones, or I'd get very sick. The hormones would keep my breasts there even if the silicone was taken out, and I can't stop taking the hormones. I'd probably die if I did."

"Oh."

God, I felt awful. I'd come here to give this guy, this *woman*, a big lecture about shaping up or shipping out, then decided not to for my own selfish reasons. I mean, I wanted him to stay fucked-up to keep Lee and Diane here in Buford with me. But now, if I had a magic wand, I'd go *ping!* and change everything for him, change him back to a man, and he could figure out with hindsight if he wanted to be straight or gay or whatever, but he'd know not to have any operations. At the very least I'd give him a new TV so he can watch *Benson*. But I don't have a magic wand. Even the stick I hold my tent of silence up with is imaginary.

"So what are you gonna do?"

I really wanted to know. He didn't say anything for a while, then he says, "Burris, I truly believe I'll kill myself if things don't get better."

He said it just like that. He's looking straight at me, not at the calendar, and there was no dramatic pose or anything.

"Yeah?"

"Does that sound selfish?"

"How are you gonna do it? I mean, if things get really bad."

"You don't think it'd be selfish of me to leave Diane, who's stuck by me?"

I hadn't even looked at it that way, but now that he's mentioned it, I think Diane would get along better with Lee if Gene wasn't around. But if she and Lee start getting along together again and there's no Gene to keep them in Buford anymore, it'll be bye-bye, buddies.

"I really don't think you should kill yourself, Gene."

"It's not an easy decision to make. I'd have to think about it very carefully. Look what happened after the last big decision I made."

"I see what you mean. I don't think you *should* kill yourself, but if you did, how would you do it? Just out of curiosity."

"I don't know. I haven't thought about it. It's an awful thing to think about."

"Yeah, it is. I think poison and stuff is risky, unless you're a druggist who knows exactly what he's doing. If you gave yourself the wrong dose you could suffer a lot before you died, you know, squirming around on the floor in agony."

"I'd never do anything like that, take poison."

"I think the surest, safest way is still the good old pistol to the head. Got a gun?"

"No, I don't. I used to own a .45, but I gave it to Lee."

"You could borrow it back."

"I don't *want* it back."

"Okay, I was only saying *if* things got really bad."

"I'm not a Catholic or anything, but I think killing yourself is a terrible thing."

"So you're definitely not gonna do it."

"I didn't *say* that. I said I *might* if things got very bad."

"Well, if you *do*, the .45 is your best bet. It'll leave a little mess, but that won't be your problem. It'll be the Green Acres manager's problem."

If it would've made the manager's cleanup problem worse, I'd have tried persuading Gene to commit hara-kiri or swallow a hand grenade. But like I said, it's in my own best interest to keep him alive. *Her* alive. There should be a word you can apply to humans that doesn't mean male *or* female, a nice word, not like *it*. It has to be dignified. Guys like the manager are its.

"Did you sell a lot of outboard motors?"

"Yes, I did. Everyone thinks there's no water in New Mexico, but it's not true. Just around Tucumcari there's Ute Lake and Conchas Lake. I sold a lot of outboards. I was just about to start getting Windsurfers into stock as a kind of sideline when I decided to sell the business."

"Windsurfers are big now."

"I know. It's just incredible no one thought of putting a sail on a surfboard before. Whoever thought of it must've made a million.'

Gene got pretty chatty after that. He talked about a lot of stuff back in Tucumcari and how he met his wife Cathy and got married, et cetera, only that didn't happen in Tucumcari, that happened in Gallup before they moved to Tucumcari, which is where Diane got born. He says in Gallup there's a high school yard with an elm in it that Gene planted when he was just a little kid. He was picked out of the whole school to be the one that planted this tree, which is huge now. He knows because he went back and had a look at it a few years ago. It seemed pretty important to him, so I listened while he talked about it. I think Gene's been starved of conversation, what with not being welcome over in Lee's trailer whenever Lee's there, and he probably gets tired of talking with just Diane through the day, and not having the TV anymore must be pretty hard to take too. He talked plenty about his outboard business and how he got an award one year from Evinrude or someone for selling more outboards in an inland town than any other dealer. Retailers on the coast have got an advantage being next to so much water, so inland outboard retailers get put in a different category, and guys selling in small towns like Tucumcari get put in another category. Gene won in the small inland town category. He was proud of it, all right, you could tell by how he talked. Frankly, I was getting a little bored by then. If it wasn't for his amazing sexual problem, Gene'd be a pretty boring person. I pretended to be interested, though, because he cheered up plenty with someone there to listen.

Then there's a knock at the door. Shit! It could only be Lee or Diane, and I don't want them to know I'm within miles of here. Gene got up to answer it.

"Don't say I'm here," I whispered.

"Why not?" he says.

"Just *don't* . . ."

But he's already opening the door, the stupid prick.

It's Diane. Surprise, surprise. She came in and says, "I thought I heard voices," which is a big exaggeration because Gene was doing *all* the talking in there, believe me. "Hello, Burris," she says next.

"Hi."

"Lee's gone drinking," she says to Gene. "I was going to invite you over to watch TV. I don't want to interrupt anything."

"Oh, you're not, Dee," says Gene. Dee must be his pet name for her. It's kind of embarrassing to have intimate stuff like that flung around under your nose. "Burris and I were just shooting the breeze."

Shooting the breeze? Gene's been watching Roy Rogers.

"Well, why don't the both of you come over. There's a movie just about to start."

So we did. Diane didn't ask me what the hell I was doing there or anything, just acted like it's perfectly natural to find me over in Gene's trailer. We watched *Castle of Doom*, which I can't be bothered talking about. It wasn't as hilarious as *Death's Head Zombies* the week before, but at least we didn't switch channels halfway through to watch *Benson*. The movie ended, and Gene said he's tired and went back to his own trailer, but not before Diane got his car keys off him to drive me home. I didn't even know Gene had a car. I just assumed he came to Buford on a Greyhound or something. He said good night to me, and I did the same.

Then Diane drove me home. Gene's car is an old Chrysler in pretty nice condition, a '78, I think.

"Thanks for paying Gene a visit."

"I thought he might like some company," I said. It's easy to tell a lie if it helps people think you're a good guy.

"That was kind. I was expecting you at our place, but then Lee came home and said you weren't coming."

"I wasn't invited." Take *that*, Lee.

She didn't say anything, then she says, "How's he been at the plant?"

"Not much fun. He won't clown around anymore. He's not too happy, I guess."

"No," she says, then, "he doesn't usually go out drinking. He's not the drinking type—not in bars, I mean."

"Well, he'll probably be home by the time you get back."

A minute later we were on the Interstate, and when we went past the Starlite, I told her about how they're going to tear it down and how I've got myself booked into 107 on the last night.

"Why?" she says.

That's when I realized Lee hadn't told her about Room 107, and I got mad at him. When you tell someone an important thing like that, you expect he'll at least tell his wife about it. But he hadn't. He probably thought it was so *un*important he forgot about it. I call that pretty fucking insensitive. So I told Diane about 107 and what it means and everything . . . and guess what—she thought it was just the greatest thing she'd heard all year!

"I wonder if it's the same bed still," she says. "Wouldn't that be incredible, to be the last one to use the actual bed you were born in! I really envy you."

She was practically getting off on the whole thing, which was very gratifying. I really liked her for that. Up until now I kind of thought of Diane as a part of Lee, if you see what I mean, but the way she got enthusiastic about 107 made me look at her with my third eye, the one that sees Truth, and she's nothing like I thought she was. I mean, I always liked her and everything, but now I *really* like her. In fact, you know what she did? She went and stepped right into Lee's shoes as the person I care about most. Isn't that crazy? It took about thirty seconds, and all because she thinks the 107 deal is great. It's not that I *abandoned* Lee, it's just that he's been so *distant* lately, with his problems, et cetera, and I wasn't feeling as close to him as I did a couple weeks back. And I wasn't so sympathetic about Lee's problems anymore, now that I talked with Gene and don't think he's a creepy pervert or anything. It's strange how things work out. Lee told me not to come around tonight, and because I didn't go to the trailer park in the usual way, I found out the Starlite's coming down. If I had've been with Lee in the Dodge I probably wouldn't have seen the sign, but because I was on foot I saw it and got Room 107 on the last night. And because I went around to the trailer park, anyway, and ended up talking to Gene and then Diane without Lee around, I've got a whole new way of looking at them both. Tonight my third eye got pried open by what I thought at first were bad circumstances, but look at the terrific way everything turned out—the 107 thing, talking with old Gene and finding out he's a human being, falling for Diane . . . Strike that! Appreciating Diane more than I did before.

She dropped me off and drove away. We didn't say anything special, just "Thanks for driving me home," and "You're welcome," ordinary stuff. Peggy was watching TV. Uncle Ron and Auntie Nancy were in the White House garden when I walked in. A reporter asked Ron a question, but I didn't catch it. Ron didn't seem to catch it either. He stood there with his arms hanging straight down by his sides the way they do, and this big smile on his face, and didn't say a word. Then Nancy leaned in close to him and whispered. The mike wasn't supposed to pick up what she whispered, but it did. She whispered, "We're doing the best we can." Then she straightened up again. Ron's smile got even bigger. "We're doing the best we can," he says.

Way to go, Ron!

8 Saturday night was a big night for Buford. There's this local band called DNA that's been around for years, but now they've hit the big time with a gold album called *Double Helix*, a nationwide number-one track from it, "Ace Face" and a video on MTV. I bet before too long Revlon or Max Factor or one of those big makeup outfits will use the tune and hook line from "Ace Face" to sell their stuff. They'll pay DNA a million bucks for the rights to the song, and DNA'll take the cash and hear their best number murdered, but they'll have the million to dry their tears with. I just bet it happens. Anyway, this Saturday night they came back home after a cross-country sellout tour—I mean, all the tickets were sold. The other kind of sellout'll come later—a big successful tour, and they're going to play in their old haunt, Poco's, in Wilmington, just to show that fame hasn't spoiled them and they haven't got big heads or anything. Me, I don't give a shit. What I did instead of rushing down to Poco's to watch DNA be humble, I went for a walk up along Harland Heights.

This is real concrete pineapple country. They're everywhere, on gateposts, beside doorways, standing in the corners of gardens like fat little guardsmen with feathered helmets, pineapples, pineapples everywhere. Hawaii may be the biggest pineapple producer in the world, but Harland Heights has got to have more of the concrete variety than anyplace else on the planet. Jesus, I hate concrete pineapples. I really *hate* the fuckers. The houses up around here are in the six-figure category, and you can just bet the first number isn't a one. Big ranch-style houses with lots of lawn that needs a mower you sit on to mow them, and signs everywhere that say NEIGHBORHOOD WATCH AREA, which means if your face doesn't fit, they call the cops, and THIEVES BEWARE—THESE PREMISES PROTECTED BY GAUNTLET SECURITY INC. Everything here is very fucking neat, the houses, the trees, the lawns—the street even. I looked everywhere but couldn't see a single McDonald's takeout box or squashed cola can or used zoob tube. There isn't even any dogshit up on Harland Heights. I bet if a dog took a dump up here, someone'd call the cops and they'd rush out to scoop the poop and pound the pooch. Gimping along Overlook Avenue, I really felt at home, like a turd in a Gucci shoe. If it had've been daylight, I would've been spotted and the red alert sounded—"Intruder! Intruder! Intercept and apprehend!" But no one seemed to notice me. There were plenty of parties happening up that way, with lots of Le Barons and Lincolns and a few Mercedes parked along those half-moon gravel driveways big houses have, and always, *always* out on the front lawn there's a welcome lamp that looks like a street lamp from the 1800s, but you can tell it isn't a genuine antique because there's *always* a little brass eagle sitting on top to give the thing *class*, yes sir. Those little brass eagles with the opened wings make me want to puke almost as much as concrete pineapples.

I kept walking, walking, swinging the short leg, not thinking much about anything—that is, trying not to think about Lee and Diane. I've got to stop thinking about those two so much. And Gene, don't forget old Gene. Yes, *do* forget old Gene, *and* Lee, *and* Diane. Forget, forget, forget. I'm almost out of Harland Heights now, entering Comstock, not so ritzy but still plenty rich, and with the same view across the town. It's a nice view, so you have to pay for it. I stopped awhile to look at the lights winking and blinking below. If I look right across Buford and squint my eyes . . . yep, there it is, way over on the far side where the Buford Thruway turns back into the plain old Interstate, the pink-and-green neon sign of the Starlite. Only three nights to go. Zip-a-dee-*doo*-dah! I feel good knowing I've

got a date with destiny in 107. Hot dog! I'm too excited to just
stand there. Walk, lad, *walk!* You know you can do it, boy!
Walk to me! Roddy McDowall topples into Walter Pidgeon's
arms. *How Green Was My Valley*. Walk, Burris, *walk!* I walked.
There's a police siren drifting up from the town, too thin and
far away to sound urgent. Is it getting louder? Maybe they're
coming for *me*. Maybe some rich fucker saw me through his
triple-glazed window while he was checking out the alarm
system and ran to the phone. "Police! Police! A gimp has been
sighted on Overlook Avenue! Please hurry! He's right outside
my *home!*" Nah, it's getting fainter. I'm safe. I can walk on
without hurrying.

Then I saw it. Welcome lamps, brass eagles, concrete pineapples, they all vanished, blotted out by the monstrosity in
front of me. Words aren't enough to describe what I felt. I had
to stop and look at this *thing*, slap in the middle of some
asshole's lawn. It was *awful*, just the worst thing you could
think of to put in front of a house. Are you ready for this? It
was a waterwheel. Yeah, a fucking miniature waterwheel, about
three feet high, with this miniature mill and millrace all set
beside this fucking *pond*. There must be a little electric motor or
something inside the mill that's turning the wheel, because the
pissy little stream dropping over the blades wouldn't turn a
leaf. There must be a hidden pump sucking water out of the
pond and pulling it up to where the sluiceway starts, then it
flows along the little sluice ramp on stilts till it empties over the
wheel. And on the other side of the pond there's another
miniature, one of those covered-over bridges you get in New
England, the ones that look like long sheds, but this one doesn't
even cross any water, just sits alongside the edge of the pond
looking completely useless. I'm surprised there isn't a model
railroad that runs around the edge of the pond to link everything up. It was revolting enough just as it was, but the thing
that made it really puke-making was the fact that there's a
spotlight trained on it. A *spot*light! The morons who live here
want to make sure everyone passing by *notices* their pride and
joy. *Look* at our wonderful waterwheel. *Admire* its scaled-down

perfection. *Envy* what you see. Don't you wish *you* had one? I wish I had a stick of fucking dynamite, pal. What a disgusting fucking abortion to ram down Joe Public's throat. I hated it so much I got the shakes, that's how mad I got, and I had to gimp away at double-quick speed to get myself calmed down. Jesus, some people don't deserve money, really they don't.

I kept going through Comstock to Belvedere, which sounds kind of wealthy but isn't. The thing I like in Belvedere is the playground, which has got this actual jet fighter from the Korean War sitting up on steel rods in a big concrete block. It's a snub-nosed Sabre jet, just the shell of it, no engines or guns or anything, and it's been coated with around fifty coats of khaki to weatherproof it. The perspex cockpit bubble's gone, but there's a metal seat welded inside so you can sit where the pilot sat thirty-plus years ago to blast shit out of those slant-eyed, atheistic Reds. When I was a little kid I used to love that plane. I'd sit in it long as I could, until some other kid wanted his turn. There's even a joystick in there, but it's welded in one position. All the instruments are gone. There's just this wrap-around dashboard thing with lots of spooky holes where the altimeter and horizon-finder and all that stuff used to be, but you could fill in the holes easy enough just by imagining. I haven't been near the old Sabre in a couple years, but no one's around tonight, so up the ladder I go, up and over and down into the cockpit.

Shit! Some prick ripped the seat out and there's just a cross-bar to sit on. How'd he do it? That seat was *welded!* Bastard! How fucking *stupid*, to steal an ordinary metal seat from where it was doing a useful job. I hate vandals. It wouldn't worry me if vandals got lined up and shot. I can't think of anything dumber than a vandal. I got really pissed about that missing seat. That crossbar bit into my ass like teeth. Never mind, I told myself, you're back in the pilot's seat and cruising above the 38th parallel looking for MiGs. There's just the continuous, rolling boom of the engine behind me spewing out superheated air, pushing me along in a slow bank to the right. Where are those commies lurking today? I shot down fifteen yesterday, but those fiendish yellow bastards can whip up a new jet practically overnight. I think they build them out of flattened beer cans on a bamboo airframe and fuel the fuckers with soy sauce. My wingmen today are Jake and Bill and Barney, and we're all red-hot for a scrap with the slants. Just let 'em try messing with us and it's American bullets for supper. *Rata-tatatatatatatata! Kablaaaam! Kablooooey!* Another MiG bites the dust! Eat lead, ya stinkin' Red! More satisfying than a Chinese meal, yuk, yuk, yuk, but if ya want seconds, I got a cannonload of dessert just waitin' for ya, ya slant-eyed commie monkey!

I really used to think stuff like that back then, Flight Lieutenant Burris (Daredevil) Weems, the gung-ho gimp, age twelve. I had so many red stars on my plane it was embarrassing. When the President gave me a medal he asked how many there were, and I said, "Mr. President, enough to make widows weep from Korea to Tibet." He thought that was pretty good. Even a smart twelve-year-old like I was is very often a total fuckhead. Nowadays I'm more mature about war and stuff. It's got nothing to do with my dad getting killed, because that didn't *mean* anything to me, seeing as I was too young to know him. No, it's just plain common sense makes me want to stay out of the armed forces. They teach you all kinds of nasty shit like in *An Officer and a Gentleman* when the tough sergeant tells the rookies the Navy's going to teach them to be aviators that'll *obey orders* without even stopping to think about it, even if it means blowing away women and kids. I thought that was pretty revolting, but I bet it's exactly the way they talk and think.

I'm not a pacifist or anything. I mean, if someone pushed me I wouldn't go turning the other cheek or anything. You end up with sore cheeks that way. But I wouldn't hit back right away, either. What I'd do, I'd try to talk my way out of it. People that go around hitting other people are generally pretty dumb, so I'd use my nimble tongue to dazzle my way past their fists, blind them with the illogicality of fighting to win an argument when sweet reason could do the job without anyone getting hurt. And if that approach didn't work, I'd pull out my gun and shoot the stupid fucker dead. There are too many stupid fuckers in the world. So I can't call myself a pacifist, but to join the army in peacetime and risk getting told to go kill people is just crazy. Okay, the Japs and Krauts asked for it, starting a war like they did, but today no one's trying to take over the world that I can see. Wars today are because people *think* different from each other, that's all.

It really pisses me when I see some kid outside the recruiting office downtown, standing there with his eyes on those posters with the square-jawed he-men on them. He thinks he'll look like them if he signs up, with perfectly regular features and an expression that says, "I've been trained to kill, so don't fuck with me." He thinks the military life is glamorous, wants to be one of THE FEW—THE PROUD—THE MARINES. Yeah, that's for *me!* There'll be even fewer come Warday, feller. Can't he *see?* Doesn't he *know?* Don't go in . . . ! He went in. Now he'll get to be a man among men. They'll ask him why he wants to join and he'll say, "Uh . . . patriotism, sir. My country needs me." I bet recruits say exactly the same thing in Russia, just crank out that fucking *word* again and again, like unfurling a flag or something. Patriotism, patriotism—my country, right or wrong. It doesn't make any *sense.* Okay, you're in the army or the Marines or whatever, and the President says you have to go fight the Wickywackywoos in a far-off land. You go, you fight, you get a leg blown off, your best buddies get killed, then they elect a new President and this guy says, "Come on home, the war never should've got started! The Wickywackywoos are okay!" So your buddies died because the first guy, the one you swore allegiance to, thought the Wickywackywoos were assholes who needed a good stiff dose of good ol' U.S. *kickass,* and the second guy, who you swore equal allegiance to, thinks different and says to come on home and forget the whole thing because it was a big mistake. One man thinks one thing and the next man thinks another thing. What the fuck do *you* think, Private Dogface? "Uh . . . well, sir, I'm not paid to think. It's okay with me if those guys in the White House do my thinking for me, sir. I'm just here to kick ass when I'm told." Now *there's* a *soldier!* Sign on the line and surrender your brain at the door before we issue you this butch *uniform* and this great little *gun*. There now, don't you look terrific! This year we don't like Pollywollydoodles, so go *seek! Kill!* Get 'em quick before Pollywollydoodle season's over and there's someone new to tell you what to do. It drives me *crazy! I* should be the President. I'd tell everybody to *cut out all the patriotic crap!* Right now! But I won't ever be President, which is a big loss to the nation, believe me.

My ass is on fire. This crossbar's branded me forever. I got out of the Sabre and went home, an hour's walk. The local cable channel is presenting DNA live from Poco's. They're just as boring as they ever were, but dressed fancier. I watched some other stuff on the tube till three, then crashed.

Sunday I did nothing, just lay in the hammock out back and thought about Lee and Diane and Gene. I didn't know how I felt about them anymore. Sometimes I wish I hadn't met them. When there was just me, it was simpler. People complicate your life if you get too close to them, or let them get close to you. It was very dumb of me to think I could change their situation. I don't have any influence on them. Lee's the one who'll change things down at the trailer park—if anything *does* change. It's got nothing to do with me. It never did. I just *thought* it did for a while, because I'm not used to being around people—apart from Peggy and Loretta, that is—and getting mixed up with the Green Acres bunch must've thrown me off-balance temporarily. But I'm okay now. I know I don't mean all that much to them. I've quit agonizing over everything the way I was doing last week. It's a waste of time. I thought those three people were spinning around me like little moons, but really they're three stars clustered together, circling each other like in a binary system, except they're a trinary system—if there is such a thing—and I'm just a wandering comet that's drifted across their path on a trip from nowhere to nowhere. I'm a galactic wanderer with a tail a million miles long and a head with no substance at all. I thought about being a lonely comet all afternoon, just a streak of dust on a black marble floor that extends forever. I made myself very depressed. I felt better after a pepperoni pizza. Don't laugh. If it wasn't for things like pizza and a good movie now and then, the suicide rate would skyrocket.

Monday morning. I didn't want to see Lee. I just wanted to forget about him. I wanted to be on my own again. When the horn sounded out in the street, I practically had to drag myself outside and climb aboard.

"Hey, Burris. You get any on the weekend?"

Sometimes he acts like a moron deliberately. He *knows* I didn't get any, he just wants to get a rise out of me. I could've said something like, "Had to beat 'em off with a baseball bat," or "Plowed myself sore," or something. But I didn't feel like it. I'm pissed at him about Friday night. I waited for him to say something about how I went out to the trailer park, anyway, invited or not, but he didn't say anything about it, not on the drive out to Servex, not during the morning or at lunch break, not a single word about it all through the afternoon. First off I thought he's playing a game with me, one of those dumb games where one person waits for the other person to say or ask something the first person *knows* the second person wants to say or ask. I thought he didn't want to give me the satisfaction of knowing that my surprise visit on Friday night is a subject worth talking about, but the funny thing is, he hasn't got a secret grin on his face the way you'd expect if he truly was playing a wait-for-the-other-guy-to-break game. Not only wasn't he talking about my Friday night visit, he wasn't talking about very much at all. People playing the waiting game pretty often try to disguise the fact that they're playing the game by talking a lot, but always in circles around the subject the game is all about. But Lee wasn't doing that. After that first terrifically original line he didn't bother making any more wiseass cracks about my nonexistent sex life, or about anything else. Maybe he just didn't care if I was out at Green Acres or not, which is kind of an insult, like nothing I do could possibly *matter*. I watched his face. He never seemed to look at me, but he wasn't cranky or anything, just did his job and spoke my name a couple times just in ordinary job talk. "Gimme a hand here, will you, Burris," and "Rolling around to quitting time, Burris," stuff like that. He wasn't giving anything away, and it annoyed the hell out of me.

Then I figured it out. He's not asking about Friday night because he *doesn't know*. Diane and Gene didn't tell him I went out there! That changed everything. I thought hard about the new situation. Those two must be mad at him about something, not to tell him about me this way. Maybe he came home real drunk and beat up Gene, or beat up Diane! He better *not* have! I looked at his hands. No swelling or scabs, but Friday night was three days back now, so that doesn't prove anything. But I'm sure he doesn't know I was there. It's like a secret between Diane and Gene and me. Then it hit me—it's *Lee* who's the wandering comet, not me! If a guy's own wife and parent-in-law don't tell him important stuff, it means he's in the doghouse. It means they don't want to share things with him anymore, and if that's how they feel, it can only be because Lee did something bad. He *deserves* to be in the doghouse, I bet.

This big revelation came to me just a few minutes before we shut the bander down, which is something I don't know why we do because the next shift just switches it straight back on again ten minutes after we're gone. I went with Lee to get washed up, and looking at the back of his head and his skinny neck and no shoulders when he went through the washroom door ahead of me, I started feeling sorry for him. Diane and Gene must really be down on him about something, not to tell him about important stuff like my surprise visit. I wonder what he did. Now that I knew he was under the pooch porch, I looked at things differently. That's what *always* happens, because I've got this dumb *ability* or something to put myself in his shoes. In *any*body's shoes. Watching him work up suds between his hands, I felt very sympathetic toward him, it's hard to say exactly why—I mean, he hasn't been treating me like a friend ought to just recently. But I can't help it. I'm all heart, I admit it. What I wanted to do, I wanted to go over to him and say, "It's okay, Lee. Things are tough for you right now, but you've got me to lean on," something corny like that but *sincere*. I felt very sincere watching him shove his hands under the blower and rub them dry. He looked like a little old man when he did that, rubbing his hands that way, and I wanted to reassure him like crazy about everything, only I didn't know what to say.

We went out to the parking lot same as usual, and he says, "Another day, another dime."

"Yeah."

I wanted to say something like that, too, unoriginal but funny anyway, but I couldn't think of a single thing. We got in the Dodge and he fired it up, and we laid the usual smoke screen to the gate and out onto the highway. Sooner or later he'll get pulled over by a cop, the way he pumps out smoke like that. We rode along with Lee whistling a little bit, not a tune or anything, just sounds. In a movie that kind of thing means the whistler is scared, and he's whistling to try and show he's not. But Lee didn't look scared. He didn't even seem to be *there*, if you know what I mean.

"Want to see something really disgusting?" I said.

"If it's an appendix scar, no."

That was just exactly the right thing for him to say. It sounds like the old jokey Lee is back.

"It's nothing like that. It's up in Harland Heights."

"Where's that?"

"Hang a left at the next light."

He hung a left and we started climbing.

"This better be good. I mean bad, disgustingly bad. Is it one of your girlfriends?"

"Nope."

"Can you guarantee I'll be truly disgusted?"

"Your money will be refunded if satisfaction is not achieved."

"Can't say fairer than that."

I directed him through to where Harland Heights turns into Comstock, along Overlook Avenue, which now I come to think of it is a dumb name—the Avenue part, I mean—because an avenue is supposed to have trees on both sides, isn't it? Overlook has got houses down one side and the actual overlook on

the other—I mean, thin air and a view. It's those idiot town
planners with their names-in-a-hat policy again, I bet.

"Stop!"

We stopped.

"Well?" says Lee.

I pointed. He looked.

"Jesus Christ . . ."

"Ain't it a beaut?"

"Great God Almighty . . ."

He was overdoing it kind of, but that made me feel good.

"I told you."

"You said it'd be disgusting, not fucking abominable."

"You should see it at night. They shine a spotlight on it."

"You're stretching my brain, Burris."

"It's true! You can see it up in the tree."

"Hold my hand, Mother, I'm dying. . . ."

"Did you ever see anything more revolting?"

"Not outside of the bowl, buddy."

"If I was a neighbor I'd blow it up."

"That fucking thing is *garbage*."

"I bet the guy that put it up has got an electric train set in the
basement. I bet he's a retired insurance salesman that puts one
of those Casey Jones hats on his stupid head and makes trains
go around and around in circles down there in the basement."

"I bet that's exactly the kind of cunt he is."

"Yeah."

"I can't stand cunts like that, Burris."

He wasn't kidding, either. He was really staring at that
dumb waterwheel like it was the worst thing in the world.

"Me neither."

"They make me puke."

"Me too."

"I really don't like that thing."

"It's a dilly, all right."

"Thanks for showing me."

"That's okay. I knew you'd appreciate a true work of art." We
got rolling again, but somehow all the fun of it had gone.

"I got drunk pretty bad last Friday," says Lee.

"Yeah?"

"I went out. Sometimes that damn trailer really gets in my craw, you know. Ever been to Lucy's Bar down on Wilmington?"

"No."

"They've got this big neon cocktail glass outside. The olives flash on and off. The first time you see them they're above the glass, then they're gone, then they're *in* the glass, then they're out of it again. It's a great sign. It's a fucking *swell* sign."

"Is it okay inside?"

"It's a dump. That's why I went there."

There's a real edge to his voice now, kind of ugly.

"It's a faggot pickup joint," he says.

"In Buford?"

"Come on, Burris, they're everywhere. There's even one in little old Tucumcari, maybe more than one, but one for sure that I know."

"Why would you want to go in a place like that?"

"I observe," he says, and he makes it sound like a scientist watching something wriggle around in a test tube.

"Well . . . why?"

"Fruits are interesting characters. Even the boring ones are interesting. You go in those places and get talking with the fruits and you'll be amazed at the stuff they tell you. Even when they figure out you're not like them, they keep talking. They generally like to talk about what they do. They're exhibitionists, most of them."

"Are you interested in them because of Gene?"

"That's exactly right. Old Gene opened my eyes. Before him, I thought only those cute little pixie types were homos, but they can be just about anyone at all."

"I guess I don't know much about it. . . ."

"I know you don't, ol' pal, ol' buddy o' mine. You keep it that way. It's very fucking *unsavory*."

"Yeah, AIDS and all."

"Right, AIDS, and the shame of it is, it's spreading to the rest of us now. If it only killed fruits, I'd say let 'em die, why find a cure? Don't get me wrong, I'm not one of those idiots that says it's God's revenge. God's got nothing to do with it. God's got nothing to do with anything. It's just a disease you get if you shove your prick into someone's bowels. I mean, we're talking *shit* here. That's dirty stuff. *Germs*, right?"

"Yeah."

"You do that dirty stuff and what can you expect but some kind of dirty disease. I'm not talking *moral* dirt, I'm talking *dirty* dirt, germs and bacteria, that kind of dirt. I don't sit in judgment over anyone. It's just dirty, that's all. Know what else those guys do?"

"No."

He told me some other stuff which is pretty unbelievable and must hurt like crazy if they really do it. He was starting to spook me with all this talk about fruits and germs and dirt. I wanted to tell him that Gene told me he'd never done anything sexual with guys, but that would've meant admitting he told it to me last Friday night when I went around there, which Lee doesn't know about and which I didn't want him to, don't ask me why, maybe because he's got me too scared to defend someone like Gene, who isn't one of *us*. I know it sounds stupid for me to be scared of Lee, but I was. Sometimes I think I must be a coward. But he's got this *look* on his face, very *intense*, and he's working his lips like he's chewing tobacco, which he isn't.

Then a weird thought came into my head—maybe *Lee's* gay! Maybe he's one of those guys that tries to fight it by being very *anti* all the time. The fact that he's married and hates Gene doesn't mean a thing. It was a very scary thought to have, sitting right next to him like that—I mean, it wasn't scary to think he's *gay*, it's scary to think he doesn't *know* it, doesn't even suspect that all this talk about fruits and disease and all is a way of hiding the truth from himself. If it's true, then this guy has got problems that have got practically nothing to *do* with the fact that he's living in a shitty trailer in a town where he doesn't want to be, with a parent-in-law he doesn't like. That stuff is nothing more than *annoying* if the real problem is deep inside Lee—I mean, about him being wedged way back in the closet and denying he's even *in* there. How come I didn't think of this before? It's another terrific example of Weems hindsight, which lets me see things very clearly, third-eye clearly, but too late, or at least *not soon enough*. I felt stupid about not figuring it all out earlier. Poor Diane. Does she know she's married to a closet case? Imagine having a father that turns himself into a woman, and a husband that's gone and buried himself in the closet! Maybe she *does* know Lee's that way, knows it even if Lee doesn't. Would she love him anyway? Maybe, what the hell do I know? And how about that time Lee said he should talk to Dr. Ruth about a sex problem, then turned around and tried to make out he was just kidding. Wouldn't a closet case have trouble relating sexually to his wife? I bet he would. Hey . . . maybe Diane's a *lesbian!* They're supposed to get along pretty good together, homos and lesbians, even *get married* sometimes to fool people into thinking they're not gay! Or was it years ago they used to do that, before Gay Liberation and all? But it *fits*, it definitely fits! Why didn't I see this before? All *three* of them are weird!

"I saw old Gene one time."

"Huh . . . ?"

"One time in Tucumcari. Saw him go in that gay bar."

"Gene?"

"You bet. Before he had the operation."

He's lying. He's got to be. Gene told me the exact opposite, said he'd never done stuff with guys.

"Yeah, he went right in there. I waited around awhile, parked outside, and he came out a half hour later with another queen and they went off together in Gene's car. I followed them to this guy's place. They went in and I waited again. They were in there three, four hours, then Gene came out and drove away and I followed him home, so it was Gene, all right."

"I don't believe it."

"Say what, ol' pal?"

"I don't believe any of it."

"Yeah? Why not?"

"He told me he didn't do stuff like that."

"Bullshit, he did."

"He *did*."

"While you were watching fuckin' TV?"

"Not *then*. *Last* Friday night."

"Burris, you weren't even *there* last Friday night."

"I fucking *was!*"

"Bull*shit*, you were."

"I went to see Gene by myself, and then Diane came over and we went back to your place and watched *Castle of Doom*, her and me and Gene, while you were out at a gay bar trying to pick someone up *yourself!*"

"Whaaaat?"

"You can quit acting straight around me, I know the *truth*."

"You calling me a faggot?"

"Yeah! And just leave Gene alone!"

"Jesus . . . you think *I'm* a fuckin' *queen*?"

"Yes, I *do!* You only act like you do because you don't want to admit it!"

"Christ! Now you're a goddamn psychologist!"

"Just quit telling lies about Gene, that's all!"

"It's *not* lies, it's the *truth!* He used to *fuck* guys!"

"He did *not!* He *told* me! He said maybe he should've, instead of having the operation, but he *didn't!*"

"I know what I saw. . . ."

"And you said *yourself*, that time you drove me home after I met Gene, you said he used to dress up in drag and stuff, but he *didn't fuck guys!* I remember you *saying* it."

"I was being *polite*, for Chrissakes. It was bad enough I had to tell you Diane's father's a fucking *woman*. I couldn't tell you he used to spread his ass too."

"I don't believe you."

"You don't, huh? Well, fuck you, Burris."

"Fuck you too."

"And you think I'm a fruit like Gene."

"I think you're a fruit *not* like Gene."

"Different fruit, same tree."

"Yes."

"Well, that pisses me right off, pal. I don't like that one little bit."

"Well, I'm very sorry about that, but you shouldn't tell lies about other people."

"If I didn't need both hands for the wheel, I'd take your fucking head off."

"You don't scare me. You're too skinny to do anything."

He hung a left real fast, making the tires squeal.

"So you paid old Gene a visit last Friday."

"Yes, I did."

"And saw my old lady too."

"Yeah."

"And all three of you had a wonderful time watching TV and talking about what a cunt Lee is, I bet."

"We didn't mention your name once, so don't flatter yourself."

"Oh, I don't flatter myself. I don't do that, no way."

He hung another squealy left.

"Where are you going?"

"To hell in a hand basket," he says, and gave out this big whooping laugh, real crazy-sounding.

"Where do you think you're *going!*" I said, getting scared all over again.

"To the big rock candy mountains," he says, and whooped some more.

"Stop and lemme out."

"Can't do it, buddy. This train runs express."

Another left. We're headed back toward Overlook.

"Just stop the fucking truck and lemme out!"

"No way!"

"I wanna get *out!*"

"Tough shit. You should've thought of that before."

Here comes Overlook . . . He did a right that left rubber behind us at the corner, and now we're heading back the way we came.

"Let me out, please," I said, trying the cool approach this time.

"You can leave anytime."

He's doing fifty, at least.

"Look, just let me out, please. I just want to get out if you don't mind."

"You'd miss all the fun," he says.

God, he looked creepy. He's got this big grin on his face, and his eyes are all screwed up behind his glasses, and his hat's pulled down so low over them he has to tilt his head back to see where he's going. I practically shat my pants, I'm so scared, because on one side of Overlook there's this slope, not a cliff or anything, but it's got to be around forty-five degrees, and a car going over the edge'd keep right on going down to the bottom a couple hundred yards later and maybe'd turn over a few times on the way. But he didn't swerve over to the slope side of the road, just kept on the way he's going, so maybe he's not feeling suicidal, which was the big thought in my head right then, but I'm still plenty scared, too scared to talk, even.

Then we're coming up to the place with the waterwheel, and he took us off the road and across the curb, a smooth curb, not a ledge, and then we're racing across the lawn and he spun the wheel and aimed the Dodge and ran smack into that dumb miniature mill and *kapow!* smashed the entire thing to pieces with the near-side bumper and somehow managed not to let the front wheel go down into the pond, then we're heading across the lawn again and *bump!* across the curb, and he's pushing the gas pedal way down till we're doing sixty to get out of there before someone sees it's us that created the racket.

"Jee-*zuz!*" he says. "We creamed that fucker good! You feel her smash up when we hit? I bet it looks like a fuckin' *bomb* hit it!"

"Slow down!"

"That'll teach 'em to put up something like that. Jesus, they were asking for it, *begging* for it."

"You're way over the limit! Slow *down*, willya!"

In the movies the wheelman always panics after the bank holdup and drives the getaway car so fast, he crashes or runs a red light or something, and lets the cops see he's speeding, so they come after in a big chase and it always ends in a hail of lead.

"Slow the fuck *down* before a cop car sees us!"

He eased up and we dropped back to thirty. We're out of Comstock, practically out of Belvedere.

"Wasn't that a great feeling, though?" he says.

"Yeah, terrific. I'd like to get out now."

"Relax. We got away."

"Fine. Just let me out at the corner."

"I'll take you all the way home. No reason why I shouldn't."

"You don't have to. I can walk."

"Why walk when you can ride?"

"I *want* to walk."

"Just you stay sat, Burris," he says, and his voice is all cold. I stayed sat. We didn't talk. Finally we stopped outside 1404, and I got out fast. I didn't say anything, just walked away. He drove off. I didn't even turn to watch the Dodge go down the road, just slammed into the house and went to my room and lay down on the bed and listened to the way my heart's going *biddabun, biddabun, biddabun.* He really had me scared back there. What a crazy shit! I bet someone saw the truck after he wiped out the waterwheel and reported it. I bet the cops are already searching for a beat-up pickup with the worst paint job in town. Lucky there wasn't any other traffic around when he creamed the wheel, no one that could've chased us and gotten Lee's plate number. That crazy fucking bastard! All because I found out the truth about him. I *think* I found out the truth about him. Maybe I got it all wrong. Maybe he just doesn't like anyone that deviates from the norm, like the Bible-thumpers in *The Chrysalids* that took out after the twelve-toed girl. Maybe he's just plain prejudiced. But he's smart! How can someone smart be prejudiced? And he carries an umbrella and walking cane on his rifle rack! How can someone wacky as that hate someone sad and pathetic like Gene? None of it makes any sense. I'm *shaking* and I can't stop.

Talking it all out has helped. I still don't understand Lee, though. I don't know if he's straight or gay or what the hell he is. And did I *really* think Diane is a lesbian? Nah, not really. Well, maybe . . . I don't know anything anymore. *One* thing I know, the only thing in *my* closet is T-shirts. No one catches Burris Weems bending over, no sir. I may be skinny and gimpy, but I'm *all man*, and if you dare say anything different, I'll cry all over my purse, ha, ha. Kidding aside, I know I'm straight because I've got this picture on my wall, this big color poster of Charlotte Rampling in *The Night Porter*, which is a movie I can recommend if you have trouble sleeping at night, but Charlotte looks pretty good in these baggy pants held up by suspenders and these long black gloves that go right up to her elbows and this Nazi officer's cap with the skull 'n' bones on the front. That's all she's got on, but it's not a nudie picture or anything because she's holding her arms across her chest so you can't see anything. She looks pretty good all right, and I wouldn't think so if I was a closet case, now would I?

Sieg heil, Charlotte!

9

Tuesday. Lee didn't show up at 8.30, which didn't surprise me. What *did* surprise me was, Diane did, in Gene's car. I got in.

"He's gone," she says, driving off.

"Gone where?"

"Who knows?" she says, and turns a little bit toward me.

She's got this black eye, practically purple.

"Awww, shit . . . did he do that?"

"No, I hit myself in the eye tossing pancakes."

So she wants to make a joke of it. That's pretty brave, I think.

"He came in late, pretty drunk. I asked where he'd been, just a simple question, not being bitchy about it or anything, and he hit me. Then he got a suitcase and filled it and left. I didn't try to stop him. You need two eyes to get around."

Another joke. She's a trooper.

"Did he tell you about the waterwheel?"

"The what?"

I told her.

"This I've got to see."

I showed her how to get there. I wasn't in any big rush to get to Servex. After a while we're cruising along Overlook.

"There it is."

I should've said, "There it *was*," because he really did cream that thing. The waterwheel and mill just aren't there anymore, except for a few little sticks of timber scattered around. The sluice just empties into thin air, and the electric motor that turned the wheel must've been knocked clear into the pond. I bet the owners were pissed, but Lee was right about one thing—they deserved it. We cruised on by, going slow so Diane can get an eyeful, but she hadn't ever seen the wheel when it was there, so the element of contrast is missing. We speeded up and drove away.

"Will he be coming back?"

"I don't know. He went away once before and didn't come back for six weeks."

"What's Gene think about it?"

"He blames himself. I've told him he shouldn't, but he does. That's the one really bad thing about Lee going away."

"Uh . . . won't you miss him?"

"I need a little space to breathe. Everybody does, sometime. If he comes back, he comes back. If he doesn't . . . *c'est la vie!*" she says, and throws one hand up in the air and waggles it about, very French. She's still trying not to make a big thing out of Lee going away. She's got real guts. I really admire Diane.

"What are you gonna do now?"

"Wait and see."

"What if he doesn't come back?"

"Then I'll make other plans."

"Do you need any money?"

"I've got a little to be going on with."

"I've got some if you need it."

"No thanks, Burris. That's real kind, but I won't need it. Gene has some money too. We'll get by."

"Okay."

"Hey, tonight's the big night."

"Huh?"

"Room 107! You didn't *forget*, did you?"

"No."

I *did!* I *forgot!* My brain is being eaten away by worry!

"I bet you're pretty excited about it."

"Yeah, it'll be an experience, all right."

"Got anyone lined up for company, or is it a solo thing?"

"Oh, solo I guess. I think an experience like this is something you should do on your own. It might have less . . . uh . . . meaning with someone else there."

"That's true."

"Did you put a steak on your eye? That's what they do in the movies, put a big steak over it."

"I can't afford steak. How 'bout chopped liver?"

We both laughed at that one. She's got class, Diane. Lee must really be a prick to hit her and leave like that. What an asshole. I wouldn't do a thing like that. A girl like Diane deserves better. I'd be really good to her. We'd have plenty laffs together like just now, cracking jokes together while we watch TV and eat pizza, like I do with Loretta, but with Diane it'd be different, because after we digested our food and turned the TV off and went to bed it wouldn't be to fall asleep, it'd be to have sex with each other. I'd like that. I think that'd be just the greatest. I can't think of a better thing I'd like to have than sex with Diane Trimble. I'd lick her genitals if she wanted me to.

"Here we are."

She pulled up outside the Servex parking lot and I got out, then leaned back through the window. "Thanks for giving me a lift."

"No problem. Want me to pick you up after work?"

"Uh . . . no, no thanks. I'll catch the bus. It comes right by here."

"Okay. Well, don't work too hard."

"I won't."

" 'Bye."

And off she went. I felt like shit. Of *course* I wanted her to drive me home. I wanted her to drive me *crazy*. But all she's being is friendly, I can tell, and it's pretty fucking mature of me to be able to see that. An immature guy would try to put a few moves on Diane, try to take advantage of the situation. Not me, pal. So from now on it's the bus for yours truly.

I went in and I'm eleven minutes late. You can't fool a time clock. I went to the bander to start it up, and the foreman comes over and says, "Get movin'!" I looked at him. He's a real dopey-looking bastard with these piggy little eyes. "Waddaya lookin' at! Get movin'!"

I gave him a salute, a real snappy one. "Yes, *sir!*" I said. "Movin' right along, *sir!*" And I moved right along, past the foreman, past the bander, past the pallets . . .

"Hey! Where the fuck ya think ya goin'!"

. . . past the pallets, past the loading bay . . .

"Hey! Fuck *you!*" he yells.

Another snappy salute.

"Yes, *sir!* And fuck you, too, *sir!*"

. . . past the loading bay, ducking around the forklifts, and soon was free, free! *free!* I gimped across the parking lot under a different sun.

For the rest of the day I did what I always used to do over vacation—I went to the movies. They have early matinees all summer while school's out, so I squeezed in three. *Cocoon* wasn't bad, apart from the sappy happy ending, *Pale Rider* was nothing new, and *Rambo* was just the absolute pits. Then I pushed my eyes back in my head and went home. I didn't tell Peggy or Loretta about Lee leaving Diane, or about me leaving Servex, or about what I intended doing the rest of the night. Peggy asked me into the studio to give my opinion on her latest line in velvet paintings, which is clown heads, very orange and white and red.

"They're pretty good, but don't you think they'd be more commercial if they were crying?"

For a few seconds she thought about it, then she saw I'm being sarcastic again. "Thank you, Burris," she says. "You may get the hell out of here now."

Which I did. "What'd you think?" Loretta wants to know.

"I think I prefer the tigers."

"Hmmmm. You better be nice to Peggy for the next few days."

"Why?"

"I told her I'm thinking of marrying Pete. She didn't take it too well."

"*Marrying* him?"

"I like the guy."

"Okay."

"Is that all you have to say on the subject?"

"Congratulations."

She expected more, it looked like.

"I really mean it. Congratulations, Loretta. Pete's a great guy."

"I said I'm *thinking* about it."

"Oh."

"Peggy doesn't approve."

"Doesn't she like him?"

"She likes him fine. Peggy doesn't approve of marriage."

"That's because she had a lousy one."

"We don't *know* that, Burris."

"What about his kids and all?"

"They're okay. They like me, I like them."

"Are you gonna have more? If you get married?"

"Maybe just one, to see what it's like."

"Does this mean you'll be moving out?"

"If I go ahead with it, yep, the big push."

"Awww, shit . . ."

"I'm twenty-one, kid. Time to leave the nest."

"Fuck."

"Can we put a stop to the language, please? You're not impressing anyone."

"But then there'll be just me and Peggy."

"It won't be such a bad setup."

"Yeah, but . . ."

"Look on the bright side. You can have my room. It's bigger than yours."

She's right, and there'd only be half the amount of cigarette smoke in the place. But it didn't make me feel any better. Shit! Fuck! Why'd she have to tell me *now?* This is supposed to be my night of nights, my rendezvous with 107, my heavy date with destiny, and first Lee screws things up for me, now Loretta. Where's all the *good* news? There must be good things happening out there, but they keep passing me by. They come toward me then split like a divided highway around a traffic island where I'm stood like a stuffed cat, and the good things stream past me on either side and merge somewhere down the road. Whatever the opposite of magnetic attraction is, I've got it. Good things get pushed away from me, repulsed. Yeah, I'm calling myself repulsive.

Loretta gave me a lift downtown at nine o'clock. She thought I was going to a movie. If I saw another movie today I'd go blind. She was headed for Pete's. I didn't ask if she's planning on giving him the Big Answer or not.

"I might not be home tonight," I said.

"How come?"

"I just mightn't be home, is all."

"Is there a girl involved?"

"Yeah, I'm seeing this hundred-dollar hooker, an all-nighter." She laughed at that.

"Don't bruise your meat," she says, which is just about average-crude for Loretta.

"I just don't want Peggy getting all worked up if I'm not there in the morning."

"I'll phone her from Pete's. What about your friend that picks you up?"

"I told him not to come."

She dropped me off on Wilmington. I walked past Lucy's Bar, thinking maybe the Dodge'd be parked somewhere around, but it wasn't. The green olives plinked into and out of the pink cocktail glass up on the roof. A few people went in. They didn't look queer to me. The whole story was probably a lie. I quit hanging around there in case it wasn't and headed for the Starlite.

The old guy didn't recognize me when I walked in. He's got a brand-new shirt on, so new the back of the collar is square. It makes a kind of triangle down to the knot of his tie. It's eighty-nine outside and he's wearing a tie. His wrinkly old neck came out of the triangle like a tortoise. He should've had a little derby hat on like cartoon tortoises always have.

"Hi there, boy!" he says, very hearty.

"Hi. Can I have the key to 107, please?"

"You sure can. Just cross my palm with silver, heh, heh, heh."

He thought that was a pretty good one. I bet he uses it about twenty times a day. Nah, the Starlite only has ten rooms. He uses it ten times a day.

"I already did."

"What's that, son?"

"I crossed your palm with silver last Friday night."

"Advance booking?"

"Yes, sir, four nights back."

"It'll be in the book," he says, and starts looking for it, running his shaky old finger down the register.

"Weems?"

"That's me."

"Odd name," he says.

"I'm an odd person."

I shouldn't have said that. It started his motor up again. "Heh, heh, heh."

"Can I have the key, please?"

"No luggage?"

"No."

Just the tape recorder in my pocket.

"Got a friend coming by later on?" he says, and gives me this wink, only it turns into a nervous tic. He can't stop it and it got him mad. He turned away from me to handle it, pretending to take a long time to find key 107 on the board, and when he finally had to turn around again to give it to me the eyelid was still fluttering like a dead leaf on a speckled old marble.

"Here," he says, shoving it at me.

"Thank you."

I went around to 107 and stood by the door. Two other rooms were occupied, 103 and 110, a Buick and a Torino. I took a deep breath, my heart really knocking to get out of my chest, and put the key in the lock. *Ker-lick*. The door swings open. There it is—107. I went in and turned on the light. It's a very ugly room, very square and very ugly, I don't exactly know why. The walls are cream but they're turning yellow, and there's a kind of shadow up in the corners where the walls and ceiling meet. The air-conditioning is off, so it smells awful stale in there. *Clunk*. The door's closed now. I'm alone in 107.

First thing, air-conditioner on. It's a big metal box under the window with a wire grille on top that's very dented by people putting their asses on it, a very bad design for a utility device that's got to serve thousands of guests. But it works okay when I push down the blue button. The fan kicks on and the coolant in the tubes does its stuff. The puke-green curtains ripple and quiver. A blast of chilled air hits me in the face. God, that's good. The sweat on my neck cools, a wonderful feeling. I'm stooped over the unit like a willow over water.

That's enough for now. I turn away and look at the room again. Improvements have not taken place since I last looked at it. Take the ceiling light, for example—forty watts, so the bills don't mount up. The light barely makes it out from behind a square hunk of white plastic crimped at the corners, anchored to the ceiling by a gold knob. I can see the shadows of dead moths up there. Most of the light it gives shines upward, away from the walls and floor, but that's probably a blessing, seeing as the walls are turning yellow and the carpet's getting thread-bare along a stretch from the door past the end of the bed, leading to the bathroom. The pattern is swirling mucus blobs and vine leaves, I think, but the colors are hard to identify in this pissy light. There's another lamp on the bureau, with a lot of fancy scrollwork on the base and some sprayed-on highlights to make it look like tarnished brass, but really it's plastic, and the lampshade is white plastic with a fabric texture to it, just a vertical barrel with no top or bottom. It's another forty-watt bulb in there. The bureau itself is made from pressed wood chips covered by plastic sheeting with a wood-grain pattern on it. The sections are screwed together, not dovetailed the way a carpenter would've made a piece of real furniture. Frankly, it's a piece of shit. I opened one of the drawers and yes! they really do have Bibles in motel rooms. I always thought it was just something you saw in old movies. It's a Bible with a plastic-simulated leather cover. The pages are so thin I can almost see through them, and the print is so fine I can't even read it in this crummy light. Back into darkness goes the Bible.

To the bathroom. I switched on the strip light. It's got to be at least one hundred twenty watts, and the contrast makes me squint. There's a shower stall with stippled glass sides that get darker toward the bottom, with some kind of growth on the inside. I slide the door back, *grumble, grumble,* and look at the tiled walls. They're cream-colored, separated into squares by lines of greenish-brown grout. The bottom of the stall is tiny tiles with the same problem. I wouldn't get in there barefoot if you paid me. The crapper has a band of paper tied across the lid. SEALED FOR YOUR PROTECTION, it says. I snap the paper and lift the lid, expecting to see a turd in there, or do I mean a toad? It's empty and odorless, but filled with a million farts and rivers of shit and a waterfall of vomit, anyway. Back down goes the lid. Into the plastic bag lining the plastic waste can goes the paper strip, its noble purpose served. The basin was scrubbed just recently, you can tell by the parts not done properly. There's little spatterings of old soap on the undersides of the faucets. Tiny square blocks of new soap sit to one side, wrapped in paper. I look at myself in the mirror. The light is mounted directly above it so you can study every wrinkle and pore and broken vein and blackhead and zit while you shave, and it's set so high it gives you cheekbones even if you don't have any, and puts luggage under your eyes. Shining straight down onto my head, it shows the white scalp under my hair so clearly the area around the part looks practically bald. I look around thirty-five or forty. I turn off the light and hurry out of there. I didn't unwrap the plastic cups from their cellophane wrappers—sealed for my protection, natch. I'm not thirsty. I can't imagine eating or drinking in this place, only crapping and throwing up.

The bed. A double. I laid myself on it and heard this weird rustling, so I pulled back the nubby-patterned cover. The sheets are made from some kind of nylon, not cotton, but it doesn't rustle when I crinkle it between my fingers. I pull back the top and bottom sheets and find there's a sheet of . . . yeah, plastic, covering the whole mattress. I guess it's there to keep the come stains from marking up the flower pattern. Sealed for its protection. I smoothed everything out the way it was. I won't get into the bed, I'll lie on top. The pillows are inside plastic bags, too, then covered by nylon cases. If I got in the bed I'd sweat like a pig. The pillows rustle loudly in my ear.

I've got both of them under my head to prop it up. I don't want to look at the ceiling. Directly in front of me is the TV on a metal swivel stand. I *think* the stand is metal, but it might be heavy-duty plastic. I'm not ready to watch the tube yet. I haven't finished savoring the disappointment that hit me the moment I came through that doorway over there and turned on the light. What a fucking awful hole. I raised up my knees and looked between them at the TV the way Peggy did almost sixteen years ago, watching Neil set foot on the moon, which couldn't be a lonelier place than this room.

There's a phone on a little table by the bed. I want like crazy to talk to someone, but Diane doesn't have a phone in her trailer. I'd have to call that asshole of a manager and have him fetch her to the pay phone. No way, Rene. I'm cut off from the outside world. The wind is up, the lines are down. The howling storm outside penetrates my castle walls, a thin wailing like the hum of an air-conditioner. No one can reach me. Who'd even think to try? Now would be a good time to put a gun to my head. This has got to be the worst room in the world. This bed has been fucked on a million times. It won't be tonight. Only his own hand will hold the modest prick of Burris Weems tonight. I felt like I could sink right through this plastic-wrapped mattress, down and down to where the rock melts under pressure and runs like mercury. The bed is a raft on a stormy sea. I have to dig my fingers into the covers to keep from sliding off among the waves. Sharks are waiting for my meat, and after they've gulped down big, greedy gobs of me the rest'll sink—little bits and pieces, a hand, a foot—sink to the bottom of the deepest trench in the ocean floor where blind things crawl, hunting each other in the dark. By the time my foot reaches them it'll be squashed by pressure to the size of a fingernail. Something'll eat it without knowing it's a human foot that up on the surface was an entirely different size and shape, the foot of Burris Weems that never stood on another person's neck or left its print outside of stinking Buford.

The walls and ceiling move inward a fraction of an inch whenever I forget about them. Unless I want to be crushed I have to keep at least one eye on the room, not the room itself, which is just a square space filled with air and misery, but the surfaces *containing* the room, the flat planes that keep this room from seeping out into the world and poisoning the atmosphere. That mustn't happen. The door and window have to be kept shut tight to keep the room *inside* where it can only work its evil on *me*. I can take it. I'm a fucking hero. Do your worst, room. I spit in your eye, ha, ha! The room doesn't like me because I know it for the horrible, shitty thing it is. That's why it wants to crush me. But it can only move very slowly, shrinking, shrinking, waiting for me to fall asleep so it can close around me like a big square mouth. I have to stay awake.

TV to the rescue. I levered myself up off the bed and switched on the set. The screen swam with lines and a picture lurched up from the bottom. I pick up the complimentary TV Guide and turn to Tuesday. Reruns, mostly. *The A-Team.* "The team saves two soda-pop queens by blasting the bad guys with bubbles!" Sounds ger-rate. *Riptide.* "Nick, Cody, and Boz have to rescue a satellite before the bad guys get away and the feds close in." Oh, gosh*darn*, I've *missed* it! Will there be something good on later to compensate me for this awful loss? Baseball. Fuck off. Aha! *Twilight Zone* at eleven. Good old *Twilight Zone.* But I've got some time to kill. I watch something about grizzly bears. A big fucker bats fish right out of the water onto land. Smarter than the average bear. He eats the fish. Messy. He trundles off into the woods to lay some cable. Ever notice how bears waggle their big fat asses when they walk? End of show.

It's *Zone* time at last! Cue theme music, *doo* doo doo doo, *doo* doo doo doo . . . "That's the signpost up ahead. Your next stop—the Twilight Zone." Pan down from the stars to a ramshackle old farmhouse at night. Great! I know this one. It's one of the best ever. There's this old woman lives alone in the farmhouse, a real hillbilly slob that looks like Ma Kettle, and she hears something land on the roof, so she goes to take a look. It's a flying saucer just five feet across, and out of it come these two teeny little guys in fat space suits with helmets you can't see inside of, so maybe there's something really *horrible* in there. They look like clockwork windup toys and talk to each other in what sounds like Morse code—*dit dit dit, dot dot dot.*

Ma Kettle goes bananas and tries to kill them. The little guys fight back with ray guns that sting the old girl but don't do any real harm, she's so fucking *big* compared to them. They chase each other all around the house. Whenever she knocks one out the window with a broom or something he turns right around and starts burning his way back in again with his ray gun, and while she's swatting at him the other little guy attacks her ankle. Does she get *mad!* She throws a blanket over him and picks him up in it and swings him hard against the table a couple dozen times—*smash! bash! crash!* until he's in pieces, then she dumps him in a box and puts the box on the fire. By now his pal has had enough and goes back to the saucer on the roof. Ma Kettle follows him up there, and we hear him screaming into the radio as she bashes the saucer into junk with a hatchet. "Probe One to Base! Probe One to Base! Stay away from this planet! Inhabited by giants! Unsuitable for visitation! We're finished . . .!" And as Ma Kettle gives the saucer's dome a final whack the camera tracks down its crumpled side to the words *U.S. Air Force—Space Probe One.* It should be NASA, not U.S. Air Force, but who's bitching? The point is, the little guys that looked like windup toys were Earthmen, and Ma Kettle, who we were rooting for all along, was a big old giant on another planet somewhere out there . . . *doo* doo doo doo, *doo* doo doo doo . . .

Now it's a *Tonight Show* rerun from last year. Johnny Carson interviews Susie Suck, starlet who never quite became a star, and now it's too late, doll, because you're getting broad in the keister. She hasn't been on network TV since she was in some god-awful miniseries a couple years back, *Forevermore*, or was it *Forever, More?* Most likely it was, because it was about this very poor girl who marries this millionaire and becomes a very rich bitch. Susie Suck talks about how she's matured over the years and how the bright lights and razzle-dazzle of the Hollywood publicity machine mean so *little* to her now that she's received *enlightenment* or something. Her life now revolves around her home and her daughter, Tara, which is just as well because she was a lousy actress—I mean, she couldn't express emotion if you told her to use her contract for an asswipe. Pruning the pot plants is definitely something she's better at than acting. We see some home movies of Tara, very cute. Everybody knows her father was Roger Ramrod, Beverly Hills producer who just loved Susie's bod but couldn't establish long-term *rapport*, Susie being about as intelligent as a kumquat. Johnny nods his head a lot while she tries to talk about how meaningful her life has become, a piece of body language that regular *Tonight Show* viewers know means he's bored shitless. I guess he doesn't make up the guest list. But Johnny's a professional and politely asks questions to fill the gaps that yawn like Grand Canyon between what Susie *wants* to say and what she actually says.

At last it's over! Bring on the safari guy that's on the show every now and then. This time he's got an ocelot, this beautiful cat from South America. Everyone oohs and aahs. This ocelot is *some cat*. You look at an ocelot and you *want* one. Other cats no longer make it. The word for cat is *ocelot*. Susie Suck would like half a dozen, one for a pet and five for a coat. The ocelot misbehaves like crazy and digs a few holes in Johnny's jacket, but Johnny doesn't get upset. He's got fifty other jackets. Then it's a comedian. He's pretty funny. I laughed a few times. He made a big mistake at the end of his act, though. He says, "Here's one for you intellectuals. Define film noir. Anybody? No? Okay, that's a movie starring O.J. Simpson and Ben Vereen and Richard Roundtree and directed by Sidney Poitier." No response. They didn't get it, but he rescues himself by hauling up his sleeve to look at his watch and saying, "*Definitely* time to leave." They gave him a big hand for that one, the morons. End of show.

Time for the late movie—*Empire of the Ants*, in which H. G. Wells's nifty little story is thrown out the window. Back through the window comes a very long turd in the form of film on a spool. Joan Collins and others get threatened by giant plastic ants. Go get 'em, ants! I can't stand it. Down goes the sound. The ants wrap their pincers around human necks to the drone of the air-conditioning unit. I go take a leak in the toilet. My piss seems very yellow. Is it the crummy light or am I sick? Probably both. This place would make anyone sick. *Flusssssssshhhhhh* . . . Back to the other room, the *bed*room, the *TV* room, the *living* room all in one. Okay, maybe people bedded and TV'd here, but no one *lived*. *Time* was *spent* here, that's all. No one did anything you could call living, not in this cubic piece of nowhere. Is this the bed I was born in, or a different one? Know what? I don't care one way or the other. It's a bed, just a bed. The one in 106 and the one in 108 are exactly the same, filled and fouled by phantom fuckers that came and went. I'm getting poetic here. My neck is stiff from being propped up by two pillows. I throw one on the floor. Now I'm looking at the ceiling. There's a crack in it, just the faintest line running higgledy-piggledy away from the light. It's in flight from the light. Leaping light bulbs! Jumping jiminy! Great green gobbling grasshoppers! Oscillating ocelots! The room hasn't given up at all. It's inside my head, squeezing my brain. It snuck in there when I wasn't paying attention, so it's my own fault if my left and right hemispheres are being squashed together till they drip blood and thoughts. I have to stop the room. I have to repel it, drive it out of my head. I'll push it out my ears like invisible pus. Nah, I can't be bothered anymore.

Room, take over.

I fell asleep.

Bang!

Somebody just went in 108 and slammed the door. I'm freezing. There's nothing but electric snow on the tube. I rolled off the bed and shut down the air-conditioner. The fan slowed and died. The TV is hissing softly. *Click*. Silence. I got up too fast. I'm dizzy all of a sudden and have to go lie on the bed again, belly-down this time. I can hear voices, a man and woman, conversational type voices, not raised or anything. I can't make out what it is they're saying. I'm practically asleep again. Then I hear the bed get sat on. Shit. I bet they'll fuck, and I'll have to lie here and listen to it. But nothing happened for a while, so I started falling asleep again. Then it started—*knock, knock, squeak, knock, squeak, squeak, knock*—panting and moaning, a few words I couldn't make out, higher-pitched moaning, lots of grunting now because the guy's running out of steam. Will he make it? Will the lady achieve orgasm before he has to let go? Will their ecstasy be mutual? Is this the greatest, noisiest fuck that ever took place? Tune in again ten seconds from now and learn the incredible truth . . .

"Nnnnnyyyeeeooowwwnnnggghhhnnnnnn . . ."

That was it, folks, the Big O, no doubt about it. Peggy told me how when she was young, the Big O meant Roy Orbison, you know, the guy with the shades that sang *Only the Lonely* and *Running Scared.* Dead silence in 108, then a few words, a little moving about, faucet splashing, toilet flushing, then nothing. They're asleep. Lucky them. A nice screw then off to sleepy-byes while Burris Weems plays with himself, but very half-heartedly, too depressed to roll onto his back, unzip his fly, and do the job properly. I mustn't fall asleep. This is 107, room of rooms, space of spaces. It's the place of my origin. Here I crawled from the primeval ooze into sunlight and inflated those newfangled things . . . what are they called? Lungs! This is where it all began, and I *must not* waste a single minute by nodding off the way I did before. Tape recorder, tell a story to keep me awake. Another day in the life of Burris Weems, owner of the third eye, small-town mystic and prize pudknocker. I talk and talk. I tell it all. Now I'm dead from talking.

Room, I surrender.

Be gentle with me.

Ha, ha!

10 *Bang!*

The people in 108 are door slammers. I watched them leave, peeking through the curtains. They look ordinary. They got in a blue Datsun and left. It was still pretty early, the sun just clearing the roof of the five rooms facing me across the fore-court. The Buick's already gone, but the Torino's a late riser, like me. Now what? Is there anything to hang around here for? No sir, not a thing. Tuesday night rates as one of the all-time letdowns of my life. Why did I expect so much from it? So what if I was born here? It's just a room. Its uniqueness exists only in my head. I've been a real dork. I've also wasted $17.50. Also I'm starving hungry.

I went to Hardee's for breakfast. I could've gone to any of the others and got pretty much the same thing on my plate. It's hard to convince yourself you're in the middle of a crisis while you're sitting in a booth in Hardee's and cramming your face, but I really was in deep shit. I mean, what's in store for me? When school starts back, I'm supposed to *repeat*, the only kid in school who has to do it. Even the dummies—and there are plenty of them at Memorial High—don't have to repeat the semester. Jesus, it's gonna be embarrassing. I'm already a freak in that place, but at least up till now I was just a gimp. Now I'm a *dumb* gimp. Is there some way I can keep from going back, some way to escape the humiliation? I can't think of one. And what about my other problems? I thought Lee was my friend. I really liked that guy. I practically *loved* him, for

Chrissakes, nothing homo or anything, but I really felt good being around him. And how long did *that* last? A few fucking weeks, that's all. Now I love Diane. Okay, I admit it at long last. I love Diane. B.W. loves D.T. Carve it in a heart, then chop the fucking tree down, because D.T. sure as hell doesn't love me. I may be inexperienced in this stuff, but I'm not stupid. People that are married don't give up on each other overnight just because they have some dumb argument and one of them walks out. She's probably sitting by the phone waiting for a call from him right now. No she isn't. Diane doesn't have a phone. But she would be if she had one, I bet. Fuck Lee. I really hate him. He's got my girl, even if he's not even in *town* anymore. *My* girl? Grow up, Weems. You've got more chance of making it with Gene than with Diane. I wonder if Gene's *done* anything since he went to the chop shop—I mean, he told me he didn't screw guys beforehand, and I believe him despite what Lee said, but has he done anything *since?* If you get a brand-new vagina I guess you want to try it out sometime. But would any guy not drunk out of his mind find Gene *desirable?* It's a pretty horrible thought. I just can't get used to the idea that Gene's got a crease between his legs instead of a cock.

Well, that's Gene's problem. Mine are probably like peas alongside apples compared to his, but they're all *mine*, and that makes them plenty big. You'd think a shortass gimp'd have enough problems just being a shortass gimp, without falling for some other guy's *wife*, for God's sake, *and* having to repeat a semester in front of the whole school. A hundred years ago I could've just walked away from it all, got a job as cabin boy on a clipper, saved the captain's life in a hurricane and been married to his beautiful daughter as a reward. Nah, I would've been buggered up and down the fo'c'sle till I couldn't walk, caught the pox—anally, natch—and been shipwrecked on a rock in the middle of the ocean with nothing to eat or fuck but a Bible, all before my sixteenth birthday. Let's face it, there ain't gonna be any radical solutions for what ails me, short of suicide. It's a lonely town and I'm a lonely boy. That sounds like an old Gene Pitney song, or maybe the Big O. Could I be a songwriter and make a million?

Lonely town, lonely boy,
Got no girl, got no joy,
Wander down the lonely street,
Got no one you have to meet.

Sounds promising so far.

Lonely boy, lonely town,
Don't let people see you frown,

Uh . . .
Uh . . .

Roses are red and dogshit's brown.

Fuck it, there goes a million.

I ate breakfast too fast. Now on top of everything else I've got indigestion. There's just nothing heroic about what I'm going through, that's the sad thing. It's all too pathetic to be noble or uplifting. I'm not learning any lessons that'll help me become an adult and steer me through life, blah blah blah. All I'm learning is what a stupid dork I am, and it's depressing when you do that. If I didn't have any sense of humor, I'd be dead. What was Lady Macbeth talking about when she said, "Out, out, damned spot!" I'll tell you. Her dog Spot took a dump on the rug and she's kicking him over the drawbridge. No, I didn't read the fucking play, I saw the movie, okay?

It's 9.15. I went outside. Looks like another scorcher building up. So what else is new? I wandered back down to the Starlite. There's two big furniture trucks parked at the entrance and they're being loaded with beds and bedside tables and TVs. TVs! I ran in the office hoping the old guy isn't there because I need a fast reaction to this plan I've got in mind, and I'm in luck because it's the nice-looking lady that hired me the room last Friday.

"I'm afraid we're closed," she says.

"Yeah, I know. Are you getting rid of all the furnishings?"

"We have an arrangement with a secondhand dealer."

"Can I buy one of the TVs?"

"Are you the young man who was in here last week?"

"Yes, ma'am, Room 107 on the last night, remember?"

"Oh, yes."

"See, the reason I wanted to be in 107 on the last night is because I was born there."

"Born there?"

I told her the story.

"That's very romantic," she says when I finished. Me, I don't think it's romantic without a woman in there somewhere— for me, I mean.

"So I'd really like a souvenir, ma'am. My mom'd just love to have the TV she saw Neil Armstrong on while I was getting born."

"But all the TVs were replaced seven years ago."

"She won't know that. She'll get a real kick if I give her a TV and show the receipt with Starlite Motel on it."

"Well, I did already tell you we have an arrangement with a secondhand dealer."

"I know, but one set more or less won't make any difference to a guy like that. See, my mom's been in a wheelchair about five years now, and TV's all she's got. My dad died in the same accident that crippled her, and I got this limp you might've noticed. The TV we've got is just about shot, full of lines, and the picture keeps rolling. It's a piece of junk, frankly, but we can't afford a new one, not even a reconditioned secondhand one, because those guys really bump the price up for resale, way too much for us. So I'd really appreciate it if you'd sell me the set from 107, ma'am, for not too big an amount of cash."

"Well, I don't know . . ." she says, touching her face.

Then the old guy comes in from out back.

"They're chipping the shit outa that stuff!" he says.

"Dad, *please* . . ."

"Well, go tell 'em to handle it gentler! They act like it's firewood!"

She gave this little gasp, exasperated with him, I think, then went out back to see what he's bitching about.

"Morning," I said.

"I should've had that stuff appraised right before they started loading, not last month. Now the dealer can say it's our fault if it's scratched all to shit."

"Yeah, that would've been better."

"Go on out there and *tell* 'em," he says.

"Yes, sir."

We went out back together, but his daughter already told them.

"Dad, this young man wants to buy one of the TVs—"

"Fifty bucks!"

"Now, Dad, even the dealer wouldn't pay that much."

"Forty!"

"I don't think the young man *has* forty dollars, Dad."

"What've you got, boy?"

"Uh . . . I can go twenty, maybe twenty-five. . . ."

"Thirty! Take it or leave it."

"Okay."

"Cash."

"Yes, sir."

I cleaned out my pockets. The set took everything but $3.28. No sweat, I've got more cash at home.

"We were selling 'em for twenty each," he says, and stuffs my cash in his pants. "You should've bargained harder, boy. I would've sold for twenty-five."

"I guess I don't care about five bucks."

"You *should* care! A boy your age should show *fight!* You don't fight, this world'll walk all over you."

"Yes, sir, thank you. Thank you, ma'am."

I went in 107 and unplugged the set. It's a cable TV but it's got an aerial jack, so it'll work okay in the trailer picking up the regular channels. I picked it up. That fucker was *heavy*. I put it down again. Trying to get it out to the trailer park by hand would've put me in hock to a chiropractor for about fifty years. I went out.

"Uh . . . ma'am, could I leave it here for a half hour or so?"

"Bring it into the office. It'll be safer there."

So I did. Now I'm only in hock to a chiropractor for fifteen years.

"I'll be back soon, ma'am."

"We'll look after it for you."

It took a full half hour just to walk out to Green Acres. I knocked on Gene's door. When he opened it his hair's a mess, all dangling down, and he's got this fucking awful bathrobe on, bright red. He looked like some old Indian chief wearing a trade blanket.

"Burris?"

"Hi, Gene. Could I borrow your car for ten minutes?"

"My car?"

He wasn't awake yet.

"Right, Gene, the green Chrysler, just for ten minutes."

"Why do you need it?"

"It's a big surprise. For you."

"For me?"

"You bet. Can I have the keys?"

"You aren't playing some kind of joke, are you?"

"No, sir."

Oh *shit!* I shouldn't have said *that*. The old guy at the Starlite got me into the habit. And I can't turn around and say, "I mean, no, ma'am."

"Are you sure, Burris?"

He didn't notice. It's a good thing he *is* half asleep still.

"I'm sure, I really am. It's for you, Gene."

"Well, all right."

He still sounds doubtful. What a suspicious-minded character. He disappeared, then came back and opened the screen door.

"Here you are," he says, giving me the keys.

"You won't regret this, Gene."

"Make sure you drive carefully."

"Will do."

I got in the car and lead-footed to the Starlite. I notched up another ten years' chiropractic care getting the set into the backseat, then laid rubber back to the trailer park. Gene put his stringy old head out the door when I pulled up.

"Close your eyes," I told him.

"This is just ridiculous," he says, trying to sound scornful, but really he's tickled, I could tell.

"Close 'em or you don't get the surprise, and quit looking in the car!"

He closed them, stood there on the little steps outside his door, and I wrestled the set out of the Chrysler and held it in my arms like a baby.

"Open up."

He did and looked at me. Something was wrong. His face didn't look like it's supposed to.

"Is that for me?"

"No, for your canary. Yeah, it's for you."

"Oh," he says.

Definitely something wrong here.

"It's breaking my arms. Can I bring it in?"

"I suppose so."

There's enthusiasm for you—I *suppose* so. What's wrong with him? I struggled up the steps with my arms screaming. That thing must've weighed sixty pounds, easy. I put it on the table. "Boy, that burns me up," says a voice, Dick Van Dyke if I'm not mistaken. I turned around and Gene's other TV is working fine. Dick sits down at his desk, flabbergasted or sore about something.

"It works," I said.

Very smart, Weems. Very *observant*.

"Yes, it's even better than before it broke down."

"Lee said it was totally screwed . . ."

"I think he said that out of spite. Diane had the repairman come out and look at it. The bill was only thirty-four dollars."

"We're gonna hafta do something about this," says Marty Brill.

"Any suggestions?" asks Dick.

"Murder?" says Marty, and laughter explodes right out of the can.

"I guess I should've told you," says Gene. "I feel awful."

"Nah, it's my own fault. I should've made sure you junked the old one first."

"The color's much better than before, don't you think?"

"I never saw it working till now."

"Oh, of course. Have you had breakfast?"

"Yeah, thanks."

The situation could've been worse. He could've been watching You-Know-What. I sat down. "Know anyone who wants a cheap TV?"

"No," says Gene. "It was very generous of you. I could kick myself for not telling you."

"Ah, well. I'll take it home and put it in my room. There's only one set at my place."

"That's a good idea. You can watch TV in bed!"

"Yeah."

I only get in bed for two things—sleep and pudknocking.

"Maybe Diane knows someone around here that needs one," I said.

I really don't want to take it home. Also, if I can off-load it onto some other schmuck, the schmuck'll have to move it. That bastard weighs a ton if you're a little guy like me.

"I don't think she knows too many people," says Gene.

That's because she's too busy looking after Gene.

"I'll go ask, anyway."

I went along to Diane's trailer and knocked. When she answered the door, she's got a Colt .45 in her hand—the gun, not the beer.

"I thought it might be Lee," she says.

"Lucky for him it wasn't. Is that thing loaded?"

"Sure. Come in."

In I went. She put the gun on the table and I picked it up. It's a frontier-type Colt like you see in Westerns, but it's not a real .45 because the bore's too small. It's a .22 got up to look like a .45. It'd still put a hole in you, though.

"Is this Gene's gun?"

"He gave it to Lee a while back."

"It's not a real .45."

"I don't know what it is. I wish you'd put it down, Burris."

So I did. I didn't want to make her nervous. She didn't look good, like she hasn't been sleeping enough. I know what that's like.

"Would you've shot Lee if it was him?"

"I don't know. Why are you here so early?"

I told her about 107 and the TV.

"Oh, Burris, I'm sorry. You expected so much from spending the night there, and now the TV."

"Yeah, talk about bad judgment. An error compounded by a mistake. That's the story of my life."

"It was sweet of you to think of Gene. Have you had breakfast?"

"Uh . . . no, I guess not."

"I'll make us both some."

Yeah! This is more like it, with me watching her move around in the tiny kitchen section fixing cereal and toast and coffee and juice. I don't mean I liked it because she's doing all the work and I'm sitting on my ass, none of that sexist scrap. No, I liked it because I just plain like looking at her. I would've liked it if she stood there doing nothing at all. For once she isn't wearing those khaki overalls with the zip pockets, and it's a big improvement. She isn't wearing anything special, just ordinary jeans and a T-shirt, but it's a big improvement. She *has* got tits, I can see them now, but they're little pointy things like those shiny paper hats little kids wear at birthday parties, and her ass is kind of wide and flat and squared off at the bottom if you know what I mean. But I didn't care about stuff like that. I couldn't give a shit. I'm in love with her. She's the girl for me, dammit! Her hair looked kind of mussed and greasy, too, but who cares? Love is blind, so hand me my shades and cane.

"There you go."

She put breakfast on the table and we sat there and ate it together. Being married must be like this, munching away together with your hair sticking up on end because you haven't combed it yet. We didn't talk much, too busy eating, and then she says, "Burris, it's Wednesday. Why aren't you at work?"

"Oh, I quit yesterday. It's no fun without Lee."

"What's your mom going to say?"

"She'll bitch a little, I guess."

"I hope you know what you're doing."

"I always know what I'm doing, Diane. I knew what I was doing when I rented 107, and I knew what I was doing when I got that TV. I *always* know what I'm doing."

She laughed at that. Jesus, she looks terrific when she laughs. She's got this crooked little eyetooth back along her gum that you only see when she laughs. It's a pointy one, and the rest of her front teeth are kind of rounded, even the other eyetooth, so it stands out some.

"You're looking at my fang," she says, and quit laughing and pulled her lip down.

"No, I wasn't."

"You were. I can't help having that awful thing."

"It's not awful."

"It's a *fang*."

"It isn't. I like it."

"No, you don't."

"I do. I think it's . . . cute."

"You don't at all, but it's very nice of you to say so."

"Fang you very much."

She spluttered coffee everywhere. I thought she was mad at me, but she's laughing! She really flashed the old fang at me, which made me feel pretty good. It's great when somebody thinks you're a funny bastard, especially if you're in love with the person the way I am with her. I made a couple more cracks, but they weren't up to fang standard, and we finished eating. She looked a whole lot better now than when I came over, and I told her so.

"It must be you," she says. "You're what my grandma calls a tonic."

"That's because I keep my emotions bottled up."

That one had her howling again. She's really starved for humor, this girl, and those little pointy tits jiggled around like they're laughing too. After things got calmed down I said, "I guess I better take the TV out of Gene's trailer."

"I'm really sorry you spent money that way."

"Like you said yesterday, *c'est la vie!*"

"Want a hand getting it in the car?"

"Nah, it's not heavy."

But she helped, anyway, holding doors open and stuff.

Gene says, "I feel bad about this, Burris, I really do."

"Don't sweat it, Gene. It only cost a few bucks."

"I want you to know I appreciate the thought, anyway."

"Sure thing. I'll bring the car back later. So long."

I got in and fired it up, then the other door opened and Diane got in.

"I'm coming too," she says. "I need to get out of that trailer."

"Okay."

And off we drove. I felt like I'm the king of the world. This must be what it feels like to be married, to drive along in your car with your girl next to you. It wasn't my car and she's not my girl, but I felt pretty damn good about it, anyway. When we got to my place, she helped me with the TV. There wasn't anyone home and we put it in the living room. I would've put it in my room, but I didn't want Diane to see that picture of Charlotte Rampling on the wall. She'd probably figure I lie there looking at it and jerking off or something, so I hustled her straight out to the car again.

On the way back she says, "I want to go for a drive."

"Where to?"

"Anywhere. Just a drive, I don't care."

So we cruised on past the turnoff to Green Acres and kept on going along the Interstate. We had the windows cranked down and the car had a breeze rushing through it that made you shout to be heard.

"Feeling better!" I asked her.

"Much!" she screams.

"I wish we could just keep on going!" I hollered.

"Me too!" she hollers back.

Talking was too tough, so we just drove. The logical place to go was the state forest, so we went there and drove all through it. There were plenty of sightseers and we had to go slow a lot of the way, but we didn't care. They've got about a billion trees there, and a lake, all of it pretty nice. We stopped in the middle where they have the restaurant and ate lunch, then we drove back to Buford again, still not talking much, but we didn't need to, anyway. Diane had this kind of half smile, half squint on her face that made her look very dreamy and far away. She even fell asleep on the way home, slumped sideways against the door pillar. She looked like a little kid like that. I wanted to reach out and touch her, but she's too far away. In a subcompact I could've done it easy, but Gene's car is one of those old wide-bodied types. So I didn't touch her the way I wanted. She woke up when we hit the Buford city limits and looked around all blinky-eyed.

"I fell asleep."

"You sure did."

"Did I snore?"

"Yeah. You showed your fang too."

She leaned over and punched my shoulder. "I did *not*," she says. That punch was the greatest thing I ever felt. I grinned like an idiot all the way back to the trailer park. I could've stopped by at my place and let her drive herself home from there, but it didn't cross my mind. It just seemed natural to stay together.

"Oh, shit," she says when we pulled up next to the trailer. "I haven't got any food. Let's go to the supermarket."

So I backed up and we went to Food City. Even goofy stuff like steering the basket around the aisles was fun because I was with Diane. We got a whole lot of salad stuff and some up-market frozen dinners, also a bottle of Smirnoff. "I'm tired of beer," she says. "It's giving me a pooch," meaning a gut, not a dog, but she looks okay to me, with just the right size bulge above her jeans for me to lay my weary head on.

We drove back to Green Acres and she put the frozen stuff in the oven and we chopped up the salad stuff together, which was a lot of fun, believe it or not. It's the first time I chopped salad in my life. We had a couple nips each from the Smirnoff too. I never had vodka before, either. It's like drinking Listerine, but you feel *real* good a little while after. But I didn't drink too much of it. I didn't want to say anything dumb or fall over and look like an idiot. Diane put away plenty, though, nip, nip, nip all the time the stuff was cooking. Then it's done and we pulled it out and I went over to get Gene, who was watching *Sesame Street*. He came back with me and we ate, ate, ate. I was starving. That meal was just the best.

Afterward we sat around and yakked about nothing. Gene had a few snorts of Smirnoff, too, and pretty soon loosened up and didn't even bother straightening his skirt when it got hiked up around his thighs. He's forgotten to sit like a woman, too, and his legs are open with the toes pointing out. He looks like a drunk old whore that doesn't give a fuck about anything. He and Diane started talking about Lee, which they probably wouldn't have if they were sober, and Gene says, "He left because he hates me," which is very true, I think.

"No, no, *no*," says Diane. "He's been working up to this for a long time."

"Since I went to the gender clinic," says Gene. He used to call it a hospital like everyone else. Now it's a gender clinic. He's drunk, all right.

"*Before* that," says Diane. "You remember how crazy he used to be when we were in school? It just got worse, that's all."

"But what *made* him worse? *Me*."

"You know he always had trouble with Vern. That's what made him the way he is, not you. Fathers and sons are always screwing each other up. Aren't they, Burris?"

"I guess so."

What would *I* know about fathers? She's drunk too.

"They didn't get along at all," she says to me. I didn't ask, but she's telling me, anyway. "Vern's divorced, so there was just him and Lee living in the house, no other brothers or sisters. It was just impossible."

She says how Lee and Vern used to scrap like cat and dog all the time and how Vern yanked Lee out of college after just six months and made him get in the construction business whether he wanted to or not, which is kind of crazy because most parents want their kid to graduate from college, and how everything really went to shit after that. But she didn't say how Vern felt about Gene, which is a big hole in her analysis of what makes Lee tick, because Vern sounds to me like the kind of guy who'd just hate for his boy to marry someone whose father traded his dick for a vagina. Vern would've seen that as a personal insult, I bet, and screwed Lee up about it if he wasn't already. And an even bigger hole, like about the size of a moon crater, is how Lee's been acting toward Gene, which she also didn't talk about. So really all she's doing is trying to convince Gene his operation has got nothing to do with her marriage running on the rocks, which is very noble of her but is also a ton of horseshit. Lee hates faggots, and although Gene, strictly speaking, isn't a faggot, Lee hates him, anyway. That's a fact. I don't know why he does, he just does, and if you leave that bit out, then everything else you say about the situation just falls apart because it's full of holes. Diane knows it too. She's too smart not to know she's talking horseshit, or semi-horseshit. I mean, I'm sure Lee *was* weird before Gene had the operation, but that's only part of the story. The reason Diane's talking semi-horseshit is to spare old Gene's feelings. She's his daughter, after all. Gene can't handle hard facts. He shouldn't *have* to handle assholes like Lee hating him for having a vagina where he used to have a cock and balls, but he *does* have to handle it. And he can't do it. He just can't look it in the face. I mean, he *knows* Lee hates him, and he *says* so, even though Diane keeps saying it isn't true, but he can't adjust to it and overcome it, can't say to himself and the world, "Lee doesn't like it that I turned myself into a woman? Well, *fuck Lee!*" He can't do that, and it's because he isn't proud to've done what he did to his body. If he was proud and happy to be a woman, there'd be no problem, I bet, he'd just tell Lee to fuck off, but in his head he *agrees* with Lee that he did a horrible, disgusting thing in changing himself, so he can't fight back. I don't know, maybe Diane shouldn't encourage him to think he's not connected with Lee's leaving. Maybe that kind of talk just helps Gene bury his head deeper in the sand. Maybe it's none of my business. I can't drink Smirnoff *and* work out their problems for them. Shit, I can't even work out my own problems. Yes, I can, I *can* work them out, by which I mean *understand* the problems, but I just can't seem to change anything. But at least I'm better off than Gene. I don't think he understands himself at all, sometimes. Down the hatch! Watch out below!

Things got worse. They talked and talked and danced around and around a bush they won't admit is there. It's a waste of time and words. Gene's gone and fucked up his life, and there's no way to unfuck it. That's it. That's all there is. It's very simple. But too depressing to talk about, so they dance around and around it, talking horseshit. I kept out of it. They wouldn't want to hear what I have to say on the subject—in fact, I bet they'd hate me if I spoke my mind. My third eye would've burned them up, fried them with Truth, especially Gene. He wouldn't be able to handle what my third eye could tell him. So I didn't say anything. I kept right out of it, just sat there fueling my eye with vodka. Nothing will be resolved here, my eye told me, and I agreed, and gave it another little nip.

The sun-ray clock on the trailer wall says 11.10. They've talked for hours! Why don't they see what a waste of time it's been? Because they don't have third eyes, that's why. I stopped listening to the conversation a long way back. I just looked at Diane. She's a doll. I mean it. I love her. I want to see the fang again, because that'd mean she's smiling. But the fang was way back in her mouth, hidden by all the horseshit she's trading with Gene, horseshit sprayed with pity to make it smell better, but horseshit anyway. I forgive her for talking horseshit because her motives are good. I'd forgive her anything. I want to clamp myself onto her like a frog with fuck fever and fuck her to death. She doesn't know how much I love her. She's too busy horseshitting with Gene, reassuring him with horseshit. Gene's babbling about his manhood now, his *lost* manhood. "How could I have *done* it?" he keeps saying, very drunk. Then he says, "I never should've read books about it. If I hadn't read books about it I never would've been able to make the doctors think an operation was *right* for me. I was too clever. Whatever they asked me, I knew exactly what I had to say, knew just what the right answer was to make them think I should have the operation, all about the woman inside me wanting to be free. . . . Oh, *God!*"

And he collapsed all over the sofa and started howling, just dumped his drink all over himself and fell down sideways and hid his face in his hands. It was a pretty shocking thing to see, even worse than when he cried last Friday night over in the other trailer. Then he was just kind of sniffling and snuffling and leaking tears down his face, but now he's really howling and making these little kicks with his feet that are sticking out from the end of the sofa, *kick kick kickety-kick*, like a little kid having a tantrum. It looked kind of funny, I have to admit, even if it does sound heartless. Those big bunions he's got looked so stupid knocking against each other. Did I say we all had our shoes off, it's so hot in there? Well, we did. If I wasn't so drunk I probably wouldn't have thought it looked so funny. I didn't laugh, though. I said something useful, like, "Take it easy, Gene." That was my big contribution to the proceedings. Diane went and bent over him and held his shoulders and said over and over, "Don't cry, Daddy. Please don't cry, Daddy," which should've been pretty funny, too, but wasn't.

"Help me, Burris," she says.

I hauled myself up and waited to see what she wants help with. It's Gene. She wants to take Gene over to his trailer and put him to bed. It was a tough job, but we did it. It would've been tougher if he was a fighting, raving-type drunk, but he went quiet as a stopped clock the second we picked him up off the sofa, one on either side of him, and started out the door. His legs walked, but his face had gone to sleep, all vacant-eyed. Whoever was in there pulled down the shades so's he wouldn't have to see or hear or *know* anything anymore. We got him in his own trailer and wrestled his clothes off down to his slip. He really *has* got breasts. They look okay, too, from what I can see outlined by the slip, a better shape than Diane's, frankly, but what makes them look weird is this bony chest in between, all ribbed like an old washboard. Finally we got him arranged in the bed and left him there.

On the way back to Diane's trailer she says, "You'll have to stay here. I can't drive you home, I'd crash the car."

"That's okay."

Those are the words I spoke with my mouth, but in my head I said, "Great! That's exactly what I want! Now I can get to sleep with you because there's space in the bed with Lee gone and the sofa's too small, anyway, and when we're in bed together, I'll fuck you like a frog! I love you, love you, love you . . . !"

Jesus, I didn't know how drunk I was till I started to get undressed. That vodka comes up to you like a friend, then clubs you over the head. My head was an oyster. It sounds crazy, but my head was this big oyster that opened up whenever I said something, then closed again, just this big rough knobbledy oyster with a big blob of snot inside it that's my brain, I don't know why, and my third eye is the pearl.

"Got a pearl in my head," I said, and the hinge at the back of my neck let my oyster head open up for the words to come out.

"There's Anacin on the window ledge."

She thought I said a *pain* in my head. She wants to fix my pain. I'll let her. She can fix my pain, all right. I got down to my shorts, then stopped and sat on the sofa to watch her undress. She hadn't closed the concertina wall or anything, just shucked off her jeans and T-shirt. No bra. No need for one. She put the light out. I'm still sat on the sofa. I can feel where Gene spilled his drink. I took my shorts off. Now I'm naked. What to do next? I got the shakes. She didn't say good night. Does that *mean* something, like she's waiting for me to come over there and get in bed with her? Christ, what do I *do*? Why doesn't she give me a signal? Why doesn't she heave a sigh and say, "I can't sleep," which'll be an invitation to talk, and when you talk with someone, you don't do it from opposite ends of a trailer, no you don't, you get close to each other so you don't strain your voice box. So say it, Diane, say you can't sleep and I'll be right there. I'll jump like a frog to land beside you on your bed, and I'll *ribbit, ribbit, ribbit* in your ear about how crazy I am for you, and you'll wrap your legs around me and fuck me like a rattlesnake. Please, *please* gimme a sign . . . please? I sat there, waiting, waiting . . . God, I'm drunk. I can't feel my feet. You have to be drunk not to feel your feet anymore. Don't just *sit* there! Right, you're right, I hafta *do* something, make a *move*, anything that'll get me from here to there.

"This sofa . . . way too short . . ."

She didn't hear me because I squeaked it. Try again.

"God, this *sofa* . . . I can't *sleep* . . ."

Silence from the bed. I wriggled around on the sofa to make out like I'm thrashing restlessly in a brave attempt to fall asleep on something about as comfortable as a box of pine knots. I'm really faking it. So far only my butt has made contact with the highly flammable synthetic-plaid upholstery.

"This sofa's impossible, Diane . . . Diane?"

I finally figured it out. If I hadn't been drunk and also an idiot, I would've noticed sooner. Yeah, you guessed it. We've all seen this movie before. She's asleep—snoring, even. She really does snore. It doesn't sound too bad, though. I got up and went through to the bedroom section. I cracked my shins on the way because it's dark and I'm very drunk. She's asleep, all right. She isn't covered or anything, it's too hot for that, and she's got nothing on, not even panties. There's a tiny scrap of light coming through the venetians, and she's definitely got no panties on. I leaned over her and breathed in. She smelled wonderful, a kind of sweaty, socky, farty smell. Frankly, it made me very horny. I wanted to get on the bed and hold her, just hold her is all. I wanted that very badly. I didn't do it, natch. You can't do stuff like that to sleeping people. They might wake up suddenly and be completely traumatized by the experience. So I just stood there and breathed in that unwashed-girl-on-a-hot-night smell. It was friendly. It would've made a dog wag his tail. It also made me miserable. Another Big Night bites the dust. Is a pattern being established here?

I went back to my end of the trailer. *My* end. Jesus. I couldn't sleep, drunk or not, so out came the tape recorder. Did I tell you it's a Sony? My tape recorder is a Sony. It's very good. I heartily recommend Sony products. Send me a check, Sony. I've told my Sony everything from the time I woke up this morning. What a sorry fucking tale it is. I could let myself get depressed about the way things have gone, but I've got too much character. Strength through Adversity, that's my motto. What would that be in Latin? I should have a shield made up, the Weems crest. It'd have a dog on it like Buster, humping the ground up in one corner, and down in the other corner there'd be a TV set, all on a black velvet background.

Musculum Negativus.

Something like that.

11

When I woke up my head felt like a rock in a rock quarry with some guy hammering a wedge into it. I won't drink vodka ever again. After I learned how to stand up I went along to the bedroom and there she was, the girl I love, ass in the air and drooling a little on the pillow. She quit snoring at last, though. I can see one of her little tits squashed under her arm. A tit that size can't fight back. I wanted to kiss her all down her bumpy spine and rub my face against her shoulder blades, which are standing up like dorsal fins she's so skinny, and you could've played her ribs like a xylophone. I really thought I was gonna get laid last night. It was very disappointing. Maybe I should've just jumped on her and seen what happened, but I didn't have the nerve. Have I got the nerve now, even though my head's throbbing like crazy and I can't see straight? Yeah, I have, dammit! Here goes nothin' . . .

I lay down next to her on my side so's I could look at her face and neck and hair and her ear too. You don't usually notice ears, but when a girl's got hair short as Diane's, noticing the ears is unavoidable. Lucky for her she's got nice ones, small and neat with just the right amount of lobe, not big and blobby or anything. No earrings, but the insides could do with a scrub. It's kind of waxy and yellow in there. I'd like to lick them clean, really sink the old tongue in and get that gunk out. It'd taste bitter, I know, because I ate some of my own earwax one time just to see what it's like. You couldn't make candles out of it. I could smell her skin. She's sweated a lot in the night, same as me, and she looks kind of slick. There's bits of fluff in her hair from the crappy pillow, and she's got this very small zit needs squeezing on her chin. I bet when she opens her eyes the inside corners are full of crusty stuff. I had to dig my own out already. Her mouth's open a little way and she's breathing through it, not through her nose. That's probably why she was snoring last night. She's got dragon breath, but everybody does first thing in the morning, so I don't care. Neither of us cleaned our teeth before we crashed. I leaned over and kissed her on the cheek, very soft so's not to wake her up. She went, "*Nnnnnpphh,*" and turned away, still asleep. Okay, stay sleepy, I don't care. I'm lying beside you where I want to be. God, my head hurts. Even being next to Diane can't make me forget my head. That kiss felt pretty good, though, even if it was a bit slimy because she hasn't washed her face yet. I fell asleep again.

"Hey."

My shoulder's being pushed. Diane's pushing it.

"Who said you could get on the bed?"

She didn't sound sore, just kidding me. She still sounds half asleep.

"No one. I just felt like it."

How's that for repartee.

"I've got a headache," she says.

"Me too," I said, and squinted up my eyes and rubbed my brow to show how bad it is, then I leaned over and kissed her on the mouth. She didn't stop me so I kept at it, doing the best I know how, a combination of sucking and brushing, kind of. I had a hard-on, too, a real log. She still wasn't saying no, so I started using my hands to grab her ass and stuff and *bingo!* her tongue's in my mouth, squirming around in there like a spastic snake and her little tits are squashed flat against me and the log is prodding at her pubic hair, kind of chafing, and that's when magic time happened. It went in, I don't know how—I mean, she wasn't on her back with her legs open or anything, she's on her side same as me but it went in, anyhow, and when it happened we both quit moving for a second or two, like we're saying to each other, "Oops! How'd that happen? Oh, well, now that it's in there do we keep going or stop right now?"

We kept going, kind of pushing nice and gentle at each other, but it wasn't too comfortable sideways like that, and some of her hair's gone and fed itself into the crease and is rubbing the side of my dick till it hurts. Take the initiative, Weems! Now or never! I took it, I really did. I rolled her over on her back. She didn't mind at all, and her legs went around me like I wanted, and the log which up till then was only in a little way went sliding home to glory. What an amazing feeling! It's nothing like jerking off, *nothing* like it. *Humpety-humpety-humpety* . . . What a feeling, and these very sexy sounds were coming to me—*schlop, shlup, schlap, schlop*—from down below where everything is slippery and tingling, and Diane's going "*Nnngh, nnngh, nnngh* . . ." with her eyes shut tight and her fang showing, enjoying it, I hope. I know I am. I feel terrific! I feel like King fucking Kong! *Humpety-humpety-humpety* . . . Incredible feeling! Wait . . . something's gonna happen . . . something's gonna happen . . . I can hear another sound now, kind of a "*Hrrrrrrr-nnnnnnnnaaaaaggggghhhhh* . . . ! It's *me!* I'm making that sound! Then someone pulled a plug in my guts and everything from my chest to my knees all of a sudden got sucked out through my dick like bathwater down the drain, swirling and tugging till every little bit was gone and I'm flat and empty as a beer can on a Saturday night, puffing and panting like an old donkey engine, lying all over Diane and gasping for air. I still had my headache and it's pounding like a bastard.

"I can't breathe . . ." says Diane.

I slid off her like a dead mackerel and lay on my back—*in*hale, *ex*hale, *in*hale, *ex*hale. . . . God, I felt good! I've actually gone and *fucked* someone at last! Put it right in and come in there and *every*thing! I'm not a virgin anymore! Unfurl the flags! Break out the booze! Let it be known throughout the realm that Sir Burris of Weems, he of the dog and tube shield, hath scored mightily with the maiden of his choosing. Who'll be the first person I tell? That's important, telling someone. It couldn't be Gene. "Hey, Gene, I just fucked your daughter." No I didn't. I didn't fuck her. We made love. I'm in love with her. I don't think she's in love with me yet, but if I'm careful not to do anything dumb, I bet she falls in love with me, especially after all her problems get solved and she can concentrate on appreciating what a terrific person I am, also how fantastic a stickman I am. I *know* I was a great lay because *I* enjoyed it. That's how I felt for at least a couple of minutes. What made me think maybe I wasn't such a hot lay was when Diane rolled over on her belly again and put her hands down out of sight under her and the next thing I know her ass is jiggling, jiggling like crazy, and her head's turned away from me and she's going, "*Nnngh, nnngh, nnngh*," the way she was when we were screwing. What's *happening* here? I didn't say a word, just watched. Jiggle, jiggle, jiggle, goes her ass, and it got me feeling horny again, watching her buns kind of slap against each other, made me want to up and do it again, with her on top this time, and a couple other ways I heard about. Then the nickel dropped. She's masturbating! Diddling herself . . .! I didn't bring her because I'm a lousy lay that came too soon, and now she has to finish herself off. So *that's* how girls do it. I always thought they had to use candles and dildoes and stuff. Well, well, well. Live and learn. I felt pretty stupid about not making her come, but I'm only a beginner, after all, not an expert cocksman or anything. I still felt too *good* to get depressed about the first time not being perfect. I'll learn, and when I do, she'll beg me to quit before she goes out of her mind with ecstasy, et cetera. That's how it'll be, and that's for sure.

"*Nnnnnnnnngggggghhhhhhmmmmmmmm* . . ."

Thar she blows! Her buns clenched one last time, real hard. You could've cracked walnuts between them. Then they relaxed so much, I could practically see her little browneye, and she's puffing and panting like me. I put my arm across her back and my nose against her shoulder, and both of us nodded off again, just like that.

Knock, knock, knock!

We both came awake, jumping like rabbits.

Knock, knock, knock!

"It's Gene," she says, whispering.

"Shit . . ."

"Ssssshhh . . ."

Knock, knock, knock!

"Diane, are you awake?"

It's Gene, all right.

"I'm still in bed!" Diane calls out. "I'll be over in ten minutes!"

"Can I come in?" says Gene.

"No! It's a mess! I'll be over in ten minutes!"

Gene muttered something or other, most likely saying it's *always* a mess in here, so what's the big deal about it this morning, but he went away. Diane gave me a big shove.

"Quick. Get dressed and go."

"Go . . . ?"

My precious darling is telling me to *go?*

"Go! And don't let him see you. Go around the other side of his trailer."

I got dressed fast. I haven't even got my shirt on when she pushes me out the front door. "Hurry!" she says. I tried to get a kiss out of her at least, but the screen door's already banged shut behind me. I've watched this scene a million times in the movies. Usually the guy gets out the back window with his shoes in his hand while the husband is coming in the front door. I guess I can't blame Diane for giving me the bum's rush. Gene's her father, after all, even if he does wear frocks. She wouldn't want him knowing about her sex life—I mean love life.

I pulled on my shirt and went around the edge of Green Acres so Gene wouldn't see me. The sun's pretty high, so it must be at least eleven o'clock. My head still felt like a split rock, and I was hungry and thirsty. Correction—I was *starving* and *dying*. I headed for the Interstate and a burger breakfast, but before I got to Wendy's, which is the nearest food joint, I heard the sound of a bulldozer. I knew what *that* meant, and put on a sprint that sent little bolts of lightning from my heels up into my skull. When I got to the Starlite it's already half gone, looking like Europe after World War II, with walls but no roof anymore, and even those walls are crumbled at one end. They didn't need a wrecker's ball for something as small as the Starlite, just sent this dozer straight through. It was like a dirty yellow monster, a big square dinosaur with shovel jaws that eats the corners of buildings with one bite and lets the rest collapse around it while it goes crawling on through the clouds of dust to eat the next corner—*chomp!*—and down comes more ceiling and roof and wall—*ker-rash!*—and there's even more dust swirling around this big yellow monster snorting and chugging and roaring up and down through the gears, backing up, then moving in for the kill again.

I stood and watched, and it seemed to me that something was missing. What is wrong with this picture? I knew the Starlite was coming down today, so I'm not surprised to see the dozer there, but there's something missing from what I thought I'd feel when it came down. Then I nailed it—I don't feel any *regret*. You'd think I would, but I guess after spending Tuesday night in 107 and finding out what a dump it really is, and buying a TV from it on Wednesday morning that's a complete waste of money, and spending the rest of that day with Diane and getting drunk on vodka for the first time that night and Thursday morning losing my virginity, there isn't a whole lot of emotion left inside me to feel anything much about the old Starlite. I just stood there and watched it get eaten by the monster, and the thought that went through my head while I watched was: So what?

So nothing. So I went in Wendy's and ate like a pig, then I called Peggy from the pay phone outside, and Jesus, was she ever mad at me.

"Just where have you been for the last two days!"

No good morning, Burris, or anything polite.

"I stayed with some friends. I forgot to call."

"You did *not* forget! You didn't *bother!*"

"Well, I'm sorry . . ."

"Sorry doesn't make it right, not by any means."

"I guess not."

What the fuck does she want—blood?

"And where did this TV come from?"

"That? Oh, that's a present from a friend. He doesn't want it anymore."

I don't know why I said that.

"Burris, I'm only going to ask you this once, and I want an honest answer. Did you steal that TV?"

"Awww, come on, Peggy. Nobody'd steal a beat-up old TV like that. It's only worth twenty bucks. My friend didn't want it anymore, so I said I'd take it. I'll put it in my room. I meant to yesterday, but I was in a hurry."

"Doing what? I rang Servex and they say you don't work there anymore."

"Uh . . . that's right. I quit. They hassled my friend Lee and he talked back and got fired, so I quit. It was like a protest over the way they treated him."

"Hassled him about what?"

"Oh . . . stuff. They didn't like his attitude. He's got a bad attitude, they said."

"You're such a little liar, Burris. I asked to speak with him and they told me he didn't show up for work Tuesday. They didn't fire him at all, so don't give me any more lies or you'll be *punished* for them."

"How?"

I really wanted to know. What's she gonna do, stop my allowance? I don't get one. Hit me with the flyswatter like she used to do when I was little? She can't catch me now, and anyway, I'd take the flyswatter off her in around two seconds and break it in half like an arrow. No, I wouldn't—it's plastic. But there's not much she can do to me, so I wasn't scared. How can a guy that's just had his first fuck be scared of anything?

"I'll get you for this, Burris."

"Betcha don't."

Jesus, was I cocky. You don't sass Peggy like that when she's real mad. Now she really *will* try and get me. But who gives a shit? Not me, not while my dick's still gummy from Diane.

"Come home *right now!*"

"No."

"I'm warning you, Burris."

"I hear ya, but I'm not coming home. I've got friends in this town, see. They'll put me up, so it's no good you getting all worked up about things."

"If you don't get your tail home *right now* you're in deep trouble, mister. I mean it."

"I know you do, but listen, if I come home there'll just be a big fight and I don't want a fight, so I'm gonna stay away a few days till you get calmed down."

"You're going to regret this, Burris."

"Hey! Guess what! They're tearing down the old Starlite. You can hear the dozer from here."

I held the phone out to pick up the roaring.

"Hear it? There isn't much left now, just a couple walls and the sign."

"That does it! You're on shit street."

"It isn't my fault they're pulling it down. . . ."

"I'm calling the police and telling them to pick you up."

"Are you? Well, in that case I'm leaving town. 'Bye."

And I hung up. She can really get on my nerves sometimes, Peggy. Now what? I didn't have any plans except to go back to Green Acres tonight and do some more fucking. That stuff's *addictive*. What a great day today is! It's already ninety-one and climbing. Who cares! It'll make us good and sweaty so we slide around on each other like otters on a mud bank. Sex, sex, *sex!* There *is* a God, after all. Natural selection wouldn't have bothered inventing something so terrific, too busy increasing the length of tails and making us stand upright and all. The Big Guy said, "Let there be fucking, that my people may have entertainment before TV comes along." And *lo*, there was fucking. I'm gonna fuck with Diane till we're sore. Fuck, fuck, fuckety-fuck is what we'll do till the seventh day, when we'll rest, which is very sensible because on the eighth day it'll be *back to fucking!*

The dozer driver quit for lunch and went in Wendy's, so I went back in there after him. When he sat down I kind of slid in the booth opposite him and said, "Excuse me."

"Yeah?"

"I was wondering, how do you rate working as a demolition man?"

"I rate it fine," he says. He's got a double cheeseburger.

"Would it be too personal a question if I asked how much money you get for this kind of work?"

"Eighty a day," he says. *Chomp!* He's only got half a double cheeseburger now.

"Eighty *bucks?*"

"You bet. Trained operator. Dangerous work sometimes."

"Where'd you learn to do it—drive a dozer, I mean?"

"Army."

"Oh. Do they have bulldozer schools, apart from the army?"

"Beats me. Maybe. Pay to learn, same as you do a tractor-trailer rig, I guess."

"You're probably right. I'll look into it. Well, thanks for answering my questions. I didn't mean to interrupt your lunch."

"Pleasure," he says. *Chomp!* That double cheeseburger is *history*.

Well, that passed a pleasant ninety seconds. What next? She won't really sic the cops on me, I bet. Peggy doesn't like cops. She doesn't like anything in a uniform except maybe the mailman. I've got an entire afternoon ahead of me. Movies? There's one or two left in town I haven't seen yet. Check my pockets. Uh-oh. I have a cash-flow problem—my cash has all flown away. Was *thrown* away on that fucking TV. I've got to go home for more. I've got around $200 in my room, all that's left of my wages from Servex. Peggy didn't charge me rent or anything the few weeks I was working, so I haven't spent a lot. She's not so bad, just a pain every now and then. There are worse mothers I could have. Just to show you what a dedicated mom she is, when I was a little kid she used to pick thread-worms out of my ass—you know, those little white, wriggling bastards kids get. I had to bend over and she'd pick the fuckers out. *That's* dedication! But I always wondered why she didn't just get some medicine and dose me. Could it be some Freudian thing, picking worms out of your own little boy's asshole? Hmmmmmm . . .

I went home. Peggy's car was in the driveway, so she's in the house. How do I get in to rescue the cash without her spotting me? Think, Burris, *think*. Anyone who's clever enough to get a girl to fuck him should be clever enough to steal his own money. I thought hard. The obvious way seemed the best. Seeing as our place doesn't have air-conditioning, the windows are kept open. That's how you tell poor places—open windows in summer. The trick was to reach my window without her seeing me, which isn't as easy as it might sound because I don't know where in the house she is. There's at least three windows she could spot me from. I decided boldness was the thing. Yesterday I would've crawled along the flower bed to reach my window, but yesterday I was a virgin. Today I'm a man. Men stride up the walk with a swagger, so that's what I did, a tough job for a gimp. And when I reached the porch I chickened out and got on my hands and knees and crawled along the flower bed and around the corner to reach my window. Bravado is just sheer recklessness sometimes. The important thing is to get the money, not work on my image. Okay, I've reached my objective. My window was open as usual, and I got in easy. We don't worry about thieves. We've got nothing anyone would want to steal. A thief'd look at 1404 and say, "Nah."

Now I'm in. A quick listen for approaching footsteps. Nothin'. Okay, let's grab da cash an' scram outa here, fellers. I kept it in a drawer in the dresser, right down at the bottom. Open the drawer, reach in, feel around . . . not there. Not *there!* I pulled it all the way open, yanked out spare socks and shorts and various assorted crap, flung the stuff everywhere, but it's gone. My money's *gone.* How . . . ? Who . . . ? That *bitch! She's* found it and taken it! My own mother *stole my money!* There's a kind of thrumming sound in my head, like a rope vibrating in the wind. I could feel my skin get cold even if it's a goddamn oven in there. Rage, I thought, this is what rage feels like. Fuck her! Thief! She had *no right!* I'll get her for this. I bet she did it right after I phoned, came in here and stuck her nose in everywhere, looking for my stash. She knew it'd be in here somewhere because I don't have a bank account. The bitch, the fucking *bitch!* Okay, this means war.

I slammed out of my room and went straight to the studio. She's in there like I figured she would be. She didn't even turn around when I came in, so she's expecting me, natch. I couldn't even talk, I'm so mad.

"Lose something?" she says, very cool and sarcastic.

"Give it back."

"To what are you referring?"

She still hasn't turned around. She's painting another fucking clown. The clown's laughing over her shoulder at me.

"I want my money."

"When I get some explanations."

"I want my money."

My voice didn't sound like me. It sounded like someone else.

"Not until you answer a few questions."

"What questions?"

My voice is dead, flat and dead. It's spooky.

"Where have you been since Tuesday night?"

"Fucking my girlfriend."

"Let's moderate the language, chum," she says, very pissed.

"Engaging in coitus with a person of the opposite gender."

"Thank you. And who might the lucky girl be?"

"You don't know her."

"I *know* I don't know her. I want to know who she *is*."

"Diane."

"Diane who?"

"Trimble."

"Isn't that the name of your friend that got *fired*?"

"His name was Lee."

"Don't be a smartass, Burris. His name was Trimble, yes?"

"Yes."

"A married man, you said."

"To Gene."

"Pardon me?"

"He's married to a girl called Gene. Diane's his sister."

"And they live in a trailer park somewhere, yes?"

"Yes."

"And that's where you've been since Tuesday night."

"Right. I'd like my money now, please."

"Don't rush me, Burris. I get aggravated when I'm rushed. Where did that TV come from?"

"Room 107, Starlite Motel."

"You said they pulled it down."

"I said they *are* pulling it down right this minute."

"And you stole a TV while they were demolishing it."

"I *bought* a TV from them before they started."

"And you've been taking this Diane to the Starlite."

"Yeah."

"You'll have to find somewhere else now, won't you?"

I don't think she even remembers what room 107 *is*. She would've *said*.

"I guess so."

"Stop growling like that. Speak normally."

"Can I have my money now?"

"There was quite a bit there. You can't want it all."

"I do. I want it all. Where is it, please?"

"I'm becoming aggravated, Burris."

"I just want my money."

She painted a bit more, then says, "What kind of girl is she?"

I almost said, "Two tits, one cunt," just to shock her, but I can't talk about Diane like that. I'm in love with Diane. I don't even want to *talk* about her with this *thief*.

"She's Lee's sister."

"Burris, I asked what *kind* of girl she is."

I thought about it. "Nice," I said.

"Would I like her?"

"No."

"Why not?"

"She's younger than you."

I don't know why I said that. I'm not even sure what I *mean* by it. Peggy quit painting and turned around. She'd had her back to me all this time.

"What did you say?"

She's mad now, really mad. But it didn't start my guts fluttering the way it usually does to see her like this.

"I said I want my money."

I'm losing control of my lips. The words are getting lop-sided, kind of. The thrumming in my head is getting louder too. She's not gonna use the flyswatter on me this time.

"I want an explanation for your last remark."

Thin lips, the usual sign she's good and pissed. Let her be.

"I just want my *money!*"

"And I have told you you will not *get* your money until you explain that last remark and I'm satisfied you aren't *lying* anymore!"

I picked up a picture. It was a mountain scene. I smashed it down over the back of a chair. The chair went through the picture. No more mountains. I picked up a Kenny Rogers. Here's a picture that really *deserves* to die.

"No!" she says.

I killed it.

"Stop that!"

She can only holler. She won't come near me. She's *scared*. I picked up a Jesus Christ. *Crunch!* He'll be back in three days.

"In my bag! In the living room!"

I walked out like a robot, found the bag, got the cash and crammed it in my pocket. Then I went to my room and got all the tapes I've made, three so far, just in case she finds them and plays them, and put them in my pocket too. Peggy's crying in the studio. I can hear her in there. My mom is crying. I made my mom cry. Am I nuts or what? How could I do what I just did? What's the matter with me, anyway? I went back to Peggy. She's standing over the smashed pictures. She looks about sixty. I felt like a cockroach.

"I'm sorry . . ."

"Get out of my sight."

She tried to sound tough, but you can't do that when you're crying. The fact that she tried to and didn't make it made her look even more broken-down and old. I made my mom look old.

"I'm sorry . . . I didn't mean it . . ."

I want her to say it's okay. I want to see the pictures mended by running the film backward. I want her to call me names and then say everything is okay again. We'll both calm down, and I'll light a cigarette for her and she'll say, "Burris, you really are an unspeakable little asshole sometimes," and I'll say, "Yeah, I know, but underneath it all I'm awful cute," and we'll both laugh like hyenas. But it won't happen. Things went too far this time. I'm a cockroach, a scuttling, stinking cockroach for making this happen.

"Just go away . . ." she moans.

She *moaned* it. I made my mom cry, then I made her moan. How could I do a thing like that? I think I need help. This is not normal behavior. I felt like the king of the world a few hours back, and now I'm a cockroach.

"Honest, I didn't mean to . . ."

She turned her back on me. I don't blame her, but it hurt pretty bad, anyway, like a giant boot coming out of the sky and stomping me flat. What do I expect? I'm a cockroach. Take a hike, Mike.

I went away.

I walked around.

I felt like shit.

It's too hot for walking. I went to the park and sat by the statue of Thomas Keckley. There's a brass plate tells how old Thomas carved this place out of the wilderness in 1806 with just his wife and brother and started a town, which originally was called Keckleyville, but after Thomas died in 1834 they changed it to Buford. I think they were just waiting for him to drop dead so they could get rid of that crummy name. It's bad enough living in Buford with having to call it Keckleyville. Thomas looks a little like Daniel Boone, with this long flintlock rifle and fringes all down his sleeves and this noble gaze that's supposed to look like he's viewing the distant horizon or something, but really he's gazing across LaVista into Krazy Kurt's Discount Store, looking for bargains like everyone else.

I got out my Sony and started talking. Everything is a mess. I'll have to stay away from home a few days now. I can't believe I did what I did. Is the heat driving me crazy? I'm ashamed of myself. There's a squirrel a little way off, jumping across the grass like he's on springs. His fur's gray, with some red mixed in. Do the red-and-gray types interbreed? I guess they do. I always thought squirrels were cute until I saw a dead one that had a chunk of fur pulled out of its tail. The thing I always liked about squirrels was the tail, all soft and fluffy-looking, but on this dead one I could see that the actual tail under the feathery brush is long and skinny and pink, exactly like a rat's tail. Squirrels are rodents, did you know? So it's true when they say a squirrel is just a rat with a bushy tail. Another thing about squirrels is, everybody says they bark. People say it, and you read it in books. "The squirrel's angry bark is heard when its hoard of nuts is approached," or whatever. But squirrels *don't* bark. Bark is the *last* word you could give to the sound they make. Squirrels *squawk*. They sound more like a bird than a dog. A bark is Arf! Arf! or Woof! Woof! Squirrels don't sound anything like that. But people have got used to this dopey way of describing the noise a squirrel makes. They don't *question* it, just like they don't question most things. Squirrels? Oh, they bark, of course, everyone knows that. Bull*shit* they bark. They fucking *squawk*. Next time you hear a squirrel making a racket, ask yourself if it sounds like a bark or a squawk. You'll see that I'm right. I don't mean to be pedantic or anything, I just wanted to get that off my chest. The subject of squirrels is closed.

Bong! Bong!

That's the town hall clock sounding off. It must be ninety-five by now, easy. I really stink. I haven't had a shower or changed my clothes since Tuesday, including socks and underwear. That's a long time in summer. Pretty soon, if I walk in a store the crowds'll part before me like the Red Sea before Moses. Aaaaaagghh! Everybody retreat! It's Burris Weems! Sometimes I think my life has always been that way. Okay, I'm stretching it again, but honest to God, I feel like I've got leprosy sometimes. The thing is, I feel like I gave it to myself. How do you explain that? It's very weird. Just lie back and relax, Mr. Weems, and tell me about the first time you dreamed of having anal intercourse with your teddy bear. I have to *think positive.* I've got a girl that lets me put my body in her body, which is nothing less than a medium-sized miracle, frankly, and there's lots of other stuff to be positive about. I can't think of any offhand, but they're bound to be out there, those positive things, it's the law of nature or something—I mean, for every shitty thing there has to be a good thing, right? Now that I come to think of it, I don't see why there should be. There aren't equal amounts of ocean and land, are there, so why should there be equal amounts of good things and bad things? Answer me that, Professor. Shit, I don't care if the world *is* nine-tenths garbage. I've got a girl and that's all I need right now. Everything rests on Diane, rests on her furry little head. She's smack in the center of everything, like the hub of a wheel, and I'm all around her like the rim, and the spokes are how I reach her. I'm talking bullshit. But it's true, she's all I can think about. Even when I'm not actually thinking about her, she's *there* somehow, kind of hiding behind the stuff I *am* thinking about. You know how God is supposed to be everywhere, but isn't? Well, Diane is everywhere and *is*. She's my highway madonna with a hubcap halo. I can't wait to see her again tonight. Maybe we'll chop up some more salad. That was kind of fun. And then, to *bed*. I really want to feel that terrific feeling again, all slippery and grippy at the same time. An hour ago I smashed Peggy's paintings and made her cry, and now all I can think about is making it with Diane. Love is kind of sick in a way. Is that the same as saying love is a sickness? I heard that somewhere, or read it. Love is a sickness. Maybe it's true. If it is, I'm a dying man.

Medic! Medic!

12

Something terrible has happened. Everything is changed forever. It happened at Green Acres. Wait . . . *wait!* Tell it all. Deep breath. I was in the park. Yeah, the park, with a whole afternoon to kill before I saw Diane again. Solution? What else, I went to the movies. I saw the new Bond flick. It's the same as the old Bond flicks. When I came out it was 5:30, so I strolled across town to the trailer camp and knocked on Diane's door. No answer. Maybe she's over at Gene's, so that's where I went. Gene was in, but at the same time Gene was *out*—I mean, *out to lunch* about something. His mouth's hanging open and he can't focus his eyes on me, just stands there in the doorway like he's just that second been hit in the back by an arrow or something.

"What's up, Gene?"

He opened the screen door and let me in, still not looking at me. Diane wasn't there. Maybe she's at the store. Gene's car gets kept around the back of his trailer, so I didn't see if it's there or not. She's probably getting stuff for us to eat tonight. Gene flopped down on a chair and leaned his head on his hands, elbows on the table, still with that arrow-in-the-back look.

"Hey, Gene, something wrong?"

"They went away," he croaks.

"Who did?"

"Both of them."

"Both of *who?*"

I hate it when someone isn't specific.

"Lee and Diane," he says.

It's specific, but it's bull.

"Lee went last Tuesday, Gene. Where's Diane?"

"She went with him."

"No, she didn't. She was here this morning . . . I mean, yesterday."

I didn't want him thinking I was still here this morning, for Diane's sake. You've got to be careful around parents.

"Lee came back," he says. "They both left."

He still isn't looking at me. He's talking to the table in this soft, spooky voice, like he's dazed or something.

"Wait a minute. *Lee* came *back?*"

"This afternoon."

"Where's Diane?"

"I'm *telling* you, she *went*. They *both* went."

"Went where?"

I felt like throwing up.

"They didn't say. Tucumcari, I don't know . . ."

I wanted to kill him for telling me this stuff.

"Have I got this straight? Lee came back and he and Diane went away and won't be back? I mean, they've left Buford for *good?*"

"Yes, *yes.*"

He sounds like he's having trouble breathing. No, it's *me* I can hear. I sound awful, like a dog choking on a bone. I looked around the trailer. It was full of Diane because she wasn't there and never would be again. Lee came *back*. They're *together* again. *Gone.* My guts were like a blocked U-bend in the TV ads, with this disgusting black stuff clogging the bottom of the U, waiting for Drano to dissolve it away. Diane is *gone*. She's *left*. With *Lee*. Lee's her *husband* and I'm a cockroach. She stomped on me. How could she make love with me and a few hours later *leave* with a guy that beat her up, a guy she was ready to use a gun on? *What has happened here?* I'm drowning in black sludge, gagging on it. There's so much sweat on my forehead it's soaking my eyebrows. I can smell myself. I smell like a dog. I *am* a dog. I'm Buster the ground-humper and come-eater. She picked Lee. She dumped *me* and picked *him*, went away with that no-shouldered four-eyed faggot-hating bastard asshole cunt of a fucking bastard shit fuck cunt bastard asshole fucker. I can't *breathe* in there. . . .

I left Gene with his elbows on the table and went . . . *ran* to Diane's trailer. The door opened when I turned the knob, so she's *got* to be there. She would've locked up if she went away. Gene's got it all wrong, the stupid idiot. I went in and the place is tidy, no clothes scattered around, no dishes in the sink, no crap everywhere. It's an empty trailer. The bed sheets are gone, the towels, the sun-ray clock . . . The door key's on the table, left there the way you leave a motel key behind when you go. The asshole manager probably doesn't even know they've gone. They took everything they owned. *They*. Her and *him*, the one she prefers to *me* . . . I bet she left a letter! She wouldn't just leave without some kind of explanation. Okay, she's gone, but at least she's left me a Dear John, hasn't she? I looked everywhere for it. The letter wasn't there. I bet she left it with Gene! I raced back over there. He hadn't moved an inch.

"Did she leave a letter?"

"Letter?"

"Did she leave a letter for me?"

"No."

"How about a message for you to give me?"

"No, nothing."

"*Think*, will ya! She must've said *something*. . . ."

"She said . . ."

"Yeah?"

"Said I had to come to terms with my life. Lee told her to say it, I know. . . ."

"But what'd she say for you to tell *me*?"

"Nothing. She said I had to come to terms with my life. That's what she said. He made her say it. She wouldn't have said something like that just on her own, not my Diane. . . ."

His mouth opened and shut like a ventriloquist's dummy, and the words all came out in the same tone, at the same pace, like words on a tickertape.

"I leaned on her too long, that must be it, leaned on her, depended on her for support all this time, made her leave home to be with me when I should've been learning to do what she said, come to terms, it's the only sensible thing, but I couldn't, I tried but I couldn't, not yet . . ."

I wanted him to shut up, close that mouth with the wrinkles in the top lip, shut it and lock it and throw away the key while I try to *think* about what's happened and what it *means* and *what the fuck am I gonna do now?* Why'd she *go?* She opened her body and let me inside, and now she's *gone away* without leaving a letter or message or *anything.* How could she *do* that? What did I do to *make* her do it? I didn't do anything bad to her, so why'd she *do* it?

I stood there looking at Gene without seeing him, and he sat there looking at me the same way, and even though it's Diane that made us both feel this way we're a million miles apart. I couldn't stay in there another minute. I kind of lurched out and went back to the other trailer and spent the next half hour searching for that fucking *letter.* It *had* to be there. But it wasn't. All I found were some fish sticks in the freezer and a couple inches of vodka. I couldn't have eaten, but Jesus Christ, I needed a drink. Oh, you bitch, you fucking bitch, I hate you, hate your poisonous guts, you two-faced slut of a whore cunt bitch lying pox-eaten fuck cunt shitty whore . . . down the hatch . . . lying bitch of a two-faced slut bag shit-faced fang-toothed flat-ass small-tit bitch of a slut whore . . . I hope you drive off the highway and into a tree, off a cliff, smash and crash and roll over crunch flatten stomp splinter glass cut blood pump squirt bone shatter gas tank incinerate flesh melt squash guts back break skull smash, the both of you . . . fucking *cheers* . . . I wish you agony and pain and torment and horror, and I want you crippled forever in wheelchairs and blind and paralyzed and eaten up by cancer for the rest of your days, you bastards, you shits, you fucking selfish *users,* you hypocrites, you assholes, you *cowards,* sneaking off that way because you couldn't face me, and I bet she didn't tell him about fucking me—oh, no, not Diane, not such a wonderful girl as that, no sir, wouldn't dream of upsetting hubby with tales of naughtiness while he was away, wouldn't tell him it was someone that didn't beat her up or have sex problems or hate her father—oh, no, Lee might get mad and bring her right back to Papa, and we don't want that, do we, because coming back might mean running into Burris, the well-known fall-guy patsy dickhead dope fool clown eight-ball foulup shortass gimp, which might be embarrassing, mightn't it, so keep those lying lips shut tight, baby, and he'll whisk you away in his white pickup, away down to cactus country where you can snuggle up close and laugh about the way you left old Weems back there with nothing but thin air to hold on to.

Congratulations, you cunts!

I drank the whole two inches. That's quite a bit if you only drank vodka once before. I got stinking drunk and lay on the bed and used the same dozen or so words over and over in my head—shit fuck whore bastard cunt, et cetera—ran them through my head like the shortest tape loop in the world, but after a while there wasn't any anger left inside me to make the words mean anything anymore, so I quit and just felt . . . empty. I lay on that selfsame bed I lost my cherry on just this morning, this *morning*, and stared at the ceiling, watched it get darker as the sun went down and the venetian slats crawled across it, getting blurrier by the minute, then fading to gray, then black. I could hear the sounds of the trailer park through the window behind my head, radios and TVs, kids and cars, and later on when it got quiet, the faraway hum of the Interstate.

I couldn't think anymore, couldn't connect one thing to another the way you have to when you think, just lay there feeling numb, partly booze, I guess, and partly whatever the opposite of adrenaline is, pumping slowly through me, washing away all the black sludge, smoothing down the spikes inside me that stood out like porcupine quills. I'm practically anesthetized, feeling sorry for myself in a stick-out-your-bottom-lip kind of way, too chicken to think about tomorrow or the day after, uh-uh, it's all I can do to make it through tonight. I wish I had just a little more Smirnoff, just enough to topple me over the edge into sleep, so I can forget, forget, forget . . . but no deal, Neil, you're still awake and crying inside like a little kid that's had his lunch money stolen and his hair mussed and his toes stepped on for good measure. Cry, baby, cry, it's all you can do, boo hoo . . .

There's a knock at the door, then it opened and in came Gene, the last person I want to see right now. He turned on the light.

"Turn it off!"

He turned it off.

"Burris . . . ?"

"What."

"I wondered if you were over here."

"Well, I am."

"I don't know what to do . . ." he says.

"Get drunk. I just did. It feels better."

"I mean . . . I don't know what to *do*. . . ."

"Me, neither."

He's still standing by the door. He came further in. I didn't want that, didn't want him close to me.

"I don't know what you can do, Gene."

He stopped by the kitchen range.

"I have to do *something*. . . ."

"I told you already. Get drunk."

"No, I have to keep a clear head."

"What for?"

"I don't think getting drunk is the solution, Burris."

He sounds like a fussy old aunt or something.

"I just don't know what to do. . . ."

Jee-*zuz*. Just when I'm at the stage when I can start blotting things out, in comes Gene and pries open the whole can of worms again.

"Well, *I* don't know either, so will you please quit asking me? I don't *know* what to do. About *anything*, okay?"

"I just thought you might have some advice. . . ."

I wish he'd quit being so goddamn *hesitant*. It's driving me crazy.

"I'm fifteen fucking years old. What the hell do *I* know?"

"I thought we were friends. . . ."

He's just a shadow back there, a darker piece of darkness.

"We *are*, but I don't know how to solve anything for you, okay?"

"A little bit of company might help."

He sounds sulky now. Jesus, what a pain.

"Gene, I'd be real bad company tonight for reasons I can't get into right now—just believe me, you wouldn't want to be in the same room as me. We both of us are just gonna have to tough it out, okay? That's all I know."

"Yes," he says, in a voice flat as a foghorn. Then he says, "I can see you'd like to be left alone."

"I would, I really would. Thank you."

"Well, good night."

" 'Night."

He stayed where he was, not moving, not turning around and heading for the door like a normal person would've done. No, he just stayed there, waiting for me to deliver a few pearls of wisdom or something, or tell him he's got the worries of the whole fucking world on his shoulders and isn't it just the most unfortunate, terrible thing that's happened to him and it's a cruel injustice on someone who doesn't deserve it, blah blah blah. I stayed quiet. If I opened my mouth even to breathe he'd take it as an invitation and stay, pull up a chair and start puking up the garbage inside him that's weighing him down like ten yards of chain. Diane's right, he's got to learn how to cope on his own, or else he'll be like an old baby forever. So I didn't speak. He stayed where he was for at least two minutes. It seemed like two hours. In my head I'm saying, "Fuck off, fuck off, fuck off . . ." about a hundred times over, trying to *will* him away. In the end he turned and left. He banged his hip in the dark on the way out and gave this feeble little "Oh," partly surprise and partly because it hurt, and for a few seconds there I thought he'd use it as an excuse to stay and pry some sympathy out of me. I didn't even look in his direction, just stared at the ceiling till I practically burned a hole in it. Get out, get out, *get out, get out*, GET OUT, GET OOOOOOUUUUUTTT!

Click.

He's gone. Thank Christ for that. I've got enough trouble coping with my own load of shit without having to worry about his too. I'd like to go to sleep like Rip Van Winkle and wake up in thirty years or whatever it was, with a long white beard and no one around who'll recognize me. That'd suit me fine, because I don't want to see the sun come up tomorrow, because every time the sun comes up your troubles start all over again. The sun gives a new lease on life to misery, if misery is what you've got, and I've got plenty. But now that Gene's gone the spikes inside me are settling down again and the vodka is doing it's stuff, soothing me, making my head fuzzy, and I know the feeling of tiredness when it comes creeping along. Hello, tiredness, take me away. And it did.

I'm in Gene's trailer. He's sitting on a chair, looking at a TV screen with nothing on it but a hissing electrical blizzard. He sees me there and says, "The operation didn't work out, Burris. Something happened they didn't expect. It's awful. I'm ashamed. . . ."

"It's not your fault, Gene," I said, but really I'm thinking it probably *is*.

"But it went all *wrong*. . . ."

"Take it easy now."

"They said nothing like this ever happened before, Burris."

"So you'll make history."

I was trying the upbeat approach, see, trying to cheer him up.

"But this is *so* bad I can't show it, not even to the history people."

"Yeah? Are you sure?"

"I'd appreciate your opinion. You're very sensitive and intelligent for someone your age."

"I do my best, Gene, especially for friends."

Mr. Humble, that's me.

"But are you sure you want to see this? You might be shocked."

"I've been around, Gene. I'm pretty unshockable."

"All right, but promise me you won't make any loud noises and wake the neighbors."

"You mean like screaming? Ha, ha, I won't scream, I promise."

"All right."

And he scooted down low on his chair till his back is where his ass was, and his legs are straight out in front of him with the knees wide apart, and he's hauling his skirt back up his thighs, which are white with blue varicose veins, up and up till I can see he's not wearing any panties, and there it is, the vagina the doctors gave him, just like a regular vagina, a long, pulpy crease with hair around it, and I thought, What's he talking about? They did a great job, but then I see there's something wrong, because the vagina is *moving*, starting to bulge outward . . . now it's *opening* . . . something's coming out, something smooth and wet and slick-looking in the light from the TV screen, but it's not the head of a baby, it's a *parrot's beak* like in *20,000 Leagues Under the Sea* when the *Nautilus* is attacked by the giant squid and they surface and Captain Nemo goes out on deck with an axe to chop off the tentacles but one of them grabs him and starts hauling him toward the place where all the tentacles meet, this place with a slit in it, and out of the slit comes this fucking horrible parrot's beak, opening and closing, getting ready to chop Nemo in half, and it's so unbelievable I had to check it out in the library and it's *true*, a giant squid has this parrot beak for a mouth that he keeps tucked away inside himself until it's time to eat, then out it comes, and that's what Gene's got between his skinny old legs, this slit with a parrot's beak that pushes out when it's time to eat, and what it wants to eat is *me*, because Gene isn't in the chair anymore, he's moving toward me with his belly and chest pointed at the ceiling, moving toward me with his legs and arms, which are longer and skinnier than usual holding him clear of the floor like a limbo dancer, and he's coming toward me like a fucking spider with his arms and legs moving one at a time, slowly, so I'll be hypnotized by the beak opening and closing in his cunt, and he's saying soothing things to keep me where I am so's the beak can grab me, and it's exactly level with my crotch, so the first thing it'll grab is my cock and balls, grab them and tear them off and gulp them down with a few quick slashes of the beak, but I can't let it happen so easy, I just can't, only I'm frozen there, can't move a muscle, and the upside-down spider-thing is moving toward me with its cunt-beak going *click, click, click,* getting closer and closer, and still I can't move or make a sound and now the beak is grabbing me and *tearing my balls off*—

I jumped like I had ten thousand volts run through me, jumped in the air and came down with both hands grabbing at my crotch, and a scream that wouldn't come out plugging my throat like a cork. I'm scared shitless. I've rolled completely off the bed and I'm kneeling by it, shaking and twitching like crazy I'm so scared. That's the first time in my life I ever had a nightmare. It made me feel sick to think about. There's a screw loose upstairs if I can have stuff like that in my head, I mean it. I'm covered in sweat, really shaking. You read about the smell of fear, something animals can detect. Well, now I've smelled it for myself, *on* myself. It stinks. No wonder animals attack anything with the smell of fear on it. I'm ashamed to smell that way.

I took a shower. They left soap behind. There's no towel, but I dried off in the air in a few minutes and it felt good to leave my hair all wet, cooling my scalp and neck. The bad thing is, I'm wide awake now, and it's still dark, I don't know what time. I won't be able to go back to sleep, and there's no radio or TV in here, and I don't want to just sit and think about everything that's happened these last twenty-four hours. Solution? Gene—go see old Gene. Chances are he's still awake, too, the poor old fart. I was pretty rude to him before, practically telling him to fuck off. I'll go apologize, that's what I'll do. I only hope he isn't sitting in front of the TV with his legs apart and nothing on the screen but snow, ha, ha . . .

I got dressed and went over there. I didn't like putting on those dirty, sweaty clothes now that I'm clean, but I didn't have anything else. I knocked on the door but there's no answer, so I went in and fuck me if he isn't sitting in front of the TV with his legs apart and nothing on the screen but snow. Jesus . . . I'm not facing this in darkness. I turned on the light. His hand's got this huge fucking bandage wrapped around it, and he's slumped sideways in the chair with his head hanging over to the left and blood all down it. He's had an accident, I thought, then I figured he'd cut his wrist and that's why that big bundle of bandage is around his hand, but he's right-handed like most people and you cut your left wrist if you're right-handed, and the bandage is around his right hand, not his left, so he hasn't cut his wrist, and how would that explain the blood down the side of his head, anyway?

I went closer and saw what happened. He shot himself in the right temple. The big bandage is two white towels he's wrapped around the gun in his hand to deaden the noise, the same way Robert DeNiro did in *Godfather II* when he killed that old fat guy on the stairs. I unwrapped the towels. They were only a little bit scorched where they touched the end of the barrel. The gun was Gene's own fake .45 that's really just a .22. He probably needn't have bothered about the towels because a .22 makes hardly any noise if you've got the doors and windows closed. They must've left the gun behind when they went, which was dumb of them. Didn't they know it'd be a temptation to Gene? Maybe he convinced them he was okay, acted the part: "You go ahead, kids, I'll be okay, yes I'll be fine, you go on now . . ." They've killed him. And I have too. Go away, Gene, I said, leave me alone, and he did, he left me alone and came back over here and turned on the TV and wrapped towels around the .22 and shot himself in the head. I took a closer look. The hole is small and neat, not bleeding all that much—I mean, it bled some then stopped. The blood down his cheek and neck is dried already, so he did it a while ago. There's no exit hole on the far side, so the bullet's still in there. Those .22 rimfires don't have a whole lot of punch to them. Blasting through towels probably slowed it down too. There wasn't a lot of mess, no blood on the chair, even, just a little around the neck of Gene's dress. I picked up his left arm and dropped it again. It was like a hunk of cold rubber. No rigor mortis yet. I don't think that sets in till a few hours after death.

Old Gene's dead and not fretting anymore about the organs he lost eighteen months ago and the daughter he lost today. Why'd they leave the gun behind? Maybe it wasn't deliberate, maybe they just overlooked it in the rush to get packed and leave. But they took everything else, so why not the gun? Maybe Gene snuck it back over here when they weren't looking, and in the rush to get out of there they plain forgot about it. If that's what happened, it means old Gene was planning on suicide even when they were still here, hatching out the plan in his head while he watched them emptying cupboards and drawers and stripping the bed and all. Yeah, I bet that's what he did, watched them with a smile on his face to make them think he's okay, and while he smiled he swiped the gun and stuck it under his blouse or something and carried it away, getting himself set for dying. I bet when Lee came back he told Diane she's got a choice, him or Gene, and she agonized awhile and then chose Lee. I bet Gene's heart turned into a lump of coal when she told him, but he took it like a man, didn't let her know how he felt about being abandoned, smiled at her and told her she's right about him having to face up to things and not being able to lean on her forever, and they drove off, left him there with a .22 hid away, and then I came around and ended up in Diane's trailer, and he came over to see if maybe I'd talk him out of killing himself and I told him to leave me alone. So he went ahead and did it, only he didn't want to disturb the neighbors so he used the towels.

I'm to blame. Me and Lee and Diane. We killed him by turning our backs when he needed us. He should've been strong enough not to need us, but he wasn't. We all knew that and turned our backs, anyway. All three of us killed him. It's just that simple. I didn't feel sad about Gene, because in a way he's better off dead, and I didn't waste any time getting all crippled up with pangs of guilt or anything because I knew what I was going to do about this. I was going to do the *right thing*, the thing that'd kind of pay back what I owed Gene for being partway responsible for him killing himself. It was a good idea, a good plan to go ahead and do the right thing, and it came into my head like it'd always been there and just needed this opportunity to pop out in the open.

What I plan on doing, I plan on taking Gene home. I'll take him home to Tucumcari and show Lee and Diane what they did. It's the least I can do. It's not a crazy plan, it's a good plan, because it's the right thing to do. All three of us have to confront what we did to Gene, and it's up to me to make it happen. It isn't enough that *I* understand how and why it happened. The other two guilty parties have to acknowledge their part, too, have to admit they did wrong, the way I've done, and they have to do it the way I've done it, standing over Gene, seeing the actual evidence of guilt right there within touching distance. That's the way I'm going to do it, because that's the only way it can be done. Any other way is the wrong way. It's all perfectly clear and simple. I've got a mission. I've got a concrete objective. It's very important that I complete my mission. If I don't, it's an insult to Gene, and I won't ever be able to rest easy. I feel calm about all this. I know what I did wrong and I admit it. Now the other two have to admit it. It's my job to see that they do.

First I took off Gene's wristwatch and put it on. I never owned a watch before, and Gene won't be needing it anymore. Thank you, Gene. It's 3:57 A.M. I went through his purse on the table and took out the money in there, $259.43. Thank you, Gene. I took the car keys too. Thank you, Gene. I went out around back of the trailer and opened the Chrysler's trunk. Then I went back in and picked up Gene and carried him around back. He's skinny but tall, and he weighs a ton. Frankly, I couldn't do the job properly, like with a fireman's lift, I'm just not big enough, so after I got halfway to the car I had to put him down and just drag him. Sorry, Gene. I pushed him up and over and into the trunk gently as I could, then went back and got the .22 and the towels and threw them in, too, also Gene's purse. Then I packed up all his dresses and stuff in suitcases and put them in the backseat and the passenger seat. I left a big space in the backseat for the TV. I left that till last because it's a real bastard, almost as tough a job as getting Gene out there. I wanted it to look like he took off all of a sudden, the way Lee and Diane did. If I left stuff behind, especially expensive stuff like the TV, the manager'd get suspicious and call the cops, which would just complicate things and interfere with my mission.

Finally everything was in the car. I was proud of the way I got a tough job done with a minimum of noise, not letting the trailer door or the car doors or trunk slam, handling them very gently, making them go *click* instead of *bam!* I know I did the job well because no lights came on in the other trailers. I left the door key on the table the same way Lee and Diane did with theirs, then I got in the car and took a very deep breath. My mission truly starts here, when I turn the ignition key. It's mission ignition time. I turned the key. The engine turned over and caught. It's a well-tuned engine, pretty quiet. I turned on the headlights, put the car in gear and rolled out from behind the trailer, steered down the rows going nice and slow, then past the manager's office and onto the road that leads to the Interstate.

When I got there I pulled into the Amoco station and got myself a tankful of gas and checked the oil, paid for the gas, then pulled over next to the ice-vending machine in the corner of the lot. PARTY ICE 75¢ BAG, it says. There's no one around except the guy on duty in the cash booth, and he can't see me. I got twenty bags and opened up the trunk and packed them around Gene to keep him cool. It's summertime, and New Mexico is a long way away, and Detroit hasn't yet made a car with an air-conditioned trunk. Gene looked like he's sleeping there on his side. The plastic bags of ice were like a shiny blanket all around and over him, keeping him safe from harm. Don't you worry, Gene, I'll be looking after you from here on. You take it easy and I'll get you home.

I closed the trunk and paid for the ice. The guy didn't even want to know how come I need twenty bags so early in the day. I planned on telling him it's for a party tonight and I'm getting ready early, but I didn't have to say anything. Then I got back behind the wheel. It's 5:02 and time to go. I swung onto the Interstate and headed southeast, which is the direction it goes and the direction I want to go, too, and pretty soon I'm rolling along at a steady fifty-five, obeying the law and talking into my tape machine, getting it all down. My mission is under way. It's a good mission, a worthwhile one, and I'm confident I can bring it off. I feel very strong somehow. I know what I have to do for maybe the first time in my life, and it's a good feeling to have inside you.

We have lift-off.

The clock is running.

13

I've got around a thousand miles to go. It should take a couple of days, no more. Two mornings from now I'll roll into Tucumcari. I'll stay with the Interstates all the way for speed. I'm not here for sight-seeing. I'm a delivery man. The shadows were long and misty when the sun came up behind me. I'm not usually awake this early. The air was pretty cool, so cool I had to crank the window up a little. There's practically no other traffic in either direction, maybe an eighteen-wheeler snorting down the highway now and then, not much else. I shut my mind down for a while and just drove, feeding the road into the hood, grazing the white line with the left fender, steering an inch this way, an inch that way, listening to the wind flutter through the window gap. I like driving. It's still a big novelty for me. Looking out through the window is like watching a movie. I'm a camera, recording everything that comes at me from up ahead, bends and curves, bluffs and trees, billboards and route markers. I'm on Interstate 64 and I'll stay with it all the way to St. Louis, then go across to Kansas City on 70. I'm an ant on a roll of film that stretches away forever, and in two days I'll have crawled from one end to the other. Ants carry loads ten times their own weight. I'm carrying Gene. His death weighs a hundred times more than me.

Drive, drive, drive. At 7:41 I left Indiana. Now I'm in Illinois. At 9:08 I got hungry and stopped to eat. The burger bars really let you know they're up ahead. McDONALD'S—25M., BURGER KING—16M. They give you plenty of time to make up your mind if you're hungry. I was. I parked and went into Hardee's. I would've preferred to use the drive-through window, but I needed to take a dump. I did it fast and got out quick. I didn't like being away from Gene. Anything could happen. The trunk lock might develop a fault and spring open. I had to be on hand in case of emergencies. I practically ran back out into the parking lot. The trunk was shut and there was no one standing around it with crowbars.

I drove back onto the highway and pushed the Chrysler five m.p.h. over the limit to make up for lost time. Everybody drives at around sixty, anyway. Fifty-five is a dumb speed to impose on a four-lane Interstate. It's perfectly safe to travel at sixty-five or seventy on something this wide and straight. They lowered the limit to fifty-five back when the Arabs bumped up the price of oil, back when I was a little kid, but now there's a worldwide oil glut, so why make us drive slow to save gas? Everyone hates it. If I was a presidential candidate, I'd make repeal of the fifty-five m.p.h. speed limit, on Interstates anyway, part of my platform. I'd be swept into the White House on a landslide. That's a tip for free for presidential candidates.

St. Louis is *big*, even from a distance. I got there at 11:17 and got onto I-70, heading due west for Kansas City. We're in Missouri now. I got low on gas around then and pulled into a Mobil station. They've got KRYSTAL KLEAR ICE in the usual big chest over in the corner of the lot. After I got tanked up I waited till no one was around the ice chest, then drove over and dumped the old stuff just in time. It was all turned to water by then, but the bags were pressure-bonded so they hadn't leaked. I jabbed a hole in each one with my finger and slung them out of sight behind the dumpsters there. Gene's dress was cool and damp, so the ice is working okay, but I'll have to replace it more often. I packed fresh bags around him and slammed the trunk. There's a big puddle of melted ice water running out from behind the dumpsters, like blood from a wound. Pay for the ice. Time to go.

There's more westbound traffic than eastbound. It's vacation time, and Mr. and Mrs. Norman Normal plus Norm, Jr., and little Norma are striking out boldly for adventure in the Golden

West. They've got just the basic necessities with them—trailer with all home amenities, inflatable raft, trail bike, credit cards— and they're heading for the horizon along with their neighbors the Averages and the Mediums. They aren't stupid. They've planned this all year and their guidebooks are full of paper markers. They're gonna see *everything*. They've got a schedule, also a camera. They'll make Kodak even richer with their millions of three-by-five Grand Canyons and Yellowstones and Monument Valleys and Giant Sequoias with the matte finish so their friends and relations back home can handle the pics with envy and they won't get all marked up. What the fuck, I'd go see all that stuff, too, if I had the time and cash. But I'm only here to drive, drive, drive. Sometimes I forget Gene's in the trunk. I *forget!* It's like I'm driving for the sake of driving. I have always driven. I will always drive. It's all I can do. I *have* to do it. I'm driven to drive. I drive, you drive, we drive, they drive. Droves of drivers. Diverse drivers drove like demons. The wheel is melting in my hands, turning to rubber under my palms. Does rubber come from palms? Nah, that's coconuts. Rubber trees are not palms. I went up to a palm tree once. I asked it for a date, ha, ha! Rubber trees are hard to please. Rubber trees are full of fleas. Rub-a-dub-dub, keep drivin', Bub.

It's 1:10 now and the sun is a little ahead of me, throwing a lot of glare off the hood. I pulled over and opened the glove compartment. Flashlight, Rand McNally map, pocketknife, cer- tificate of title, insurance papers. There are never any gloves in the glove compartment, *never*. There's a pair of sunglasses, though, and I put them on. This very cool-looking dude looked back at me from the rearview mirror. I'm wearing Gene's shades, but I don't look like Gene. Even Gene didn't look like Gene. Gene looked like an old pioneer lady that had fifteen kids and died in a sodbuster's shack aged forty-five but looking sixty. Gene would've looked just like that if he had've worn a bonnet and gingham dress. I'm not being disrespectful, just stating the facts. I'm the custodian of Gene's remembered image. I'm the one that knows better than anyone else what he looked like. This camera never lies. This camera shoots through a third eye, one that gives added depth to whatever's in front of the lens. It's only got one setting—wide open. I catch all the light that ever spilled from the sky and pour it through the aperture of my third eye. My regular eyes *see*, but the third eye *transforms*, like one of those stereopticons with the two identical pictures mounted side by side that slide into each other and seem real when you look through the viewer. My eyelids are shutters. I blink, and a picture is recorded on a spool in my head—*click!* I take a dozen pictures per minute. I remember them all, especially the ones of Lee and Diane and Gene. I talk to the pictures, explain to them where all four of us went wrong. I analyze the whole thing brilliantly, I admit it. It's krystal klear. Only a moron would disagree with me as I drive my points home. Drive, drive, drive.

Another gas station, this time a Phillips 66. I've still got a quarter tank, but it's time to change the ice. It's *hot* out here. The bags are full of ice water again. Out they go with a finger hole to drain themselves. In goes the new ice, but these bags are only sealed with a plastic twist, so they'll leak like crazy if I leave them in there too long this time. I'll have to check them out after an hour. Missouri ice bags are inferior to Indiana and Illinois ice bags.

Now it's 6:03 and I'm coming into Kansas City. From here I have to switch to Interstate 35 and follow it down to Wichita. The glare is bad, and 35 aims itself southwest, so the sun'll still be in my eyes. Gene's shades weigh a ton because I'm not used to wearing glasses, but I have to keep them on. I've changed the ice five times now, and I've been driving for eleven hours. I'm kind of beat, but I'll try to make Wichita before I quit for the day.

7:04. Wichita's too far. My eyes are hanging out of my head and my ass is on fire. My hip's pretty bad too. Wellsville is where we'll stop for tonight. I pulled into a motel and got a room, set the air-conditioner, then walked back down the road a little way to a supermarket and got some stuff I could eat cold, some bran muffins and apples and two Hershey bars, the kind with almonds. Those babies are big. I'll save one for the highway tomorrow. I didn't want to be away from Gene too long, so I hurried on back to the motel and fed my face awhile. God, I'm tired. It's 8:32 and still light. I got in the car and went looking for an ice vendor to replace the bags for the last time today. This time I got twenty-eight bags, just to make sure, and I covered Gene but *good*. Then I drove back to the motel and took a shower that felt like liquid heaven, then I got in the bed and added a few more words to the tapes the way I've been doing all day, and now it's 9:56 and time for sleep. I haven't even watched any TV, very unusual for me. It can only be because I'm totally fucked.

3:29. I woke up and panicked, thought I heard voices outside. I peeked through the curtains but there's no one hanging around the car. I opened the door and poked my head out, just to be sure. No one. But I can hear a drip, drip, dripping from the back of the Chrysler, so I pulled on my pants and went out. There's a pool under the back axle you could breed frogs in. Shit! I opened the trunk, and the bags had all collapsed and emptied themselves everywhere. I pulled them all out, every one of them flat as a pancake or sloshing with a little water still, and dropped them in a dumpster at the end of the parking lot. The bottom of the trunk is sopping wet and so's Gene. Sorry, Gene. I figured things'd cool off in the night, but it's hot as ever. I had to drive to the same place I got the last load of ice and get more. There's only seventeen bags left in the chest, but they'll have to do. Before I loaded them in the trunk I took a traveling rug from the backseat and spread it over Gene. I've been an idiot, opening and closing the trunk all day to change the ice with Gene lying there big as life. What if someone came up behind me and saw him? I should've done this at the beginning, but I wasn't concentrating on details this morning. There's a heavy feeling to the air, like there's a big saucepan lid a few miles above Kansas and it's lowering itself slowly, squashing the air underneath it. I've gone and woken myself up again with all this activity, so why waste time trying to go back to sleep? I got Hershey bar number two from the room and started driving again at 4:21, out of Wellsville and back on Interstate 35 for Wichita. I got thirty miles down the road before I remembered I forgot to turn off the air-conditioning in the room. Oh, well, it'll be nice and cool for whoever comes in to change the sheets five or six hours from now.

Guess what. I've come about five hundred miles and I haven't turned the radio on once. Am I stupid or what? I forgot it was even there, I was concentrating so hard on driving. So now I turned it on and music fell out of the dash and wrapped itself around me. The windows are opened wide to catch the breeze and the sound of the engine was being scooped inside, so I had to turn that music way up to push it out again. The engine I can feel through my feet, but the rest of me is for feeling music through. One song after another spilled out into my lap and swirled around inside the car, like having a bunch of friends with you at a very crowded party. I drove my party across Kansas and we picked up a station from way off across the plains. The radio dial was green and yellow and friendly. If there wasn't a saucepan lid above Kansas I bet it could've picked up Radio Moondog. That's a radio station on the moon that plays nothing but the stuff I want to hear. It can reach me anywhere except under water. The DJ—that's Dog Jockey—he knows what I've heard over the last fifteen years, including oldies, and he's got a list of my thousand or so favorites, and he plays them back-to-back with no commercial interruption, great song after great song as loud as I want for as long as I want. It's a wonderful notion, Radio Moondog, but there's this saucepan lid covering everything, shutting out reception from Moondog's secret transmitter in the mountains of the moon, which is this long silver aerial poking up out of all the rocks and shadow, beaming a signal straight at my head. You might be asking yourself how come I never mentioned Radio Moondog before. There's a good reason for it. I just now made it up is the reason. Remember the tent of silence? I made that up in Wendy's. I never had a tent of silence before that. I'll probably make something else up before long. Only people who are dumb don't make things up. Not making things up is a sure sign of limited mental horizons. My mental horizons are wider than Kansas, so I make things up. But I don't cheat. If a thing is made up, I'll tell you. I'll slap a label on it that says NOT

REAL so you don't start wondering what's truly happening here and what's not.

Gene is dead and in the trunk. That's real, all right. I wouldn't kid you about a thing like that. Lee and Diane'll think I'm kidding when I tell them, but I'll bring them out to the trunk and open it up like a magician opening his magic cabinet, only they'll see Gene, not a girl in a spangled swimsuit. They're in for a shock, yes sir, and they deserve one for being just as big a pair of assholes as I am. If they deny their guilt I'll be angry, but more than that, I'll be *disappointed* in them. They already disappointed me by running off without saying good-bye, which was cowardly, I think, but it'll be worse if they deny they killed Gene, because then they'll have disappointed me on Gene's behalf, which is a serious crime. If that happens I'll remove them from my head, like snipping someone you hate out of a photograph. If they can't do what I did then they aren't worth squat, and I'll get my scissors and snip them out of my head, snip, snip, snip. But I'm optimistic. There's a fair chance they'll confess, and after they've admitted their guilt the way I've done, we'll bury Gene together. We're all the family he's got, so all three of us have to shoulder the responsibility. My third of it sits on my shoulders like a heavy cloak. It's a lot of weight to carry around, but I'm glad it's there because without it I'd be no one. With it I'm *the guy in the cloak*. No dagger, just the cloak. I don't need a dagger. I'm not afraid of anything. My mission has been a success so far, with only human weakness to delay things a bit. By human weakness I mean I have to stop the car to eat and sleep and crap. These are delays. Justice shouldn't be delayed like this, but it's an imperfect world. You have to make allowances. . . .

Somebody smashed a light bulb across the sky! There's another one, bright filaments scattering across the blackness and disappearing! Is it lightning or what? I pulled over and stopped the car, turned off the radio and got out. Jesus, it was quiet. There isn't another car's lights in sight, not a farm window or aircraft light—nothing. Then came a sound from up above me, a kind of ripping and rumbling, and another giant light bulb was smashed. Honest to God, that's what it looks like, not forks of lightning that snake down to the ground like you'd expect, it's *horizontal*, something I never saw before, like above me there's this huge sheet of glass, and someone up there is tipping these brilliant flashing things onto the glass, a big handful at a time, and they hit the glass and scatter across it, and a few seconds later the ripping and rumbling comes crunching down from above. I'm standing under a gigantic glass-topped table in the middle of a blacked-out room, and the only light is when more of these electric flashes are dumped onto the table and run to the edges and disappear. I stood there watching it for I don't know how long. It was the most *terrific* thing. Who would've thought lightning could travel sideways across the sky? Not me, I never heard of it before, did you, Gene? It's all new to Gene too. We felt pretty good about discovering something we never saw before, but we can't wait around even for something as wonderful as this. We've got places to go, things to do. Engine on, lights stabbing at the dark again. We're off.

We drove without the radio till dawn. I already had enough music in my head to keep me going, and the saucepan lid and glass table were left behind by the time the sun came up. It sat on the horizon over my shoulder like a fluorescent peach, then started floating up into the sky. The left rearview mirror beamed it straight into my eyes, and I had to reach out and adjust the angle so I can drive. Gonna be another hot one. Gene'll need more ice soon.

7:01 A.M. Wichita. More ice. Denny's for breakfast. Back on the road by 7:44. Now it's due south, still on 35, heading for Oklahoma City. We should get there by 11:00. Crossed the state line at 8:28. Oklahoma looks just like Kansas. There are signs alongside the road warning me not to speed. Oklahoma does not like speeders. Oklahoma imposes heavy fines. Not to worry, Gene, we're sitting on fifty-five like a hen on chicks. Mr. Law-abiding, that's me. Another change of ice.

11:12. Oklahoma City. We hang a right onto Interstate 40, heading due west. It cuts across northern Texas and runs into New Mexico. Tucumcari is on 40. Interstate 40 is also Route 66. Remember the old song, Gene? You're old enough to've sung it yourself when it was in the charts. But there won't be any kicks for me on Route 66, uh-uh. I'm here on business. Get down to business, Mr. Businessman. I'm getting down to business. This time tomorrow I'll confront my partners that ran out on Gene Inc. and left the company bankrupt. I'll propose a merger, like we had before. We'll be a holding company. Then we'll bury what we held.

Have you ever noticed that this country is dotted with fart zones? They're fifty, sixty miles apart on average. You're driving along and all of a sudden you smell a fart smell. Honest, it's just like a fart. It must be stagnant water or something, but every time we go through a fart zone I can't see any water around. I guess it only happens in summer when there's a lot of heat to decay things. In winter the fart zones probably disappear, get frozen up. You wouldn't know it if they didn't though, because in winter you drive with the windows up. But in summer it seems like you pass through a fart zone every fifty, sixty miles. It'd be a drag if you were with someone you didn't know too well, or someone who was kind of tense about anal stuff, someone you couldn't turn to and ask if they cut the cheese, ha, ha! But Gene and I are old friends, so we can joke about it. Fart zone, Gene! Roll up the windows! Too late, it's in the car. . . . *Aaaaaaggghhh . . . !*

1:41. We crossed the line into the Lone Star State. Remember the Alamo! That's where Davy Crockett died, way south of here. At 3:39 we passed through Amarillo. I've been noticing customized plates ever since we left Indiana. Some of them are pretty funny. There's a black guy in a white Trans Am and his plate says ST WISE. Geddit? And a little VW bug putt-putting along has got VROOM. There was one I saw back in Illinois, this sharp-looking Italian guy with a New Jersey plate that says DOO WOP. And bumper stickers are interesting too. HEY, BRUDDAH, KEEP YOUR EYES ON MY REAR END—NOT HERS! How about this one—YOU'RE UGLY AND YOUR MAMA DRESSES YOU FUNNY. Weird. Some are pretty ho-hum, like STREAKING PUTS COLOR IN YOUR CHEEKS. And let's not forget the Christian drivers—JESUS IS ALIVE! and GOD'S BUSINESS IS UPLIFTING. Boring stuff like that.

At 5:14 we crossed the state line again. Adios, Texas! It doesn't seem like such a big place when all you drive across is the square bit at the top. Now we're in New Mexico. It's only about fifty miles to Tucumcari! I thought it'd take forty-eight hours, but it's only gonna be around . . . uh . . . thirty-seven! That's because I only slept about five hours since we started. I'm not tired, though. We're too close to home for me to feel tired. I've changed the ice seven times today. Gene's cool as a cucumber back there. Almost home, Gene!

I started getting pretty excited, I admit it. My heart's all over my chest like a jumping jack, and my guts are kind of squirming around down there. Those last fifty miles even had me breathing funny by the time they're up. And there it is— TUCUMCARI NEXT EXIT. I steered off the Interstate. Good-bye, 40! So long, Route 66! Hello, Tucumcari! It's 6:18. I drove through town from one side to the other. It looks like a million other towns. One thing I noticed was a clock, and it says 4:23. Whaaaa . . .? That clock is *wrong*. No, it isn't. You know what I did? I forgot I crossed two time zones! I turned Gene's watch back two hours. Good. That gives me even more time to get things done.

Down to business. I parked by a phone booth and looked up Trimble in the book. There weren't many. I phoned the first one.

"Hello?"

It's a woman.

"Uh . . . hello. Could I speak to Lee, please?"

"Who?"

"Lee . . . Lee Trimble."

"I think you've got the wrong Trimble. There's no Lee here."

"Okay, thank you. . . ."

Click.

Try again.

"Hello."

A guy this time.

"Hello, is Lee there, please?"

"Lee? There's no Lee living here."

"I'm sorry. . . ."

Click.

Deep breath. Dial . . .

"Yes?"

A woman. She sounds friendly. She said "Yes?" with two syllables. That sounds friendly somehow.

"Uh . . . hello. Can I speak to Lee, please?"

"May I ask who's calling?"

Bingo!

"Uh . . . Burris."

"Pardon me?"

"Burris Weems."

"Weems?"

"Yeah, from Buford."

"Where?"

Jee-zuz . . .

"Buford. Tell him Burris Weems from Buford."

"I'm afraid he isn't at home right now," she says.

"Are you expecting him back sometime soon?"

No answer.

"Ma'am?"

"Yes . . . no, we're not expecting him."

"Well . . . uh . . . can you tell me where I could find him?"

"I'm afraid I don't know. We haven't seen Lee for some time."

"You mean he hasn't got back yet?"

"Back?"

"From Buford."

"I don't know anything about this Buford place, I'm sorry."

"Could you . . . uh . . . tell me when was the last time you saw Lee?"

"Lee left town almost a year ago now," she says, sounding kind of choked.

"Oh."

I'm getting panicky. Not only have I beat Lee and Diane back here, it sounds like they haven't lived here since they got married. I just assumed that when Gene sent for Diane to come help him, she and Lee were living here in Tucumcari, but come to think of it, there's no reason why they should've been. They hadn't told me different, so far as I recall, but they didn't say they lived in Tucumcari, either, just said they grew up and went to school and met each other here. And I thought Lee's parents were divorced. . . .

"Ma'am, are you Lee's mother?"

"I'm his aunt."

"Could you tell me where he went after he and Diane left here?"

"I don't know. He never wrote, never called. We haven't had any word in a year, and Diane's people are the same. I mean, her mother hasn't heard from her. Her father hasn't lived here for some time. Have you seen Lee recently?"

They won't be coming back here. Gene didn't know where they were headed when they left Buford. He said he didn't know, then he said Tucumcari, or maybe it was the other way around. Either way he was just guessing, maybe *hoping* it was here, like Tucumcari is where all three of them came from and the only way they could get together again is back here, no place else, but it ain't so, Joe. That was wishful thinking, not facts. They won't be coming back here. They could be just about anywhere in the U.S.A. I've come on a wild-goose chase.

"Are you there?"

"Uh . . . yes."

"Where have you seen Lee, and when?"

"Oh, a few months back now, up in Oregon."

"Was he well?"

"He's fine. Diane too. Excuse me, ma'am, I thought Lee lived with just his father."

"I'm only here for the afternoon, tidying up. You know how men on their own are. He's not here right now because he works most Saturdays."

"I didn't mean to bother you or anything."

"No, no, I'm glad you rang. We haven't heard anything for so long. Vern is unhappy about the way things were between them. Did Lee tell you anything about that?"

"He just said they didn't get along."

"Vern has changed since then. When you see Lee, be sure

and tell him Vern has changed. Are you going to see him soon?"

"I dunno. See, I thought I'd find him here."

"Oh. I don't think that's likely, not unless he told you he was coming back."

"He didn't do that, no. I just thought maybe he'd be here, and seeing as I'm passing through, I thought I'd drop by and say hello."

"You could come by, anyway," she says, sounding eager. "I'm sure Vern would like to know how he's getting along—and Diane."

"I don't think I can do that. I'm with some people, and they want to keep moving if Lee's not here. . . ."

"I'm sure we could accommodate you and your friends," she says.

She's reaching down the phone to grab me, hold me there till she finds out everything.

"No . . . no thank you."

I hung up. The booth is like a sweatbox. I'm slick with it. The door wouldn't open and there's no more air in there. I pulled and pushed, and finally it folded and let me through. At least the air out here is moving, chilling the sweat that's poured off me. They won't be back here. They could be *anywhere!* I brought Gene all this way to confront them, and they're not here and most likely won't ever be here again in their *lives*. It's all been for nothing. . . . I felt like throwing up. What am I gonna do now? A few minutes back I had life by the scruff of the neck, now I'm a kid a long way from home with a dead body in the trunk of a stolen car. Tucumcari means nothing more to me now than all the other towns I passed through to get here. It was supposed to be the end of the road, but it's just another dot on the line, and now I don't even know where the line is heading. One thing's for sure, I can't stay here. I've been inside the city limits maybe twenty minutes, and already it's time to leave. I can't breathe properly. The air is so hot, it's frying my lungs. I got back in the Chrysler. It used to be my chariot, now it's a hearse. I used to share it with Gene, but now I'm alone. Gene is just meat. Without Lee and Diane he doesn't have a *purpose* anymore, and neither do I. One phone call is all it took to turn everything upside down.

I drove back to Interstate 40 and kept going west. What else could I do? I can't go home. I bet the manager of Green Acres got suspicious when he saw how both trailers got vacated in a big hurry. Did he find any blood in Gene's? I didn't see any except what was on Gene, but the light in there was pretty crummy, so maybe there were a few drops that he snooped around and found. He would've told the cops, and they would've asked if Gene had any visitors, and the manager'd say there was this shortass kid with a gimpy leg, some kind of fruit pervert. They've probably already got a description of me flashing from teleprinter to teleprinter across the country, and Gene's car, too, because the manager'd have the make and model and plate number on record. Would they be looking outside Indiana yet? Maybe they're already looking in New Mexico. The Chrysler's got New Mexico plates. I better get out of the state. The shortest way is back to Texas, but I don't want to go that way. I had to keep going west, don't ask me why.

Oh, Jesus, Jesus, Jesus . . . Everything's turned to shit in my hands. For two days I was a man with a mission, now I'm a fugitive with hounds on my trail. It's making my guts turn over, I'm so scared. Why did I dream up this cockeyed scheme to bring Gene home? How is it possible that someone smart as me could've made such a colossally huge error of judgment? Was I temporarily insane or what? When I found Gene dead, I should've left quietly and never gone back. It would've been nothing more than a few seconds' airtime on the local TV news—Suicide found in trailer—*finito*. But the story's just beginning, and it's gonna be a fucking chase movie. Shit shit shit shit *shit!* I'm so worried and scared, I'm farting. I do that when I get very, very nervous. I fart and fart and can't stop because my guts are churning so bad. I'm in a permanent fart zone, carrying it along with me, the smell of fear coming out of my ass instead of my skin. The sun is ahead of me, sinking but still white-hot. Without Gene's shades I'd drive off the road. What am I gonna *do?* Drive, drive, drive; drive and survive. I can't talk anymore right now.

7:00. The sun's getting lower, turning orange. I can't talk now, either.

8:32. Albuquerque. It's not quite dark. The Interstate runs right through town, not around it the way it generally does. Lots of lights. I feel better now that the sun's going down, safer somehow. I've been driving for eighteen hours since Wellsville, Kansas, but I don't feel tired. I've got a pile-driver headache, but I don't feel like resting or sleeping. I want to be out of New Mexico before midnight. Or I'll turn into a pumpkin, ha, ha! My sense of humor is still with me, so I'm not as scared as I thought, or maybe I'm just getting used to the idea of being a fugitive. Back in Tucumcari I felt like someone pulled the floor out from under me and I went down into the crocodile pit, but now I've quit moaning and groaning and farting. Now I just drive, drive, drive. I tried the radio, but the music just annoyed the hell out of me. On the hour and half hour I've been listening to the news, but there's nothing about me. Sudden thought: Maybe they're after Lee and Diane, not me. The manager didn't seem to know they were related to Gene, but the fact that they disappeared at the same time as him is pretty suspicious. Maybe the manager won't remember me being there. . . . Nah, he'll remember me for sure after the back talk I gave him about cops' crotches and all. And the neighbors'll probably remember that Gene's car was still there hours after Lee's crappy old pickup came and went with him and Diane and their things inside it. No, it's me they're after. So why isn't there anything on the news? Maybe they're keeping it under wraps for the moment, not wanting to alert me by way of public announcements, trying to make me feel secure. No chance, Vance. I've seen that movie before. I know you're making every effort to apprehend me, news or no news. I wish I had a CB radio or something I could intercept the police wavelength with. Can CBs do that? I don't know. Maybe truckers could tell if there's a roadblock ahead.

"Breaker, breaker. This is Flarn Fish, lookin' for Arceman. You heah me out there, Arceman?"

"Iceman here, Flying Fish, on the line and hearing fine. Whatall you got for me?"

"Got a messa smokeys on I-40 jes' westa Gallup. 'Pears t'me they lookin' for someone. If I's you, I'd hang me a tight right onto 371 at Thoreau, then a lef' at Crownpoint an' head on outa the state by waya Standin' Rock. Gonna be smokey-free out thataway."

"Appreciate it, Flying Fish. Iceman out."

Only in the movies, pal, only in the fucking movies. There aren't any roadblocks ahead of me, anyway. Cops don't move that fast, computers or no computers, and they don't start murder manhunts until they're sure someone's been murdered, which they can only be sure of if they've got a stiff on their hands, which they haven't because the stiff is in the trunk back of me, which means I have to dump it. I've got to get rid of the car too. These are things I have to do, have to do, have to, have to, have to, hafta hafta hafta hafta hafta drive drive drive drive

drive

drive

drive

drive

drive

drive

drive

14

11:48. I'm over the state line into Arizona. I won't turn into a pumpkin, after all. It's Gene that's turning into a pumpkin. He's getting bigger and oranger, and bigger and oranger, and if I don't get rid of him he'll buckle the trunk and pop the lock and show himself to the world like a second sun, swelling and rising out of the trunk like daybreak. But not yet. Every car that overtakes me looks like a police cruiser in my mirrors. I clench up inside until they're past me, and they're never police cruisers. There isn't much traffic on the highway now that it's getting late, mainly long-distance haulers that have a schedule to keep. Vacationers are bedded down for the night in their trailers and Winnebagos and Kumfy Kabins and Ramada Inns. I'll keep going till the highway's practically empty. What I've got to do needs privacy.

12:19. I'm coming up to a rest area, turning off the road, driving slow. The place is deserted, just a parking lot and toilets and a few picnic benches and trash cans. I've pulled in here because stopping on the highway might make a Good Samaritan stop, too, and ask if he can help. I got out and opened the trunk. Quick as I can, before someone behind me decides now's the time for a crap, I hauled out all the bags. There's no ice left in them at all, just water, and there's plenty more water sloshing around under Gene. I flung them wherever they wanted to go—*splat! splosh! splish!* Then I got the towels and crammed them in a trash can, then changed my mind and pulled them out again. The guy that empties the bins might get suspicious of towels with blood and powder burns on them. So I ran to the edge of the parking lot, which is separated from the desert by this little concrete curb, and I jumped over it and ran a little way more and shoved the towels under some brush, then ran back to the car again. The trunk's still leaking water like crazy. I slammed it shut. Why did I leave it open after I flung the bags out? Someone could've come along while I was off in the darkness getting rid of the towels. A car standing there with its trunk open and no one around would've looked pretty suspicious. I'm an idiot. I have to *think* about what I'm doing. Think, think, *think*, idiot!

Back behind the wheel and back onto 40. Drive, drive, drive.

1:20. Almost no traffic at all. Now is the time. I've got to get rid of Gene pronto, got to *dump* him, but I can't do it along 40 because there's this wire fence all along the Interstate on both sides, and he's got to be dumped a long ways from the road so he doesn't get seen. What I'll do, I'll take the first exit I come to and dump him on some little old dirt road away from everything. Where there's a will there's a way. So they say. Hey, hey, hey.

1:32. I did it—got off 40—and now I'm on a regular two-lane blacktop heading I don't know where, but there's no wire fence alongside it that I can see, and no traffic on it, either. Do it, do it, *do it*, you chickenshit bastard!

2:11. It's done. What I did was, I slowed down and stopped, turned off the engine and got out. No noise anywhere, and no lights. No cars coming. This place is the original middle of nowhere. I got back in the car and started it up but turned the lights off. I couldn't risk getting seen. I know there's no one around, but a smart person takes precautions anyway. I swung off the shoulder and started bouncing across the desert. There's a three-quarter moon, and I could see where all the runty little bushes are, mesquite or whatever, and at five m.p.h. there wouldn't be any accidents, but I drove with my head out the window just to make sure, because if I get stuck here I'm in shit city for sure, and another thing, I can't use the brakes because even when the lights are off, the brake lights work, otherwise brake lights'd be useless in the daytime, right? So I can't use the brakes. Someone back on the highway might see those red lights off in the sagebrush and get suspicious. Is sagebrush the same thing as mesquite? Tumbleweeds are the ones that roll along with the wind. I drove at least a mile from the road. Every time I told myself I'd come far enough, I made myself drive a little further, and a little further, and a little further still.

Far enough. I bumped to a stop and killed the engine. Silence. I got out and opened the trunk. Out came the blanket. And there's Gene. And without the blanket to keep it in, a smell came out like a swarm of bats. He stinks. Maybe the ice helped keep it down, but he's definitely started to turn. Also, he's shat himself. I didn't know a dead body could do that. Maybe it's got something to do with the muscles relaxing totally after rigor mortis has gone. Most people think rigor mortis is permanent, but it isn't; it goes away after eight or twelve hours, something like that. I saw it on *Quincy*. The stiffness of the stiff was crucial to solving the case, and that stuff about rigor mortis going away after a while kind of stuck in my head. But I've never seen anything on *Quincy* about corpses shitting themselves. It's interesting in a disgusting kind of way, but I guess it isn't exactly a subject for prime time, even on a show about a county coroner. Anyway, Gene stinks, frankly. I had to be careful how I picked him up. I didn't want a dead man's shit on me. I know that sounds callous, but would *you* want a dead man's shit on you? No you wouldn't, so don't sit in judgment. I couldn't get him out by lifting, I'm just not strong enough, so in the end I had to haul one end of him over the rim of the trunk, then the other, till he topples out onto the ground like a sack of turnips. I didn't want to touch him anymore, so I let him stay right there. There's no better place to put him, anyway, just more flat, sandy desert with mesquite bushes all over. He's okay where he is. What I planned on doing was, I planned to make it look like suicide, which is what it was, anyway, but I had to make sure that's what it'll look like if he's ever found. To do that I had to touch him again, after all, because when you die, the blood in your body sinks to the lowest points and collects there, and seeing as Gene's been lying on his left side for forty-eight hours, you can bet that's where his blood's pooled. They'd get suspicious if they found him on his right side like he is now, and his blood over in the left side. You have to think about stuff like that. So I turned him over and arranged him pretty much the way he was in the trunk. Then I put the gun in his hand. Then I took it out of his hand, wiped my prints off it with my shirt, then put it back in his hand to put *his* prints on it, then shook his wrist so the gun fell out of his grip and landed a few inches away, the way it would've if he'd truly killed himself here. With any luck they won't find him for a long time, and the business about the pooled blood won't even count because he'll just be bones. They'll wonder what a male skeleton is doing in a dress, but I can't cover every angle. I've done it. I've dumped the body.

Time to go. I looked up. It's true what they say about desert stars. You can see thousands more out here than in town because the air's so clear. When I was a little kid I read a book about astronomy, but I just couldn't get hold of how big the universe really is, all that stuff about billions of galaxies rushing away from each other like dots on the skin of an expanding balloon, and the concept of the light-year knocked me right out. I had to reduce it all, make an infinite universe compact again, but without making it small, so what I did was, I put the entire universe, all those billions and billions of galaxies, in a jar, an ordinary glass jar with a screw top, like a jar of floating diamond dust, and put the jar on a shelf in the pantry in the castle of the fee-fi-fo-fum giant that lives at the top of Jack's beanstalk. I could accept an infinite universe so long as it was inside the giant's jar, stuck way back on the pantry shelf, glowing and sparkling there in the dark.

Time to *go*. I crawled the Chrysler back to the blacktop without lights, then swung onto the road and turned my lights back on. Thirty seconds later I'm cruising along as though my side trip into the mesquite never happened. It only took a little while to get back to Interstate 40. I'm still heading west. I just now ate the Hershey bar I had left over from yesterday, just a sticky brown goo studded with almonds. I never tasted anything better in my life. I'm proud of the way I thought everything out and went through with it without losing my cool. The car's still a problem, though. A forensic expert could still find evidence of Gene's stay in the trunk, so I have to get rid of it as soon as I can. Forensic science is what catches criminals today. I bet the blanket is full of stuff from Gene's body . . . *and I left it back there!* I didn't mean to do that. I was gonna throw it away miles further on down the highway. Shit! Would a suicide have a blanket with him? Probably not. Suspicious . . . Maybe he *would* have a blanket with him. Who knows what goes on in the minds of suicides? Come to think of it, how'd he get there, miles from anywhere? They'll ask that for sure . . . *and I left tire tracks!* His car couldn't have driven itself away! Double suspicious! They'll know he was dumped . . . unless rain washes the tire tracks away meantime, or the wind does it. . . . That's what'll happen. Rain and wind. They'll figure he hitched out into the desert, then wandered off the highway with a blanket and a gun and blew his brains out. Is it believable? I dunno. It's gonna have to do. Hafta, hafta, hafta *doo* doo doo doo. . . .

3:18. Flagstaff. I've been awake and driving for around twenty-four hours. I'm so tired I could fall asleep at the wheel, but I won't, and I won't stop here, either. I'll keep going, and not on 40. I've been on 40 for too long. Time for a new direction. There's a signpost up ahead . . . your next stop, *The Twilight Zone.* No, I'm kidding. It says PHOENIX—17 SOUTH—NEXT RIGHT. Okay, Phoenix it is. Hanging a right. So long, Flagstaff. So long, 40.

6:11. Phoenix. A big place. Now I truly am falling asleep at the wheel. Pulling over at the first motel I see. Desert Motel. I bet there's plenty called that down here in cactusland. Going inside now.

6:17. But really it's only 5:17 because Arizona doesn't put its clocks forward an hour in summer like the rest of the country, don't ask me why. The night clerk couldn't tell me, either. When I registered, I saw the clock behind him is an hour slow and I told him, being a pedantic bastard as usual, even if I'm half dead, and he told me what I just said about Arizona time, but he doesn't know why they stick to Standard Time all year round. So, anyway, it's 5:17—5:18 now—and I dunno if I can take my duds off or not, I'm so beat. I forgot to say I gave a false name and wrote that I'm driving a Ford with a number nothing like Gene's. They never bother checking stuff like that. It'd be a police state if they did. It's a shame I didn't do the same thing at the motel in Kansas, but I was a different person then, a man with a mission, a fucking *crusader* or something. I wasn't feeling scared about anything then, just careful, obeying the speed limit, et cetera, and feeling so fucking self-righteous about taking Gene home, I saw myself as . . . I dunno . . . invulnerable, maybe. I definitely had God riding shotgun in the passenger seat, if you know what I mean. I was doing the *right thing* back then, so nothing could go wrong, so why use a false name? Too late now. Jesus, I'm tired. I'm set to be snuffed out like a candle wick sputtering in its own pool of grease.

Knock! Knock! Knock!

I came awake in a flash, but the door's already opening. A Mexican lady poked her head in and saw me. "Excuse me," she says, and backed out again. I forgot to put the *Do Not Disturb* sign on the door. Bright sunshine outside. I felt like shit, but got dressed and left anyway. Two women were piling dead laundry in a mobile basket, wheeling it from room to room. They didn't see me leave. I drove downtown and ate. I should've showered before I left. My head's itchy. I haven't washed my hair since Thursday night in Diane's trailer, and now it's Sunday morning. Things to do today. Dump the car. Change my appearance. Buy a bus ticket out of here.

I drove around till I found a Mega-Mart, parked and went in. I came out again with a paper bag, inside of which is a new T-shirt, new socks and shorts, a cheap electric hair clipper, scissors, hair dye, a hand mirror, comb, razor and shaving foam, the Acme Disguise Kit, guaranteed to fool even your closest friends. Then I drove around till I found the poor part of town, which I won't embarrass the city fathers by naming, ha, ha, and I parked the car in an alley and unscrewed the plate with a nickel. I put the plate and everything from the glove compartment into my Mega-Mart bag and walked away. I left the window open and the key in the dash. There's a TV and four suitcases inside. It'll all be gone inside an hour, the Chrysler resprayed a different color by sundown.

Back to the center of town. It's already past noon. My legs are killing me. I've got out of the walking habit just lately. I got another motel room, the cheap kind. I'll only be here a little while, but I have to pay the full daily rate. I need privacy. I couldn't do what I'm going to do in a public washroom. I locked the door and got everything laid out around the bathroom basin. First I took all my clothes off, then I started. I held the clippers in one hand and the mirror in the other and angled it so I can see my profile in the big mirror over the basin. Contact! *Bzzzzzzzzzzzzzzz* . . . I shaved both sides of my head from temple to neck. It was easy with the gizmo. Look, Ma— *ears!* There's a strip of hair left down the center of my scalp like a hedge that needs trimming. I combed it out and used the scissors to crop it down to a couple inches so it stood up like the mane on one of those ancient Greek horses, except at the back where I left it long, like a tail. My arms were aching by then from holding things up in the air around my head for so long. I rested ten minutes then got going again, this time using the razor to shave the shaved parts *real* close. I didn't have any accidents. You can't cut yourself with a bonded razor unless you're a complete klutz. But I'm not through yet.

I got in the shower and washed my body and what's left of my hair. It made me feel clean and good. Then I got out the hair dye and read the instructions. It says there's enough in the bottle to use on the amount of hair indicated in the picture, which shows a girl with enough hair to hang herself. I've only got a fraction of that, but I used the whole bottle, anyway. It took around thirty minutes because you have to let it soak in. I sat on the toilet seat with my head in a towel, and waited, listening to the air-conditioner, almost nodding off to sleep. Time's up at last. I rinsed my hair and took a look in the mirror. *Wow!* That is *not* Burris Weems, it's Johnny Puke, king of punk. The strip was red as a rooster's comb. It didn't look like hair at all. No time to waste admiring myself. I swept up every bit of hair with my hands and some damp toilet paper and dumped it in the john, then I tore up all Gene's Chrysler papers, tore them into little bits and dumped them in there too, then launched it all on a long trip through the sewers. I got dressed in my new duds and my old pants, then put everything except the empty dye bottle and Gene's plate back in the Mega-Mart bag. I bent the plate practically double and took it and the bottle and the messy towel out to the trash cans and got rid of them. Then I went back in, put on my shades, picked up my bag of goodies, and left.

All that took a long time. It's 3:43 P.M. now. In the room I looked up the Greyhound depot in the phone book. There was a map in the back so I know where to go. I got there at 4:11 and went to the ticket counter. The girl there took one look at me and this expression of disgust came over her. You could see it come down over her face like a storefront grille.

"Yes?"

Very cold. She's some square person, all right.

"When's the next bus to L.A.?"

"Seven-fifteen," she says.

I got a ticket. She didn't want to touch the money, wanted to pick it up with pastry tongs, but she didn't have any. She also hates me because I'm short, not a real *man*. It was pretty funny. People looked at me like that all the way from the motel to the depot, and the way I look isn't even original or new or anything. What a bunch of dickheads people are—ninety percent of them, anyway. I bought a stack of newspapers and sat down to read them. Nothing about a body found out in the desert, no have-you-seen-this-man pictures of me. I'm safe for now. No body, no car, new identity. In L.A. I'll start a new life. I'll *embark* upon a new *life-style*. Life in the fast lane, baby. I've already got the haircut for it. After paying for my ticket I've got $237.51 left out of my Servex wages and Gene's cash, plus the clothes on my back and my Mega-Mart bag of stuff. I'm definitely traveling light. This had advantages and disadvantages. It means I've got practically nothing to lose, but it also means I can't afford to buy very much of anything. From what I've heard, $237.51 will keep me alive in L.A. for about seven minutes. This is a problem I'll solve when I get there, but I definitely, *positively* won't be selling my tight little asshole, no sir. I'll get regular work if I have to. Trouble is, no one's going to hire me for regular work with a haircut like this. Relax, Max, there'll be something.

I dumped the papers and walked around the depot awhile, then got bored looking at people waiting around for buses and went outside. It must be close to a hundred today. I haven't had lunch yet and I'm starving. I went down the street a little way and found a diner. I had a Pepsi and a Danish. Then I had another Danish. It filled the hole in my gut but didn't do a thing to beat the heat. It's hot, Dot. It's sweaty, Betty. I'm dyin', Brian. I got another Pepsi. Cheers, Geraldine. Will she do better in advertising than she did in politics? The nation anxiously awaits the outcome of her daring switch. Yawn. Burp. Fart. Do people really drink one particular brand of fizzwater instead of another because of the face beside the can, the face with a dopey smile and a hand under it pointing to The Product? Yeah, I bet they do. It's almost enough to make you turn commie. A police cruiser went by outside, drifted past the window like a mirage, but my pulse only went up half a notch. You ain't got nothing' on me, flatfoot. I dunno nothin' 'bout nothin'. Gimme my rights. I wanna lawyer. I guess we'll have to let him go, Sergeant. We have no concrete evidence except the concrete around the victim's feet, a most unusual case—the concrete was in the shape of pineapples. A menace to society is turned loose every 3.7 minutes, and the hands of the police are tied by bureaucratic red tape. And very fetching it looks too. Time is on my side, Clyde. Unless Gene gets spotted by one of those police radar planes that fly along the highway interfering with the right of citizens to drive in excess of fifty-five m.p.h. He's a good mile from the road, but if the plane's high enough, they might see him lying there. What color was his dress? Pale blue. How pale? Will it blend in with the dust and mesquite? Maybe. And the blanket was a brown-and-green plaid, pretty good camouflage. I should've covered him with it and to hell with making it look like suicide. Or maybe things are better the way they are. Coyotes have probably ripped his dress off by now, anyway. Gene's probably loping across the desert in a

dozen different bellies. I bet they didn't eat the bags of silicone
in his chest. I did my best, Gene, but I fucked up. Sorry.
Better luck next incarnation, and this time try and make up
your mind which sex you want to be and stick with it, okay?

I'm just so glad to be out of that car, away from the whole
mess. It's a miracle I wasn't nabbed, taking a body across eight
states like that. The Big Mission. Hello, I'm your friendly
iceman. We deliver promptly, with a smile. *The Iceman Cometh.*
We were all set to do that play last year, but the principal
vetoed it, said it was too pessimistic for kids to read. Mr. Brock
the English teacher was pissed about that. We ended up doing
Our Town, a real slice of the old apple pie. One of these days I'll
read the *Iceman* play. I'm pretty pessimistic by nature, so I
could handle it. I hate it when they pick you to play a role in a
play, trying to make you "join in." I always read the lines like
they're in Arabic or something, and they drop me fast and pick
someone else. But some people really go ape for that stuff—
exhibitionists, mainly, like Connie Russell. She thinks she's
destined to be a big star because she always gets picked for an
important role, like in *Our Town* she's this girl that's getting
married and runs around like a headless chicken on the wed-
ding day. She really throws herself into it, I'll give her that, but
seeing as she's got eyes that look in different directions she'll
either have to have surgery or suck plenty of dick to make it in
Hollywood. Memorial High was full of dippy characters like
that, forming bands and making big plans to be celebrities
someday. It's kind of pathetic and kind of brave, too, I guess.
I'm no different. I think one day I'll be famous. The only
difference between me and those other jerks is, I don't know
yet *how* I'll achieve my incredible goal. I mean, I don't know
what I wanna *be*. It's a big problem, I admit it.

The girl who served me is looking at me all the time, but not
the kind of look that says she wants to screw me or anything,
uh-uh, it's the kind of look that says she's waiting for me to piss
on the floor or eat a live bat or something. It's the haircut. It's
very effective at making people think I'm someone completely
unlike the real me. But that's why I did it, right? Right. Or is
she looking at me because I'm talking into my Sony? Shit, I

didn't even *think*, just went ahead and started talking into it. I
was doing it pretty softly, though. Did anyone hear anything
incriminating? Nah, there's only a few other people in here,
none of them close to me. It's Sunday and ninety-plus. Who's
interested in anything on a day like this?

I left anyway, and started gimping along the street. That's
another thing I'll have to try and disguise. The cops'll be
looking for someone with a limp. *If* they're looking for me,
which they're *not*. A cab drove by and for a second there I
thought it was Loretta behind the wheel, but it isn't, it's
someone else. Maybe they have lots of lady cabbies in Phoenix.
I wonder if she made up her mind to marry Pete. I won't ever
know, not if I make a run for L.A. I'll be a fugitive. I won't
even be able to call home because the line'll be tapped. I won't
know what's happening with Peggy and Loretta, and that's not
good. Wait a minute. I don't *know* I'm a fugitive. I don't know
anything. If I *am* a fugitive, I'll have to scram to L.A., but if I'm
not . . . if I'm *not*, I can go home. I can *go home*. I won't have to
sell my ass on Sunset Strip. I can go home instead. *If* I'm not a
fugitive. Why did I disguise myself before I knew one way or
the other? I must've panicked. That's the only explanation.
Jesus Christ, I don't know if I'm coming or going. Drivers are
looking at me. I'm standing in the middle of the sidewalk with a
paper sack in one hand and a tape recorder in the other. Am I a
fugitive or not? If not, I can just go on home. Go back, Jack.

I ran—I mean, *ran*—till I found a phone booth. I fed the slot,
dialed the number, rapping my knuckles on the glass. Come
on, come *on* . . .

"Hello?"

It's Loretta. She's at our place for once.

"Hi, it's me."

"Burris?"

"Nah, Errol Flynn."

"Burris, where the hell have you been since Thursday? Peggy
says you had a terrible fight with her and left."

"Yeah, that's right. I'm really sorry about it now. It was
dumb, what I did. I apologize."

"Don't apologize to me, apologize to Peggy."

"Uh . . . is she there?"

"She's over at Mack's. I'll give you the number."

"That's okay. Has anyone been asking after me?"

"Like who?"

"I dunno, *any*body. Has anyone been making inquiries or anything?"

"Burris, are you talking about the police?"

"Shit, no! Why would I be talking about the police? I meant, have any friends been asking about me, where I am and stuff?"

"I thought you were *with* your friends. That's what you told Peggy."

"Yeah, I meant *other* friends."

"No one's been inquiring. Where are you, anyway?"

"No police or anything?"

"You *are* in trouble, aren't you."

"No! Peggy said she'd sic the cops on me, that's all."

"Well, she didn't. You should know her better than that."

"I was just wondering. Hey, did you decide to get married?"

"Not yet. When are you coming home?"

"I'll be back in a couple of days."

"Where *are* you?"

"Right there in Buford . . . *here* in Buford. I just need to do some things before I come home, okay?"

"I think you should give Peggy a call and talk with her first."

"Sure, sure, I'm all out of time now. Great talkin' to ya, Sis."

"Burris, don't *ever* call me Sis."

"Okay, Sis. Be seein' ya!"

I hung up.

I ran back to the Greyhound depot.

"When's the next bus to Buford, Indiana?"

She took her time looking at the sheet.

"Fifty minutes. Change at Flagstaff."

"I wanna change my ticket."

"I don't know if there are any seats left."

"Couldja find out for me, please? I'm in a hurry."

She took her time again, but there's a seat. I had to pay over a hundred bucks extra. It's a whole lot longer trip from here to Buford than here to L.A., but I don't care. I'd pay a million.

I'm going home. Home is where the heart is. Home, sweet home. There's no place like home, Jerome. I can't believe I was actually planning on going to L.A. What the fuck would a guy like me do there? You've got to be totally weird to exist in an environment like that. I'm a small-town boy, Joy. I'm a back-woods kid, Sid. I'm a down home cat, Matt, no longer a roamer, Homer. I feel great! I'm going *home*. There's no one after me. The manager didn't find any blood, he just figured his tenants left in a hurry; so what, they paid till the end of the week already, so who cares? There's no evidence of suicide or murder or anything. No one's looking for anyone and I'm going *home*. I felt so happy, I even liked the snotty bitch behind the ticket counter. I'd have licked her genitals if she asked me nice, I really would. But she probably figures I'm such a punk pervert I'd only do it if she's got the flag flying. Well, maybe I would at that. I'd do just about anything, the mood I'm in. I walked around and around, looking at my watch, looking at the clock, sucking that Greyhound toward me by willpower, wanting it to get here so I can start back home. C'mon, *c'mon!*

Drive that bus, Gus!

15 It's night, 3:37 A.M. if you want to know. We're out of Arizona and halfway across New Mexico. As a matter of fact Tucumcari is the next stop, about an hour away. I felt better when we crossed the state line, and I'll feel safer still when we're past Tucumcari, too, don't ask me why. I can't truly relax until Texas, which'll be about an hour before dawn.

Everyone's asleep around me but I'm talking soft, anyway. There was a guy sitting next to me from Phoenix up to Flagstaff, which is where I changed to an eastbound bus practically right away, but no one's next to me now, so I've got plenty of room. I even tipped the armrest up so I could get really sprawled out and comfy, or as a TV newsperson would put it, I maximized my ongoing comfort situation. It's pretty damn maximized, let me tell ya. I'm too happy to sleep, though. The lights are out except for those blue strips in the roof and an orange light over the door to the john down the back. I'm halfway down the bus on the left. I've got a window seat, lucky me, but it's not much use at night. The guy that was next to me till Flagstaff didn't dare turn his head to look at the scenery before sundown because he thought I'd figure he was staring at my haircut and I'd whip out a chain or straight razor and take his ears off or something. Some people are very easily intimidated, and it's all because of the garbage they read in the papers and what they see on the tube. I don't care. I don't want to talk to anyone, anyway.

These Greyhounds are *some bus*. From the outside the motor sounds like a tank, with that whistling roar really big motors have, but inside it's a whisper, more of a vibration than a sound, and the seats are okay and it's air-conditioned too. There's nothing beyond the window but blackness. I can see myself looking back at me, a blue Mohican. I look like a different person. Maybe I *am* different. I should be, after what's happened. But I don't feel it somehow. I just feel relieved that it's all over. I think I went crazy for awhile there, from the time Gene told me Diane was gone till the time I saw the taxicab in Phoenix and thought Loretta was driving it. Two and three-quarter days of insanity, that's how I look at it. But I'm okay now, really. And the haircut's growing on me too. That was a pun, ha, ha!

I'm gonna say something strange. I love everyone on this bus. That was it, that was the strange thing. I love everyone on this bus. I don't know why I do, I just do. I haven't even seen their faces properly but I love them all anyway. They're all good people, I can tell, because I can appreciate their true natures with my third eye while they're asleep. Sleep makes them naked and defenseless. My eye floats along the aisle and absorbs their essence. If they're assholes through the day it doesn't matter, because at night their true selves are revealed to me. I know that their assholeism is only a form of fear, a suit of armor, something they can't live without. We have a busload of turtles here, turtles and armadillos. We also have some little kids on board. My eye floats above them like a tiny UFO. I see no armor. They're as trusting as puppies. One day I'll turn into a turtle like the rest, but not today. There's still a whole lot of dog left in Burris Weems, and the dog isn't Buster anymore, no sir, he's beginning to shape up and act like a real dog should, like blue-eyed Mukluk, sled dog of the frozen north, a real Jack London hero dog. Arf! Arf! Arf! Dogs bark, squirrels squawk. I love everyone on this bus. Their lives are filled with unhappiness. It stays above them while they sleep, like dark little clouds, waiting there till morning. For a second or two after they wake up the people won't be unhappy because they won't know who they are, then the clouds'll dive into their heads, entering through the ear, and they'll remember who they are and all their unhappiness will be back with them again. There's only one cure. You have to say, "Cloud, begone!" and your third eye'll swell up inside your head and push the cloud back out your ears. But it's a hard trick to do. You have to believe in the eye or it won't work. If you don't believe in the eye you may as well say, "Cloud, make yourself at home." A lot of people do that, I can tell. They'll never discover the eye. It's there inside their heads like a shriveled old pea, and it'll stay that way until they die, because they never suspected it was there, never gave it a chance to glow in the dark, which is its job. I love them because they don't know, never did know and never will. It's a shame. I don't know why things are like that. It doesn't seem fair. I'm lucky I can see the true way of things. There are no clouds in my head. Inside my skull it's like being inside a white room with a big dome instead of a ceiling. It's huge in there, and hanging in midair is the eye, never blinking, shining like the sun. The eye never feels happy, never feels sad, it just shines and shines if you let it. But if you don't, it's a shriveled old pea stuck in a corner, hiding from the clouds.

When I think like this I wonder if I'm Peggy's son at all. Maybe she was kidnapped by a flying saucer and impregnated by aliens, then made to forget the whole thing by posthypnotic suggestion. It'd explain a lot of things, like why I have a hard time getting along with the average human being, for example. Maybe my true parents are someplace else, a place ordinary humans don't even suspect is there. The aliens are testing me, waiting to see if I measure up. I'm an experiment, but there's nothing cold-blooded about it. They're rooting for me, want me to make the grade, that's why I've got a hyperactive third eye, to help me understand the true way of things. Could be they're watching over me, waiting for me to show I'm worthy of them, and when I do, they'll come swooping down from the sky and rescue me from life among normal people, take me aboard their humming saucer to meet more of my own. If I send out a message, chances are they'll pick it up. They're constantly monitoring my thought waves. This is Burris Weems calling Eye in the Sky. I know you're receiving me, but the rules say you can't aid or transmit. Okay, I understand. I'm doing my best down here, practically pumping iron with eye number three to get it in good working order.

Forget what I just said. There were never any aliens. I'm a human being and nothing but. Fantasy is for them that need it. We're alone, each and every one of us, with nothing in our heads that doesn't come from the clouds or the eye. Aliens didn't give me my eye, I came equipped with it, like a car with cruise control. It's part of everyone, that's what I think. I don't have a shred of proof, Inspector, but I know what I know. There are people on this bus who believe in God, I mean a god *that knows they exist*, a god that watches over Mrs. Shirley Nagle of 1801 Acropolis Drive, cares about her hundred and one worries, and is getting ready to receive her into the heavenly condominium when Shirley's time comes. Sorry, Shirl, there's nothing above your head but 747s and asteroids and emptiness. If your family and friends don't care about your hundred and one problems, no one does. She's not listening, *refuses* to listen. Okay by me, Shirl. Say your prayers. They'll wing their way upward and die in the stratosphere. There's a thin shell surrounding the planet and it's called the prayer zone. All the prayers ever uttered go up there and die on the edge of space and form this invisible shell, like dead polyps create coral reefs with their skeletons. It's a lonely place, the prayer zone. The only visitors are spy planes crammed with super-stealth technology zapping along the rim of the sky and *click, click, clicking* enemy troop concentrations, long black paper dart spy planes gulping dead prayers into their engines, spewing out vaporized pleas and misdirected thanks, ripping a line across the zone like a tear in silk, but the damage is always repaired by more prayers rising up to take the place of the ones that got damaged or destroyed. The PZ will always be there. It's a dumping ground for words that are supposed to be important but are only wasted breath.

Where does this stuff come from, this stuff I pour into the Sony? I don't plan saying any of it. I'm supposed to be recording what happens to me from day to day, that's all, not preaching. There's no such thing as the prayer zone. For the record, I made it up. I shouldn't be doing stuff like that. I should give the facts, just the facts. I think I'm tired after all. I'll go to sleep like everyone else. The wheels are whining a lullaby, a high-pitched hum, white noise to leave your body by. My eyes are closing. Here come the Z's, marching in line like swastikas that broke in half.

Zzzzzzzzzzzzzzzzzzzzzzzzzzz . . .

Amarillo. Out of the bus for breakfast. Lots of staring at my haircut. Had three cups of coffee and two doughnuts. When I get home, I'll start eating healthy. Back on the bus. There's a lady sitting next to me. We don't speak. I'm recording this while she takes a crap. It looks like it'll be a pretty boring trip to Oklahoma City, which is the next stop. The country is flat, flat, flat. Put my watch forward two hours, seeing as we've left Mountain Time and are now in Central Time, and oddball Arizona was an hour behind the rest of Mountain Time anyway.

2:31. Oklahoma City looks oh, so shitty. Not really, it just looks like every other city. Burger for lunch. I'm recording this while *I* take a dump.

4:45. Tulsa. I've been trying to think of something to say about the passengers, but you can't see very much of them from behind these high-backed seats. The lady next to me still hasn't said a word, just reads a book, the kind you see in the supermarket racks—*Ecstasy's Embers*, *Love's Magic Moment*, *Love's Bold Journey*, *Desire's Blossom*, *Love's Blazing Ecstasy*, *Love's Flaming Assholes*, et cetera. Other passengers come and go, and I don't see their faces for more than a few seconds. Going by bus isn't as intimate and friendly as you might expect. But maybe it's the haircut. If I was a neatnik the whole fucking bus'd probably beat a path to my seat and ask for autographs.

9:05. Springfield, Missouri. I should've taken this route when I drove down to Tucumcari. It cuts off the big bend I made by heading out to Kansas City before turning south. Too late now. All this sitting down is killing my butt, but we're about three-quarters of the way there. We've had three different drivers so far. Had another burger. The lady got off here. I hope she finds *Love's Throbbing Gristle* in Springfield. She definitely needs it. Who'll be next to me when we get back on the bus?

It turned out to be a girl. She's with a girlfriend, but they couldn't sit together because there aren't two empty seats left side by side. She sat next to me like you'd sit next to a rattlesnake. I didn't want another maximized ongoing noncommunication situation on my hands so I made an effort to be friendly.

"Hi," I said, and gave her this big grin.

She practically browned her panties, I'm not kidding. She couldn't even talk, she's so scared. I wish I had a bowie knife I could start paring my nails with or something, just to see her faint. Hey, I've got old Gene's pocketknife in my paper sack . . . Nah, leave the poor girl alone. She's wearing white gloves, can you believe it? She looks like girls looked in 1955, with a frock and all. I bet there's a Bible in her dinky little bag. I bet she uses pads instead of tampons when the flag's flying, because pushing a tampon up herself is just too darn much like having intercourse, and God might not like that. But she didn't stay next to me for long, because her friend fixed it so they could share seats by asking this nice old guy if he'd mind moving someplace else, which he was happy to do for a couple of Christian types like that. So I ended up alone again, which is the way I like it. Next stop, St. Louis. I've got a real bad headache. I'd sleep, but I can't seem to nod off. I want this trip to be *over*.

1:02 A.M. Rolling out of St. Louis. Still no one next to me. I hate buses. I'll never do anything like this again. I feel claustrophobic, shut in by the big tinted windows. I'm half awake and half asleep, and my head is hurting like crazy. I wish we'd speed up so we get there faster so I can get the fuck off this crate.

2:47. Somewhere in Illinois. I feel like I'm fixin' to die, Sy. Feel like I'm pretty near dead, Fred. See that my grave is kept clean, Gene . . . Oops! Sorry, Gene. No offense. Bury me not on the lone prairieeeeeeeee . . . Well, I didn't. I buried him in the desert. I mean, I *left* him in the desert. It wouldn't have looked like suicide if I'd buried him, now would it? Sudden thought: These tapes are evidence of my crime in transporting a dead body across state lines, which has got to be a misdemean-

or at least, maybe even a felony. Shit. I better get rid of them just in case they fall into the wrong hands, like Peggy's. I don't trust her not to snoop around in my room, not after the way she took my money. I won't burn them or anything dramatic like that. This is the age of hi-tech, so I'll just erase them, wipe 'em out. My tapes, Officer? You'd like to see my tapes? Why, certainly. This one is Beethoven's *Concerto for Spoons and Eggbeater*, and this one is Tchaikovsky's *Variations on an Unwashed Sock in E minor*, and this one's a real classic, Mozart's *Rondo for a Honda*. Take! Listen! Enjoy! No, these are the only tapes I own, Officer. I'm building up my collection, though. Next week I'm getting that great collector's item by Jimmy Joe Joplin and Billy Bob Bodine—*I'm a Horny Chicken Plucker with a Handy Wooden Pecker, So Back Off if You Got Dutch Elm Disease*.

5:05. No, 6:05, because Indiana is the westernmost state inside Eastern Time, so my watch goes forward another hour. I'm not only in Indiana, I'm home. In Buford, anyway. The Greyhound rolled in on 64 past the turnoff to Green Acres, hung a left onto Ridgeway, and followed it through to the junction of Arrowhead and Debbs, which is where the depot is. I'm the only person that got off. The whole world loves ya, Buford. I came down the steps with my Mega-Mart bag in my hand and started walking. Christ, it felt good to use my legs after all that sitting. People in wheelchairs must be in hell. I'm grateful to be just a gimp. I went gimp, gimp, gimping through the streets with this big smile on my face and sweat rolling down my ribs. It was plenty cool on the bus, I'll say that for it. There's a fat old moon over Buford to welcome me home, even if the sky's getting light. Hi, moon! Miss me? Gimp along, little doggie, gimp along. Swing that leg, Meg. Shake a tail feather, Heather. I'm bound for Westwood Drive and a soft bed I can lie down on and forget that sitting was ever invented. The birds are waking up and talking to each other. They sound like twittering, chirruping electronic alarms, about a million of 'em. Hi, birds! Get them worms! Hi there, streets and trees and houses! I'm back! Better believe it, buildings! Burris is back! No more a wild rover, Grover. Left, left, left right left! Hayfoot, strawfoot, hayfoot, hey! I hadda good home and I left, left, left! Since then I've never been right, right, right! When Johnny comes marching home again, hoorah! hoorah! It's an incredible sight, ladies and gentlemen, the likes of which Buford has not seen in all the years this reporter has been reporting. The turnout to welcome home young Burris Weems is little short of fantastic—in fact the only thing littler and shorter is Burris himself, a heroic figure nonetheless as he strides down Main Street waving to the many thousands of friends and admirers gathered here today for this amazing homecoming situation. The object of their frenzied ongoing adulation has journeyed far and succeeded against incredible odds, ladies and gentlemen, and deserves the maximum output of ovation currently impacting on this small community, a town unused to the arrival of celebrities of such stature and fame, so put your hands together for a real ongoing salute to Buford's most renowned and famous son, a hometown boy that made good in the classic ongoing tradition of guys that do stuff like this.

7:01. *Really* home. It's full daylight now. Peggy's Impala is parked in the drive. I won't wake anyone, just sneak in my window if it's open, which it is, and I'm over the sill like a thief in the night and stripping off my clothes and diving into that terrific invention that leaves the wheel standing, that cradle of civilization—the bed.

Sweet dreams, world.

I just now woke up and looked at my watch. 2:42 P.M. The afternoon's half gone. I feel good. I wonder who's home? I didn't hear anyone fixing breakfast or lunch or anything, but I slept like a lump of clay, so I wouldn't have heard a smoke alarm if it went off under my pillow. I don't feel like getting up just yet. I'll wait till I hear Peggy moving around, then I'll stroll out and act like I haven't been away at all, act like it's just another day at 1404, no big deal. She'll jump right out of her pumps, I guarantee it. Trouble is, I feel like taking a leak. I'll hang on to it a little longer. I really want to make that casual entrance. Hi, Peggy. *Yawn.* What's for lunch? I hope she's got her sense of humor back. I better be a good kid for a while after what I did to those pictures. I was a real rat to do that, but I'll make up for it. I'll even get another job for the rest of the summer! C'mon Peggy, I need to take a leak already.

I can't wait any longer. Up and into my shorts, out the door, down the hall, into the bathroom, up with the seat . . . aaaaaaaaaaaaaaahhh. . . . Flush, down with the seat again or Peggy and Loretta'll give me the usual lecture about courtesy. Out of the bathroom and into the kitchen. So where *is* everyone?"

"Anyone home?"

It sounds creepy when you do that in your own house, especially when there's no answer, so I covered up the creepiness with a few yoo-hoos, et cetera. Nope, there's no one here but me. But Peggy's car is parked right outside. This is weird. She never takes the bus if she can help it. Maybe the Impala's kaput. I looked out the living room window at the car. No new dents or anything, not on the front, anyway, but the back end looks like it's riding a little low, so maybe the springs have gone. Maybe the engine just conked out. She's been expecting it to do that for a while now. Here comes a cop car. It's stopping. Shit, it's stopping right outside *here.* . . . *Peggy's* getting out! What's happening here . . . ? She's leaning back in the car window, saying something. Now she's straightening up and the cruiser's moving off, and here she comes up the walk. . . .

I ran back to my room and closed the door like it was before. What was she doing in a cop car? Where was she coming from? Dumb question. It had to be the police station, but why didn't she go down there under her own steam? Because she wasn't there to report something, she was *taken in for questioning.* They've been giving her the third degree about the disappearance of Gene down at Green Acres and the connection with *me.* Oh, no . . . Shit! There *was* blood. The manager *did* get suspicious. Somehow they've fingered me. They know I had something to do with it. Oh, Jesus, Jesus, Jesus . . . They're *after* me! I heard the front door slam. I gotta get outa here . . . Clothes on, fast but quiet, sneakers, shades, pick up my paper sack . . . Wait! Don't panic out of here before you've got a few necessities together. Calm *down.* Open the wardrobe, take out the vinyl carryall with the adjustable shoulder strap and plenty of room inside for shorts, shirts, socks, blah blah blah, in they go, push, shove, and the paper sack goes in there too. Okay, now I'm ready. Peggy's gone to the bathroom. Now's the time. Out the window goes the bag, out the window goes me. Pick up the bag and scram, Sam, down the walk, down the drive, down the road . . .

Where to? I dunno, just keep walking, walking, walking. Why the *fuck* did I come back here? I could've been in L.A., mingling with the freaks, disappearing from view, a fish among fishes. In Buford I'm a fish among sharks. How'd they finger me? No one at Green Acres knew my name except Lee and Diane and Gene. Somehow, somewhere along the line I missed something important, some link in the chain connecting me to them, something other people knew about and blabbed to the cops, but *what?* Forget it for now, just concentrate on getting out of town. I shouldn't have disguised myself the way I did, I should've had a crew cut instead. That would've changed my appearance without putting a neon sign on my skull. Everyone I pass stares at me. There are no Mohicans in Buford, brother, and a limping Indian with his head on fire is something folks just can't help but notice. Do I hitch a ride or grab the first Greyhound? *Think.* Christ, what a fool to come home like this. Of *course* they fingered you, idiot. Cops aren't dumb. You're the number-one suspect in the disappearance and presumed *murder* of Gene. . . . I still don't know his surname, isn't that stupid? They'll tell me when they arrest me, I bet. But it can't be murder unless there's a body, and they won't find him a whole mile from the highway . . . *unless the buzzards lead them to him!* Why didn't I think of buzzards? They're in every Western, flapping down like chunks of burned rag whenever someone dies in the desert . . . unless the coyotes got to him first! They scavenge by night, so they had a head start over the buzzards. Jesus, I hope they ate him but good, dress and all. It's my only chance now. Gimp, gimp, gimp along, but not too fast. Can't afford to snag more attention than I already am. Maybe the Sony pressed in my face makes me look casual. Would a dangerous killer be dictating notes on the run? I can't put the fucking thing down anymore. The Sony's part of my hand. I'm talking into my palm and the words slide into my lifeline like cockroaches into a crack. Gimp, gimp, gimp along. You're a balloon in a pin factory, feller, threatened on every side by pricks, ha, ha! Joking at a time like this must be a sign of hysteria or something. I bet I crack a joke in the gas chamber. When the gas comes wafting up from the cyanide bucket under the seat, up past my shaky knees and buckled-down wrists, I'll open my mouth and yell so all the reporters on the other side of the plate glass window'll hear me and take down my famous last words, my epitaph: "Fart zone! Aaaaaaaaaa-aaggghhh . . . !" Enough talk for now. This is serious.

It's 4:11 and I'm in a room at Harry's Highway Haven. What happened was, I went to the Greyhound depot but there's a fucking patrol car parked outside. It *had* to be for me. They've got the place staked out. If I'd come along a few minutes later they'd have parked out of sight so's not to scare me off. Too bad you goofed, flatfoot. No way am I gonna take the bus, but I can't hitch, either, not in daylight, anyway. I'll wait till dark, then chance it, and Harry's is my hideout till then. It's a $16.50 bite out of my getaway fund, but it can't be helped. I'm in here with the curtains drawn, watching *Little House on the Prairie*. Only a desperate man would do that. Fuck it, I'm not *that* desperate. Flip the channel. *Fantasy Island*. Flip again. *Love Boat*. There's no escape. Outside, the cops are prowling for me. Inside, my brain is under attack from the networks. I'm backed into a corner here and feeling sick as a dog.

5:27. *Gilligan's Island, Divorce Court, Family Feud*. The tube is pulling this stuff in from another planet, not the one I live on.

6:03. *Munsters, Jeffersons, Brady Bunch*. The TV has stolen my muscles. I can't move except to reach out and flip channels. From my shoulders to my fingertips I'm alive, working the tube and the Sony, but the rest of me is dying.

6:51. *Laverne and Shirley, Andy Griffith, Father Knows Best*. The tube is a time warp, raking in garbage from the past. It won't ever let us forget where we come from. America, these are your roots!

7:27. *Wheel of Fortune, Waltons, Gunsmoke*. A million hours a week. It has to be filled with something. Open the vault and rerun rerun, rerun, rerun run run run run run run run run . . .

8:15. *Three's a Crowd, The A-Team, Barnaby Jones*.

8:36. *Foul-ups, Bleeps and Blunders, Jeffersons* again, *Gentle Ben*.

9:07. *Who's the Boss? Facts of Life, Dan August*.

10:10. *Hotel, MacGruder and Loud, Remington Steele*.

10:42. *Baseball, Sporting Life, Hogan's Heroes*.

I know I'll be saved at eleven. That's when *Twilight Zone* comes on. *Twilight Zone* is a raft in rapids of shit. Come on, clock hands, push a little faster and bring me the *Zone*. Now it's eleven. I flip around, listening for the *doo* doo doo doos, watching for the magic words. *It isn't on* . . . ! The *Tuesday Night Movie* is an extra-long one, and it's swamped the *Zone*'s slot! When it finishes, they'll go straight into *Magnum P.I.* Shit! Fuck! Bastards! They took the *Zone* away from me! I want to smash the screen, splinter it, shatter it. Gimme me Zoooooo-oooooone. . . . Oh, you bunch of shitty fuckhead programmers! You idiot fuckhead dickhead moron shitforbrains! You couldn't even bump it off the schedule with a *good* movie, you had to put on some fucking made-for-TV crap about some fuckhead leaving his dumbass wife but they get back together again and it wasn't even *new*, I saw it in '83, you cunts, you asshole bastards! I want the *Zone!* I want it, want it, want it, want it, want it, want it, want . . . I can't take my eyes off the screen, can't even focus. I'm plugged into the set. My third eye isn't inside me at all, it's across the room, glowing like a fish tank filled with mercury and the fish are *flick, flick, flicking* their fins a million times a minute. The mercury is seeping out a little at a time and washing around my feet, corroding the bones, seeping a little faster now because it thinks I haven't noticed, spilling out the corners of the eye like silver jelly and plopping to the floor, silver blobs that run together, massing for the big invasion. It's up to my knees now, *slosh, slosh*, seeping into my skin through the pores, eating my bones. No escape. It's trying to hypnotize me with glowing light, thinks I'm too stupid to see what it's doing, but I know all right, I know what's happening, no square eye can trick me. My third eye's back inside my skull again, a round eye brighter than the tube, and it's round eye versus square eye now, snakes of lightning zapping and crackling between them—*bzzzzzzzzzzt! zzzzzzzzzzzt!*—filling the room with silvery blue smoke, but my eye is losing, I can tell, because the bones in my legs are eaten away now, gone completely and I can't escape, and now the square eye brings in big guns. Out from the screen come the tentacles, slimy gray with suckers like onion rings along the undersides, suction cups to suck out my soul. The tentacles ooze out foot by foot from the corners of the eye with the pointy tips going this way and that, like slugs looking for food. They're not really there, I know they're not, but I can't stand to see them reach for me that way, because if they touch me I'll die, and they're getting longer and longer and I can't move and don't dare look at the screen because that's where the tentacles meet, and where the tentacles meet is something I don't want to see because that'd kill me, too, but I can't get away now, the tentacles are all around me, thick as a wrestler's leg, shifting the pictures on the walls, knocking over the bedside lamp, picking up the glass ashtray and letting it fall. They know where I am. They're playing a game, pretending they don't know I'm right there in front of the tube and they have to look for me, and all the while they're surrounding me, getting longer and thicker and slipperier and squirming around me like giant gray worms, getting closer bit by bit, but they won't take me alive, won't drag me into the set to get ripped apart by the parrot's beak in there, no sir, not while I can haul myself out of this chair they won't. . . .

I hung the Sony around my neck by the strap. It'll pick up my voice fine from there. It's a good machine. I need both hands free. Stand. It was easy. Go to the bag. Take out the sack. Dump on bed. Electric clippers, scissors, shaving cream, flashlight, mirror, pocketknife. It's got a yellow handle. Pull out the blade. Sharp. Into the bathroom. Put up the lid. Kneel. Left hand over bowl. Hold blade against wrist. Don't stop, coward. One quick slash. Go on, you fucking little coward. Betcha can't . . . Yyyyiiiiiiiiiiiiinnnnnnnyyyyyaaaaaaaaaggggggghhhhhh . . . I felt it *cutting through* things in there . . . Lots of blood coming out, *splitter, splatter, splot*, and my ears are humming, humming with blood draining from my head on its way to my wrist, red waterfall dropping to red pond, *splish, splash, splosh*, my hand's as red as my hair, keep it over the bowl, Noel, don't get it on the floor, some poor lady's gotta clean it up, so keep it where it is and squirt that stuff where it'll do no harm, all of me is going down my arm, running through my red fingers, *drippy*, *droppy*, *ploppy*, red as red down there, filled up with blood lud lud from vein ane ane feel weak eek eek can't stay knelt elt elt gotta slide lide lide to the floor lor lor my head ed ed on wall all all . . . *rumble, bumble, tumble*, next door flush ush ush bubbles come up plop lop lop in the bowl ole ole can't see just hear look up up up at the light ite ite it's round and gold old old getting closer, can't talk anymore, lips numb, communicating telepathically now, coming down closer, spinning, spinning, now it's slowing and I can see the portholes underneath, faces behind the glass, friends of mine but I don't know their names, they've come to carry me home in their flying saucer, waving to me, letting me know it won't be long now, and I'm moving out from under the light, another light coming into view, then another and another, a string of lights, I'm on a hospital gurney, being wheeled along a corridor with lights in the ceiling, lights lights lights all in a row, then through the swing doors at the end into the operating room, lights *lights* LIGHTS! burning my eyes, and the surgeon leans over me with just his eyes showing above the green mask, we're going to begin, he says, are you comfortable, yes I am, but very weak lying on the gurney, and they're doing something to my toes, something ticklish, and I raise my head a little, very hard to do, and I see what they're doing down there, and it's pulling all the little bones out of my feet, the tiny little toe bones and arch bones and the bigger heel bones, and now they're pulling out the anklebones, straight out through the skin without cutting or blood because there isn't any more blood, then the shinbones, out they come, then the lumpy knee bones, all bluish-white, not whiter than white like old desert bones, they're bluish-white and shiny new, and now it's my thighbones, out they come, it doesn't hurt a bit, then they pull out this big soup bowl of bones which is my hips, then they start on my fingers, pulling out the little finger bones, then the wrist bones, then the forearm bones, the elbows, the upper-arm bones, and now my arms and legs are empty sausage skins and they start on my ribs, out they come in one piece like a piece of sculpture, then it's my backbone's turn, this long, bony snake, then my collarbones, shoulder bones, jawbone, even my skull is pulled out through my mouth, and now there isn't a bone left in my body, I'm a collapsed inflatable man lying stretched out flat, and they're working on my feet again, rolling them up, then my legs, rolling them up like firehose till they reach my hips, then they do something very complex I can't see because I can't lift my head anymore, only feel, and I feel them tuck my rolled-up legs inside my empty belly, like folding up a sleeping bag and stowing it away inside its own hood, and then they roll up my hands and arms the same way and shove them inside my chest, and then they do something really incredible, they roll up my torso, roll it up tight and small, squashing everything inside, but it doesn't hurt, roll it up up up till it's the size of a fist, and then they take my empty head like the top of some rolled-up socks and *slip it over the rest of me* so my entire body is crammed inside my head, a heavy little package with the eyes staring upward at the lights, and then they put me on a Styrofoam tray and wrap me with Cling Wrap so I can still see out, wrap me like a chunk of supermarket meat and lift me up and carry me across to the refrigerator and open the door, huge door a mile high, and shove me inside, way down in back of the freezer with walls icy-coated and a little yellow light way, way up in the corner, and now they're closing the door, locking me in the freezer, and when the door closes I know the light'll go out and I'll be in awful darkness, locked in the freezer all alone in the dark, *don't shut it!* but they don't listen, almost shut now, and the light is already dimming, *don't shut me in here!* but they do, they shut the door and shut me in and the light is fading fast and the only way I can stop it is to call out to the little man who lives in here and switches the light on and off when the door opens and closes, but I can't remember his name, haven't used it since I was a little kid, what's his *name*, that little man who lives inside the light and turns it on and off, keeper of the light, what's his *name*, just a little yellow blob now, fading away . . .

Yehudi!
Yehudi!
Turn it back on!
Turn on the light!
Please, Yehudi
please

16 You know how at the end of the old detective movies the hero gets everyone together and explains a whole lot of stuff? Take a seat. It's November now, and the rain is really coming down outside my window. I haven't used the Sony in a long while, and I've been kind of missing it, like a big brother or something.

I think I was talking to myself all along, one half of my brain gabbing to the other half, something psychological like that. I don't think it's a sign of mental weirdness or anything, even back in the summer when I went completely overboard the way I did. I've got an interesting scar on my wrist where they stitched me up. I keep it covered with a fancy woven wristband. I don't have the Mohican anymore. It isn't practical in winter because the sides of your head freeze. I shaved myself bald, and now I've got a crew cut that's growing out. I wear a cap with earflaps when I go outside.

You know what saved me? A faulty toilet. Pretty ironic, huh? The plumbing in Harry's Highway Haven is back-to-back, see, and the guy in the room next to mine flushed his john and blood from mine came up in his, which got him worried, so he got the manager and they knocked on my door, and when there's no answer they unlocked it with the passkey and found me in the bathroom practically dead from loss of blood, which went all over the floor, anyway, exactly the way I didn't want it to. Ambulance, hospital, emergency surgery, et cetera. Then the cops came to see me. I was scared shitless. But they just said I had to attend this psychiatric counseling service for juveniles, and also I'm on probation for a year because killing yourself is *against the law*. That's some joke, don't you think? Anyway, they didn't say anything about Gene or the tapes, which were gone I didn't know where, my Sony too. The cops didn't have them or they would've said something, maybe put me under arrest. I didn't ask about them. That would've been dumb.

Peggy was pretty shook up about what I did, and Loretta, and when they came to see me I couldn't stand the look on their faces and I blubbered like a baby and said I was sorry, blah blah blah. That's enough about that. I turned sixteen in the hospital, a really terrific place for a birthday. July 20, 1969, is when Neil walked on the moon. Peggy and Loretta came in with this cake for me, not an ordinary cake, it's one of those giant cookies you can buy with iced writing on it, and it says: "16—but only just!" That's kind of witty, I think. Regular family never would've put something like that on a birthday cookie, not under the circumstances. It was a shame to cut it, but we did. Chocolate chip.

Then the guy that runs Harry's Highway Haven came to see me, the manager guy that opened the door and sent for the ambulance and all. His name's not Harry like you'd think. Harry was his brother-in-law that started the place up, then died, so now it's owned by Harry's sister Alice and her husband Rick, who's the guy that came in to see me and find out how I'm doing, and he's got my tapes! I asked if he listened to them, and he said he doesn't go for punk music. He figured a guy looking like me would have punk music on his tapes. He didn't even listen to them! So I'm safe, and he's got my Sony too. I told him I'm very grateful for the way he saved my life et cetera, which I was, and he told me you can't let life get you down, you have to fight back, something I agree with, and we shook hands, and he went away and left the tapes with me. That was a real load off my mind, having them back again, and I think I started getting better from that time on.

I couldn't get out of going to the Juvenile Psychiatric Counseling Service once I was out of the hospital, but at least it wasn't group encounters or anything embarrassing like that, just a one-on-one setup with a shrink. He asked me why I did it, and I said it was because I didn't want to repeat the last semester. He swallowed it, and our weekly sessions after that were so incredibly predictable it's almost funny, with him telling me I have to accept responsibility for my "lack of scholastic achievement" blah, blah blah and me nodding my head up and down like an oil pump, yes sir, yes sir, you're right about that, and he was pretty satisfied with the way I acted and gave me a good report at the end of summer. I bet his skull would've flipped if he knew what really happened to make me go crazy, but he'll never know, and no one else will, either. I've built a brick wall inside my head, and I keep all that stuff behind it. Nobody knows nothin' 'bout nothin'.

Oh yeah, Peggy getting out of that police car and spooking me. What that was all about was, some asshole slashed the back tires of the Impala, which I didn't notice from the living room window or when I walked past the crate when I got home early that morning, and Peggy went down to the police station to report it in person instead of doing it over the phone because she figured the cops wouldn't do anything unless she pressured them face-to-face, which is probably true. Loretta gave her a lift down there, and this cop that took her story offered her a lift back out to Westwood Drive. As a matter of fact he tried to get a date! We never did find out who slashed the tires or why, most likely just some idiot kid. But it was something as dopey as that that sent me overboard, made me think the cops were really after me.

When I got out of the hospital I went to all the newspaper offices in town and looked through their back issues. Nothing about Green Acres at all, just nothing. Now I know I'm truly safe. Gene's just bones by now. I wonder if Lee and Diane ever tried to contact him again? They never contacted me. What a couple of assholes. I still don't understand them, separately or together. It's like a jigsaw puzzle with half the pieces missing. Make that three-quarters. They've gone forever out of my life, locked away behind the brick wall, which is where they belong.

The good news is, I went along to see Rick and thank him

again for saving my life and all and got to meet Alice, a real nice lady, and this daughter they've got, Sandra. They were all kind of tense at first, talking to this suicidal Mohican, but they loosened up after I went around there a second time. Sandra and I get along okay, let me tell ya. She's pretty smart, but not one of those paranoid overachievers that go hang themselves if they get a B+, nothing like that. She goes to Memorial High too. I saw her around a few times but never took any notice before. Well, I do now. We've gotten to the feeling-up stage. I think we'll go a couple steps further before too long. She's a funky skunky punky spunky monkey. I think I love her. For a while I thought about telling her the truth, then I decided not to. It's strictly my own business, a secret thing that happened. I'm not ashamed of anything I did, I just don't want to talk about it. Sometimes days go by without me taking a brick out of the wall and peeking behind, but I know I'll never seal it up completely. The stuff behind the wall will always be there whenever I want to take a peek.

I finally made up my mind what I want to be, which is another big load off my mind. I'm gonna be an actor. I still look like Frederic Forrest in *When the Legends Die*. I saw Fred on a new TV movie the other night. He doesn't look like me because he's pretty old now, but I still look like he looked in his first movie. I think I could be an okay actor, frankly. I've been acting normal for months now, and everyone believes it, so I've definitely got talent. So I'm short—so what? Dustin Hoffman and Al Pacino are short. And John Wayne had a limp, okay? So I've got both things—big deal. It'll just make me stand out from the crowd when they're casting. Pretty boys don't make it nowadays except in soaps and other TV garbage. The big screen is ready for Burris Weems. I won't change my name, either, just to rub their faces in it a little more, all those pricks at school that think I'm a geek for trying to kill myself. When I'm famous they'll choke on it, the bastards.

Loretta went ahead and got married. She still drives a cab, though.

The TV I got from Room 107 blew up last October.

Buster the ground-humper got run over by a car, heh, heh, heh.

There's an all-new, all-color *Twilight Zone* on the tube, but the old black-and-white *Zone* is still the best.

I wish I could finish everything up neat and tidy and tie it with a ribbon, but I can't, because nothing ends that doesn't somehow overlap something else that's beginning, so I'll just give you some advice for free:

Don't ever get involved with dead people.

And avoid some of the live ones too.

Now this